"I NEED YOUR

She closed her eyes and [...] day she showed up in New [...] *True Love.*

Dear God, destiny was a sadistic fiend to hand her Josh Toby.

"Okay. I'll do it," she found herself saying. Her hand flew to her mouth. Had she really just said that? Okay, that was it: she was no longer shy. Now she was possessed by an evil twin.

Josh leaned in and wrapped her in a hug. "Hot damn!" He took her face in his hands and kissed her smack on the lips. Then he pulled back a hairsbreadth, looked her in the eyes, then kissed her again. More slowly. Deliberately.

Seconds. Minutes. Days.

He pulled back.

They stared at each other.

Her hand went to her lips. *Again.*

He leaned in and kissed her again.

ᴈᴈ ❦ ᴈᴈ

PRAISE FOR *MAKE ME A MATCH*

"4½ stars! Holquist's novel is pure entertainment from beginning to end. The interaction between the sisters is genuinely depicted, and the relationship developments are a joy to observe."

—*Romantic Times BOOKclub Magazine*

Turn the page for more reviews!

Also by Diana Holquist

Make Me a Match

Sexiest Man Alive

Diana Holquist

FOREVER

NEW YORK   BOSTON

Copyright © 2007 by Diana Holquist
Excerpt from *Hungry for More* copyright © 2007 by Diana Holquist
All rights reserved. Except as permitted under the U.S. Copyright
Act of 1976, no part of this publication may be reproduced, dis-
tributed, or transmitted in any form or by any means, or stored in a
database or retrieval system, without the prior written permission
of the publisher.

Forever is an imprint of Grand Central Publishing.

The Forever name and logo is a trademark of Hachette Book Group
USA, Inc.

Cover design by Claire Brown
Cover photograph by Herman Estevez

Forever
Hachette Book Group USA
237 Park Avenue
New York, NY 10017
Visit our Web site at www.HachetteBookGroupUSA.com

Printed in the United States of America

First Printing: October 2007

10 9 8 7 6 5 4 3 2 1

*To everyone who has ever blushed,
stuttered, or had their nose twitch like a rabbit's,
this book is for you.*

Acknowledgments

A huge thanks to Katie Delaney and the rest of the Ithaca College Theater Department, who let me watch costume designers in action.

I could never have written this book without the unwavering support of everyone at Hachette Book Group, especially my editor, Michele.

And, as always, to Ellen, Liz, and Leslie. What am I going to do without you guys?

Sexiest Man Alive

Chapter 1

"Hi! I'm Jasmine Burns!"

The naked man stared up at Jasmine blankly.

Great. She sounded like a cruise ship director on crack. She cleared her throat and adjusted her black teddy. "It's great to meet you!"

Ugh. This was definitely not working.

Jasmine stared at herself in the mirror on the far (okay, not-so-far) wall of her tiny Upper-Upper West Side Manhattan studio. *This only looks crazy,* she silently assured her reflection.

She looked down at the naked Ken doll perched on her couch.

Okay, it was crazy. Call-the-cops nuts, even.

She paced. Seven steps. Pivot. Seven steps. Pivot. Exercise #12, page 127 in her *Good-bye Shy!* workbook had made sense in theory: *Practice job interviews with a doll to focus on until the panic is gone. To achieve maximum vulnerability, rehearse the interview with both parties naked.*

Jasmine couldn't get completely naked. She settled on

a black lace teddy for herself. Ken wasn't so shy. He went all the way without complaint.

The mind controls the body. Let the panic wash over, then continue. Repeated exposure to the object of fear will dull the emotion.

So why was her terror growing? Her interview was three days, seven hours, and twenty-seven minutes away, and she was getting more panicked by the second.

Okay, so she knew why her terror was growing: Arturo Mastriani. Her (hopefully) future boss was one of the sexiest men she had ever met, and she was deathly shy around sexy men. No, not shy. The label the self-help books used these days was "socially anxious."

When she had met Arturo a year ago at the cast party for *The Cheddar Chronicles* at her friend Lucy's apartment, the right word was clearly "bananas." Jasmine had hid out in the back bedroom until the party ended. Two hours! She could still smell Lucy's lavender potpourri sachets every time she thought of Arturo.

Jasmine flopped onto her bed and stared at the ceiling of her shoebox-shaped apartment. The heel end of her single room was crammed with her elaborate queen-size iron bed, which was centered between the door to the hallway and the door to her tiny bathroom. The toe end was dominated by a lead-glass window that stretched four feet across and from the ceiling to within two feet of the floor.

And what a window. It made the narrow, tiny studio worthwhile. Magnificent, even. In a shoebox sort of way.

Despite her exhaustion, Jasmine forced herself off the bed and back to the "living room"—a flea-market, all-white couch; one white overstuffed chair; and a white coffee table rescued from a curbside trash pile, all arranged neatly at the foot of her bed. She sat next to Ken on the couch and toyed with a scrap of black Italian gabardine wool that had called out to her the day before from a sample table on 37th Street. Salsa music and car horns floated up from Amsterdam Avenue, a melody of the city she barely noticed anymore.

This shot at a real costume design job with Arturo was the chance of a lifetime. After all, the tailoring business she ran out of her apartment was an accident, not part of her plan.

Okay, so it was a wildly successful accident. A hem here, a tuck there, and within days she was in demand— the miracle worker of 109th Street. She could make a cigarette hole in silk pajamas disappear, or take in a suit better than anyone west of Hong Kong.

It wasn't a bad way to make a living. She rarely had to leave her apartment, and she liked her clients. Plus, no one noticed they were all women. When a man called, she claimed she was too busy to take the job. It was perfect. No stress.

Not that she had a problem with all men. Just appealing men. It was a minor problem. Insignificant, like a fear of snakes or spiders. A person could get by avoiding tempting men. Especially in New York, where two out of three men who (a) were tempting or (b) had anything to do with costume design were (c) gay.

Arturo, unfortunately, was (d) beautiful, straight, and terrifying.

Ugh! She had to get a hold of herself. It wasn't like she wanted to sleep with the guy.

Tell that to her nerve endings, though. Those suckers were immune to reason.

She had to get control of herself. Her graduation (MA in costume design from NYU) was five months past, and her ex-classmates were out hitting the pavement, interning and networking, sometimes in *theaters*, sometimes even getting *paid*. She let the wonderful possibility of being in their shoes spread through her.

Meanwhile, I'm twenty-eight and playing with dolls.

Naked dolls.

Maybe that was the problem. Naked Ken was too much. After all, if Ken were impersonating a famous costume designer, shouldn't he have amazing clothes?

She carried Ken to the whitewashed plywood door balanced on two white wooden sawhorses next to her window. Her black vintage Singer Featherweight 221-1 sewing machine with gold scrollwork gleamed in welcome. She ran her hand down its curves, her steel and chrome kitty. She settled into the space next to it and began to sketch.

She could do this. Costume design was her destiny. She was sure of it. She just had to get past her fear of Arturo. And she could. She would. She had to.

She took a cleansing breath and began to sketch.

One sure, practiced stroke at a time, the perfect outfit for Arturo Mastriani to interview his up-and-coming brilliant new assistant began to form on the page as if of its own accord.

Jasmine jolted awake. She was on the couch, Ken in his beautiful new clothes at her side—a tiny, perfectly behaved date.

Someone was ringing the downstairs buzzer.

Her eyes jumped to the clock: 2:00 AM. Probably Suz with a ripped seam. Jasmine had warned her wildest client and best friend that the cheap Chinese silk was too delicate to wear for clubbing, especially when Suz had insisted that she take it in to skinlike tightness.

Jasmine pushed the intercom button to the street-level door. "Suzie?"

"Jas? Let me up—quick."

Jasmine fell away from the intercom.

Amy, Jasmine's sister. In New York. In the middle of the night. Last time Amy showed up unannounced, Jasmine had to hide her from a guy named Rufus for two weeks.

Definitely not good.

Jasmine pushed the buzzer to let her sister up, then raced for the couch, tripping over the white shag throw rug. *Must hide Ken.*

Jasmine had only once made the mistake of discussing her man issues with her sister. The next day, Amy had brought home a tattoo-covered gypsy named Mario who gave "the best oral sex this side of the Mississippi." Or so Amy said. Jasmine chose not to find out for herself. It was bad enough imagining what Mario's gypsy brethren were up to on opposite banks of that raging river.

Amy had assured Jasmine that a man like Mario would make Jasmine "shake at the sight of sexy men in a whole new way."

Jasmine shuddered—in her same old way—at the memory. It had taken her forty-five minutes of absurd chase-around-the-couch terror before she managed to shove Mario out of her apartment and toss his faux-leather pants after him.

She shoved Ken between the pillows. Kicked *The Shyness Handbook* under the couch. Scooped *Living with Social Anxiety* and *Ten Steps to Being Bold* into the crick of her elbow, then crammed them into one of a dozen identical blue forty-gallon fabric bins stacked along the wall. She was forcing the top closed when she remembered she was wearing the black teddy.

Oh, hell. Amy was going to love this.

The doorbell rang.

Jasmine could smell Amy's clove and cinnamon through the thin plank door separating them. Jasmine ransacked her apartment for her white terry bathrobe. "One sec!"

Amy pounded on the door. "Jas? You got a man in there?"

Yeah, but he doesn't have a penis. How could she lose her bathrobe in a closet-sized apartment?

"Jas! Your place is the size of a rowboat. You can reach the door from the damn pot."

Could she? Well, it was close. She spotted her bathrobe neatly folded on top of a bin of last season's wool flannels. She pulled it on over her teddy, flipped the three deadbolts, slid free the safety chain, and stood back as Amy burst into the room.

Showtime.

"Jasmine. Shit." Amy went straight to the window, threw open the curtains, and peered out. "We have to talk."

Jasmine followed her sister to the window and peered down five stories to the deserted sidewalk. The trees were just changing, and the brilliant yellow of the maple glowing in the moonlight complemented her pomegranate red crepe curtains. She sucked in her breath at the pleasure of the night-muted colors, then carefully closed the curtains. She hadn't seen Amy since her graduation from NYU last spring.

"I need cash," Amy said.

Well, might as well cut to the chase. The memories of Jasmine's happy graduation were replaced with memories of the meal afterward—Amy hadn't contributed a dime. Come to think of it, there was no gift either. "Let me put some coffee on."

Amy pulled a two-liter, almost-empty vodka bottle out of her sheepskin coat.

"Okay. Not coffee, then," Jasmine said. Amy was a social drinker, not a drunk. Jasmine's blood ran cold. Something was wrong. Amy, after all, wasn't a normal person.

Amy was a psychic.

But not just any psychic. She had one gift, besides crashing into Jasmine's life at the most inopportune moments. She could touch a person and hear a voice that spoke the name of the person's One True Love. Her soul mate. Her true companion. Her One and Only.

If you believed in such a thing.

And Jasmine did. Jasmine believed completely. Not just in Amy's power, but in destiny as a concept. In a world where attractive men reduced her to a blushing, fumbling mess, there had to be one desirable man, somewhere, who would make her whole.

But there were problems with Amy's names. If your One True Love was named John Smith, well, too bad for you; you had to figure out which John Smith was the right one. And if the right John Smith turned out to be a married pig farmer in Iowa with seven children and you were an up-and-coming New York City costume designer (and she was; she knew she was; she was going to get this job), well, then, you had some tough choices to make. Amy's spirit voice rarely served up the lover a person expected. After all, who was this fate, this voice, this power? An angel? A devil? A long-dead kibbitzing old ghost, too mean-spirited even in death to mind her own business?

Well, whoever or whatever the voice was, it had stopped talking just days before Jasmine found her sisters after a lifetime apart. They had been separated twenty-six years earlier, the ugly result of their parents' True Love–induced divorce. (A naïve child, Amy had told their parents they were not each other's One True Love. Mom and Dad promptly split to find their individual bliss.)

Amy and Cecelia, the eldest sister, stayed with their dad in Baltimore. Jasmine, a toddler at the time, was taken by their mom to Bombay, India, in search of a stranger named Emeril Livingston—her mother's One True Love. Jasmine had briefly reunited with her sisters when she was sixteen, a calamitous three months together that ended in Jasmine leaving without even saying good-bye. She reunited with her sisters again just two years ago in Baltimore. Their relationship was still on eggshells.

Of course, Amy wasn't the sort to let a few dozen trampled eggshells slow her down.

Since losing her power, Amy had been doing everything she could to get the voice to spit out more names. She ladled soup for the homeless in the moldy basements of churches (well, once anyway; the spores irritated her sinuses). She consulted other psychics (whom she then accused of conning her). She wore elaborate, ever-changing combinations of crystals. Now, obviously, she had turned to vodka.

It seemed an unlikely fix.

Amy closed her eyes and rocked. The bottle was empty.

Jasmine gently removed the bottle from her sister's grasp. "Is this about the voice?"

Amy's eyes sprang open, and she flung herself onto the couch in a dramatic display of exhaustion. Everything about Amy was dramatic. She craved attention as much as Jasmine avoided it. "Would you get in the real world, please? I told you—it's about cash. Money. The green stuff." Amy frowned, lifted her ample hips, and felt under her.

Busted.

Out came Famous Costume Designer Ken in his high-sheen Hugo Boss–style suit.

Jasmine feigned surprise.

Amy dangled him from his right heel, his double-breasted jacket flapping helplessly. "Does Barbie know about this?"

Jasmine sank onto the couch opposite Amy. She ran her hand over the angora throw she had tossed over the couch, sensing the red through her fingertips. "Oh! There he is! I was designing costumes for a new play. He's a prototype." The lie tasted stale in her mouth.

Amy leaned forward and studied Jasmine closely, as if noticing her for the first time, which was likely the case. "Look at you! What are you wearing? Under your robe?" Amy poked at Jasmine's bathrobe. "Something sexy?

Was there a man here?" She frowned at Ken. "I mean, a real one?"

Jasmine considered telling her sister that she had made the black teddy for a blind date last Thursday that her friend Suz had set up. She tried not to think about that awful almost-date: gasping for breath, her racing heart. Suz was still furious at her for disappearing on the guy mid-salad, but Jasmine couldn't help it. He had such soft, deep, chestnut-brown eyes.

Jasmine took a deep breath. The cat was already out of the bag, or, in this case, the Ken was already out of the couch. Plus, Amy was right—Jasmine was an awful liar. "Ken's part of an exercise to help me get ready for an interview. I'm supposed to pretend he's the interviewer."

Amy shoved Jasmine's shoulder a touch too hard to be entirely playful. "When will you stop reading those con-job self-help books and let *me* help you get over this stupid man thing? I know a guy who can use his tongue like—"

"No! Not Mario again. I can handle this myself." Jasmine pulled her bathrobe tightly around her.

Amy looked doubtful.

Jasmine studied her beautiful sister. The woman did know a thing or two about men. Smudged kohl rimmed her dark eyes. Her wild black hair, tangling into her legendary cleavage, was alive with her constant motion. Under her sheepskin coat, every inch of her clothes sparkled despite the dim light, as if lit by Amy's excess energy. She was the stereotypical lusty gypsy, from headscarf to toe ring.

Jasmine looked down at the plain bathrobe wrapping her straight, thin body. The only thing gypsy about her was the blackness of her hair, as if every drop of her gypsy blood were trying to escape through the top of her head to a more gypsy-worthy life in another body, leaving the rest of her pale and drained. She looked more vampire than gypsy.

"Don't you get lonely?" Amy asked.

Of course Jasmine got lonely. But it was like asking a one-legged man if he missed his leg. He did, but there was no sense dwelling on what wasn't possible. "How much money do you need?" Jasmine tried to turn the conversation back to Amy.

"Two thousand."

Jasmine gasped. "What about Cecelia?" Cecelia was their doctor sister. The one with the cash.

"She's the one I owe. We had a little disagreement."

Jasmine shook her head. Amy surely owed Cecelia more than two thousand dollars; she borrowed money from Cecelia all the time, with only the faintest notion of paying her back. This had to be about something more than money.

"I sort of pawned one of Cecelia's rings," Amy said into the silence. "How could I have known it was her engagement ring? Only someone as uptight as Cecelia would keep her diamond engagement ring in a box."

"The little toe ring?"

"No. The one Finny bought her last year. The big one."

Jasmine winced. Two thousand would only pay for the setting on that rock. "She doesn't wear it because she works in a clinic with people who can't buy their kids shoes, Amy. It's a matter of principle."

"Whatever. She's got so much jewelry she never touches."

Jasmine was about to launch into a sermon on "borrowing" when she noticed Amy giving her a sideways smile. "What?"

"Forget it."

"What?" Jasmine knew that smile. A chill ran up her spine. *Amy is a con artist.*

"Nothing. I was just thinking. No." Amy shook her head, but her smile was growing. She shrugged out of her coat and stretched her arms like a cat. A sparkly, satisfied cat. Her shirt was skintight sheer black rayon stitched through with multicolored glittering thread. Her skirt was shiny, black, flowing to her ankles.

"Okay. Here's a deal for you." Amy licked her lips. "I'll tell you the name of your One True Love for two thousand bucks."

Chapter 2

The thrill of finally knowing her One True Love's name battled with the disgust of knowing her sister was an opportunistic con artist. Either Amy had known the name for two years and not told her, or she was about to make up a name for cash.

Which option was more despicable?

"You don't know the name of my One True Love," Jasmine reminded her sister. "You lost your powers before we were reunited. Remember? You last heard the voice on September thirteenth two years ago. I came back the nineteenth." Jasmine tried not to think about how hard it had been to come back to her sisters after running away from them ten years earlier. She had barely been a teenager when she left.

"Not true. I never told you that the voice came back one last time. *For you.* I read you two Thanksgivings ago; *then* the voice faded away for good."

Jasmine's heart plunged into her stomach. One last time? For her? Or another one of Amy's lies?

Amy went on. "Cecelia had roasted that huge turkey, and you asked me to pass you the peas and *bam!*" Amy pounded her fist on the coffee table. "We both held on to those peas, and there it was clear as day! The name of your One True Love. We must have connected through the platter."

Jasmine studied her beautiful sister. "I don't believe you." Truth wasn't one of Amy's strong points.

Amy shrugged.

Jasmine's body suddenly went cold at the memory. "You spilled those peas in my lap." *Was* Amy telling the truth? She remembered Amy startling. Jasmine had assumed the platter had burned her, but it felt cold to her touch. She had shaken off her confusion in the rush to clean up the mess. "You heard the name of my One True Love as destined by Fate and all I got was a lap full of peas?" Jasmine jumped off the couch. She paced, her arms crossed. "You knew for two years and didn't tell me?" Her anger expanded through her chest, a hot orange-red gone blue around the edges. Jasmine threw up her hands. She believed Amy. She wasn't sure why, but she felt that her sister was telling the truth. The moment had, after all, struck her as so odd that she still remembered it two years later. "Out!"

Amy didn't budge. In fact, she settled herself deeper into the couch. "Gypsy hospitality rules, love."

They may have had an unconventional upbringing with their divorced parents splitting the family apart, but their mother (and grandmother, in Amy and Cecelia's case) had instilled them all with a strict sense of their gypsy heritage. Gypsy hospitality rules mandated that one gypsy give aid and shelter to any other gypsy in need, even a total stranger. But what would the Kris, the gypsy court of elders, say about having to give shelter to a blackmailer gypsy who had already stolen and pawned another gypsy's ring?

"Look, Jas," Amy said. "I promised Cecelia I would never, ever tell you your True Love's name—"

"Why?"

"Doesn't matter. Water under the bridge. Now that Cecelia's cut me off, to hell with her!" Amy wagged her eyebrows. "I know you want to know. It was *Cecelia* who wouldn't let me tell."

"Why?" Jasmine asked again. She considered her drunk, desperate sister. Her stomach churned with apprehension. Yes, Jasmine had been waiting for this moment all her life, but now that it was here, she remembered how complicated it could be. She felt sick to her stomach. Cecelia was a pragmatist. "My True Love is awful?"

"Not exactly. Actually, he's quite a looker."

Jasmine's stomach dove for cover. She let her eyes drift between Costume Designer Ken and Lying Blackmailer Amy. She had to stay focused.

I want to know the name. That was the most important thing.

Jasmine thought of the $2,324 she had in the bank. It was every penny she had made that month, and she owed $1,721 in rent next week. If she gave Amy the money, then she'd *really* have to go through with the interview. She'd have to nail it. Maybe going broke was the incentive she needed. Maybe Fate was trying to give her more than True Love.

Fate was offering up a whole new life.

If she dared.

Jasmine was bursting with questions. But where to start? "So you know him?" she asked.

"Sort of." Amy began opening the fabric bins one by one. She peered into them as if expecting something good to eat, then closed them in scrunch-lipped disappointment.

"Do *I* know him?" Jasmine watched Amy approach the bin stuffed with her self-help books. Jasmine braced herself for another argument about her "man problem."

Amy put her hand on the bin, paused, then passed over it and went on to the next. "Sort of." Amy opened the box filled with Indian doupioni silks. She selected the twelve yards of a red and black print that Jasmine had spent two weeks bargaining for from her favorite shop in Bombay and draped it around herself like a tangled sari.

"Sort of?" Pressure was building in Jasmine's head. *Tell me and don't touch my imported silks.*

Amy wrapped the fabric around her head and over her face so that just her huge black eyes showed. She knelt down regally in front of the coffee table, her back upright, her head high, playing up the moment. "Your One True Love as destined by Fate. The one man on the planet destined to be your soul mate . . ."

Jasmine leaned forward. A flutter ran through her.

Amy closed her eyes. "Two thousand dollars?"

Get rid of my savings. Force myself to get that job. "Two thousand dollars. But you've got to pay me back."

Amy opened her eyes. Two black coals blazed from the cocoon of silk. "Your One True Love . . ."

"Spit it out already!"

Amy sighed, pushed the fabric off her head, and then shrugged as if to say, *It's not my fault.* "Josh Toby, Jas. That's the thing. His name is Josh Toby."

*   *   *

Jasmine laughed. "Josh Toby?" Of all the men in the world, her True Love had the same name as the biggest movie star of the decade? It was absurd. Josh Toby, as any woman with a pulse knew, was last year's Sexiest Man Alive according to *People* magazine. His face was plastered on the wall of every thirteen-year-old girl's bedroom in America and on the cubicle walls of many a thirtysomething. He was dating Cleo Chan, the reigning Sexiest Woman Alive and star of the *Agent X* HBO series that made her almost as famous as her main squeeze.

Jasmine got the shakes talking to a doll, and she was supposed to spend her life as the One True Love of Josh Toby?

Amy shrugged the silk to the ground. "It might not be *that* Josh Toby. There must be others."

Right. Possibly. But what if it was *that* Josh Toby? Jasmine felt betrayed. How could her One True Love be someone so unattainable, so wrong? Jasmine didn't follow the tabloids, but Josh Toby was definitely not a stay-in-and-watch-DVDs kind of guy.

An image of Josh Toby's blue-purple eyes flashed in her mind from his last movie—the one with the terrorists. Well, they all had terrorists. Jasmine's stomach jumped. The man was so sexy, he was practically feral.

Amy stood, leaving the fabric in a puddle on the floor. "I know. He doesn't seem your type."

My type.

The possibility of being loved by *that* Josh Toby seeped through every pore of Jasmine's body, then drained out.

Empty.

She imagined being loved by another Josh Toby—

maybe the guy behind the counter at the dry cleaners. Her stomach curled in on itself. Not even that was possible.

She had thought everything would change once she knew her True Love's name. But everything was exactly the same. She had a name, sure, but she was still her same old self. Going out and acting on the name was impossible, whether her Josh Toby was a superstar or a schoolteacher. Face it, she couldn't even get up enough nerve for a job interview.

My job interview.

What was she thinking? She couldn't run off after a world-famous movie star sex symbol. She couldn't run off after any man. She had to prepare for Arturo. She rescued the fabric Amy had abandoned. "Well, so much for that."

Amy was back at the window. Her red fingernails tapped out Morse code for "don't be an idiot" on the glass.

"If he ends up being the guy next door, I'll go to dinner with him," Jasmine explained. She neatly folded the doupioni and placed it into its box.

Amy stopped tapping and spun around. "You won't go to dinner with the guy next door and you know it." Her black eyes were blazing with challenge.

Jasmine thought of her last blind-date-turned-two-hundred-yard dash. "I would." Cripes, her voice sounded so lame, she didn't even believe herself.

"Face it, Jas. You have a serious man problem, and it's time to kick it in the butt."

Jasmine looked at Ken. Did a grown woman playing with dolls constitute a problem? "It's just a little anxiety."

"You've been running from hot guys ever since you came back from India when you were sixteen. Remember that cutie, Luke, who lived in the apartment downstairs? The senior quarterback? We had to check to make sure he wasn't in the hall before you'd go out. *Every day*."

"It wasn't a big deal. Anyway, I paid you a buck each time."

"I had to buy candy bars for you from Joey on the corner."

"So? I paid you."

Amy put her hands firmly on her hips. "Can't you for one minute stop thinking of yourself and think of poor Josh? What if it is the movie star? That sweet guy has a tough, demanding life, and maybe you're the one woman who could help him."

"Me, help *him?*" Jasmine was flabbergasted. "He doesn't need me."

"The voice spoke *for the very last time*. There must be a reason it came back one last time just for you."

Jasmine couldn't help it. She imagined meeting Josh Toby, movie star. The lightning bolt of True Love would strike as they saw each other across a crowded, smoke-filled ballroom. Sure, Cleo Chan would be disappointed, but she'd understand the power of True Love and melt away from Josh's side, her perfectly manicured finger-tips trailing off him as he floated toward Jasmine. Violins would crescendo as she and Josh rushed out of the ball-room onto the moonlit balcony where they would swear their eternal, passionate love.

Okay, it was corny. But it wasn't *so* far-fetched. Jasmine knew deep down that she was meant for bigger things than hemming her neighbors' pants. Somewhere in a hidden part of her soul, she knew that if she had her chance, she could have the love of a lifetime with a man as dashing and exciting as Josh Toby.

Or could she? What if she couldn't? What if she was exactly what she seemed to be?

A person too afraid to go after her dreams.

Chapter 3

Josh Toby walked into the almost-empty diner with his Yankees cap pulled down low. He sported a three-day beard, a scuffed leather jacket, an unassuming flannel shirt, and faded jeans. Dark sunglasses hid his very well-known eyes.

The diner was his first test to see if he'd be recognized. Neither of the two elderly patrons reading the *New York Post* in a far booth even looked up. If he'd worn his signature black Armani suit and Italian black loafers, there'd be mobs around him by now. But instead he was playing his greatest role ever: Ordinary Guy. A nobody, sitting alone at the counter of a run-down greasy spoon on Broadway and 110th, starting from scratch.

"What'll it be?" the man behind the counter asked.

Josh was startled by how tired the man looked. Usually when strangers saw him, they put on a show, lit up like 150-watt follow spotlights. This guy hadn't given a shit since sometime last decade. Permanently on dimmer.

Josh tried not to stare. He focused on the menu. "Pastrami on rye and a diet Coke."

The man nodded, blissfully unaware that he was about to serve one of the most famous people in the world.

The diner door jangled open, and a teenage girl spilled into the restaurant. This was it. It was one thing to go unnoticed around a depressed, unkempt burger flipper and a couple of geezers at the back booth. But around a teenager of the female persuasion, he would have to be wary.

"Josh!" the girl cried.

Busted. Josh braced himself to face his adoring public. He put on his "public" face: half-smile, cocked head, raised eyebrows. But the girl sailed by him and his absurd face and sat at the far end of the counter.

"Hi, Cassie." The counterman nodded at the girl. He shuffled to Josh and put the sandwich down in front of him.

Josh blinked into the empty space where Cassie had been. *I am an idiot*. The counterman was also named Josh. He swallowed his smile.

And his pride.

He examined the sandwich. Two inches of gleaming red pastrami. *Oh, New York*. This town was humbling but worth it.

"Bad news, huh?" Cassie asked the counterman. She slung her backpack under the counter, and it landed as if it were filled with stones.

The counterman set about making the girl a tuna sandwich. He didn't answer.

"So?"

"So? It's not good. Your aunt Rini needs the operation. Fifty thou."

Josh bit into the pastrami. Nicely salted, but wet-cured, not dry, making the meat tough. Machine-cut too. Still, the taste of home. He ate for a while in peace. Blissful, silent peace. Man, he could get used to this. For a little while anyway. Not too long. His stomach clenched. What was that? Probably the pastrami.

New York always got him in the gut. Hometown nostalgia.

He pulled a worn paperback out of his inside jacket pocket: *Acts of Literature*. He flipped to an article on *Romeo and Juliet* by Jacques Derrida, the infamous de-contructionist philosopher, but he couldn't concentrate with the snatches of whispered conversation floating down the counter to him. *"Maybe more tests . . . if I sell the diner . . ."*

He itched to jump down four stools and lean into the conversation. His right leg jiggled with pent-up energy.

The clenching in his gut wasn't the pastrami.

Face it, pretty boy, you're lonely. He was used to being surrounded by people. But he had come here to get away from all that so he could work. Really work. Josh stuck his nose back in the book, but the lines blurred. His stomach fluttered at the prospect of doing *Romeo and Juliet*. No special effects. No reshoots. Just him and a few other actors on a tiny stage. His chance to prove once and for all that he could be a serious actor if given the chance.

He reached for his cell to call Cleo, then stopped. She thought he was researching a role in Afghanistan. If she knew he was here doing off Broadway, she'd freak. After all, their relationship was purely about work; they posed as lovers so they could focus on building their careers without the distractions of personal relationships. They were both seasoned veterans of every brand of gold digger. The ones who were after money or fame weren't the problem. It was the real lovers whose anger turned them into gold diggers when they realized that work *had* to come first. Always. That was what it took to stay on top. Single-minded determination, endless traveling, and non-stop promotion. Love was a fantasy for people with time and privacy.

Trouble was, now that his career had taken him as far as he could go in the world of blockbuster hits, he longed for something more, well, fulfilling. He hoped *Romeo and Juliet* would be the creative outlet he needed.

His palms itched. Who else could he call?

No. Bad idea.

The clenching again in his gut.

What the hell. He'd been thinking about them since he'd gotten to New York six hours ago.

He dialed his parents' number. They lived just twenty blocks uptown, on the twelfth floor of a prewar building on Riverside Drive. He hadn't seen them in two years. Each ring made his heart flutter.

A click, then, "Hello? Hello?"

Josh melted at the sound of his mother's voice. "Hi, Mom."

Silence. Then, "Joshie? Is that you? You know I hate being called Mom. Call me Ruth. Are you calling from Afghanistan? Your, um, person, whatever you call her—"

"Maureen? Mo? My publicist?"

"I still can't believe my son has a servant." Her voice took on its familiar edge. His mother was an old-school socialist. She still had scars from the 1968 Columbia riots to prove it.

Josh didn't bother to reply. He'd explained hundreds of times that Mo was a well-paid professional, not a servant.

But his mother only responded with a sigh and a muttered, "An honest person handles his own affairs."

"Maureen said you were in Afghanistan. We were thrilled!"

Josh perked. *Mom—er, Ruth—is pleased with me. . . .*

His mother was still talking. "And I told your father, finally, after all these years, he's getting political! Protesting violence! Your father said you were finally understanding life and using some of that fortune of yours to help the war orphans."

Josh held the phone loosely, trying to control the twisting in his gut. He looked out the window at the fall leaves floating to the sidewalk. Then he looked at the girl four stools down. She stared at her sandwich while her uncle talked. Josh felt closer to this stranger than he did to his mother. His mother would only be disappointed if he told her he was twenty blocks away studying for a role off Broadway. Just more proof that his life was frivolous and wasted. "I've got to go, M—um, *Ruth*. I'm losing the connection. I'll call you later." He clicked the phone shut before she could reply.

He felt like dirt, and it definitely wasn't the pastrami. Maybe New York was a bad idea.

He was restless. He needed to get out. But the counterman was still talking to the girl. Josh tried not to eavesdrop. *"Operation . . . no insurance . . . eighty percent chance . . ."*

The counterman noticed Josh watching them. He patted the girl's hand, scribbled Josh's bill on a pad, made his way down the counter to Josh, and slapped down the bill.

$8.25 with tax.

Josh gawked at the slip of paper. He really had to start carrying cash. Usually Mo paid the bills—if people even bothered to charge him. He pulled his wallet out of his jacket pocket. No green. He fished his finger behind the plastic window where the kindergarten pictures of his kids should have been if he ever had kids (he used his wallet so infrequently, it still had the factory-installed picture of a smiling stranger) and found his emergency American Express Card. He hadn't used it in years. It had his first initial and last name. He'd have to hope the counterman wouldn't notice.

The man ran his card and handed it back to him without even looking at it. Josh watched the girl, Cassie, who was still staring into space.

The counterman gave him the receipt to sign.

Josh shrugged. What the hell? It was more important to help out than to hide out. He filled in a $50,000 tip, added up the total ($50,008.25), and signed his name as messily as he could. Then he dashed for the door.

"Hey, wait. I think you made a mistake, Mister, uh, Toby."

"It's for Aunt Rini," he said as he slipped through the door. "Plus, you make a mean pastrami."

"Wait—" the counterman began.

"Oh, my god. That's—" the girl cried.

But Josh was gone. Already out the door and across Broadway on his way to the park.

Chapter 4

Jasmine's hands grew clammy, her breath quickened, and for the fourth time in twelve minutes, she hurried past the Royalton Hotel where she was supposed to meet Arturo for her interview in the hotel's famous lobby bar.

Okay, this was ridiculous. She just had to walk in, find Arturo, and be herself. Well, no. Not herself. She had to be the fearless, bold person she'd been rehearsing the last few days with Amy and Ken. The person Arturo would hire.

She could do it. She was going to do it. *She was going to pass out.*

She rounded 44th Street and headed up 6th Avenue. Again. Across 45th. Down 5th.

Then she was back on 44th street. The hotel, with its bright red door and stately Roman columns, loomed halfway down the block. Jasmine slowed. She had to go in this time or she'd be late. She took shallow, short breaths. Her enormous portfolio in its black leather box weighed her down as much as her dread. If only she could climb inside her portfolio case and disappear. . . .

"Jasmine Burns?" A high-pitched voice assaulted her.

Skinny, jewel-encrusted arms protruding from the sleeves of an unbuttoned white fur jacket flew around her, and the puckery suck of an air kiss floated past her right ear. The unmistakable scent of Joy (was it still the world's most expensive perfume?) drifted around her. Something hard banged against her kneecap, and she jumped back.

"It's me, Samantha! Sam Olivia!" the woman cried. "Are you here to interview with Arturo? I just left. He's a doll!"

Jasmine's hands flew to Ken, who was tucked safely in her purse for good luck. No, Samantha couldn't know. It was just an expression. She rubbed her knee where Samantha's portfolio had banged into it. "Hi, Sam."

"Oh, God, *I'll* never get the job if you're up for it. Everyone knows you're the best. I'm glad I was before you and not after." Samantha had graduated from NYU with Jasmine.

Had Samantha called Jasmine "the best"? Samantha had scored an internship on Broadway before the end of the first semester. Of course, there were rumors of her exceptional blow jobs and of her daddy's connections, but it was none of Jasmine's business. Although, at this moment, eye-to-cleavage with Sam's low-cut charmeuse blouse, she realized maybe it was her business. Sam's blazing purple-red hair clashed with the orange-red of the silver oak behind her, jangling Jasmine's already-jangled nerves.

"He is dreamy. *Italian*." Samantha sighed. "But here I am jabbering when you better hurry! Good luck, love!" Sam embraced her again, and the air kiss flew by, borne into oblivion on fumes of Joy.

*   *   *

Shyness is an abnormal fear of normal situations. Take control of the anxiety or it will take control of you. Imagine Arturo is naked. Imagine that you won't throw up on his Italian suede loafers. Imagine that you don't feel as if you're about to melt into a puddle of goo. . . .

Arturo sat at a table in the back of the bar taking notes on a yellow legal pad. He was more gorgeous than Jasmine remembered. And he was wearing almost the exact same suit she had made for Ken. She had nailed it.

Too bad she was stalled two feet from Arturo's table, unable to move. *We're done,* her legs seemed to be saying. *Here is good.* Her breath stopped too. Her thoughts were the only things in motion, swirling in endless spirals: *You don't belong here; you're better off at home; it'll be humiliating; he'll laugh; he'll be sorry he ever decided to interview you; in fact, it's probably all a huge mistake and he hired Samantha anyway and hell, now he'll be worn out from Samantha's, um, many talents. . . .*

Oh, she didn't feel well. It was too hot.

I am not going to have a panic attack.

Oh, yes, I am . . .

She could feel an attack coming like an approaching train that she couldn't stop. Her heart racing, her lungs constricting.

In a rush of determination, she picked up her portfolio and sped to Arturo's table. Then stood, mute.

Here comes the train wreck.

Her portfolio clunked to the ground, making Arturo look up. "Oh, hi. Have a seat." Gorgeous brown eyes, warm and soft. And that suit. Italian doupioni, the best. So much better than her Indian silk. "I'm Arturo Mastriani."

And I'm about to be ill. She tried to speak but couldn't.

He stared at her, confused, his smile slowly fading.

Just me and my neurosis, nice to meet you. She had to get out of there before he had a new story to tell at the next cast party—the one about the NYU graduate who barfed on his $2,000 suit. She tried once more to speak, but no words could get past her demons.

She forced her mouth into an apologetic smile, squeezed out the words "excuse me," then turned as slowly as she could and walked away. One careful step in front of the other. Slow. Easy. Once she cleared the concrete pillar and was out of sight, she bolted to the huge potted lime trees set in a dark corner, fell to her knees, and puked.

Shoot me, someone. Now.

She glanced around. No one seemed to have noticed in the hushed, lush whispers of the general fabulousness that was the Royalton. But what if someone did? What if Arturo came after her?

She had to get out. Immediately. She searched the lobby. No Arturo. She carefully headed for the door, shoving through before the startled doorman could open it. She ran down the sidewalk, then slowed to a panicked walk.

It wasn't until she was crossing into Central Park that she realized she had left her portfolio behind.

"So, so, so?" Amy splashed into the apartment, a sea of shopping bags. "How'd it go? Tell me every little thing! Did he hire you on the spot?" Amy was wearing Jasmine's pewter merino sweater, stretching it to her voluptuous proportions. Her belly-button ring stared out like a third eye.

Jasmine took in the shopping bags in shock. *I gave all my money to Amy. I lost my mind.* Jasmine ran the iron over and over the hem of a pair of slacks with a stunning black warp and brown weft. It hissed out a cloud of steam as if it were angry too.

"You didn't go, did you?" Amy asked.

"No. I didn't. I decided not to. I'm a great tailor. I'm going to expand my business. I've been here all afternoon making plans. I've already designed the business cards in my head. I'm going to call it 'Tailoring for Women.'"

"That's better than '*Tailoring for Women Because I've Got Some Bizarro Fear of Men,*' I guess. But still, pretty lame, Jas. Hey, speaking of men, where's Ken?" Amy stared at the empty spot on the bookshelf where he'd been sitting in his off-hours.

Jasmine felt her eyes flick to the window before she could stop them, and Amy was off in a flash.

She leaned as far as she could, pressing her nose against the glass. "Oh, my God! You killed Ken!" Amy flew out of the apartment, leaving the door to the hallway flapping open behind her. Jasmine put the finished pants in the smaller pile and took the next pair off the top of the big pile. Being a tailor was nice. Peaceful. She got out her seam ripper.

Amy returned two pairs of pants later, out of breath, holding a dirty Ken like a sword. "Now look here. Don't murder innocent dolls. That's some scary shit, Jas."

Jasmine slashed at the threads of a hem with swift, certain swipes. She would accept the Smith wedding job she had turned down last week. Then she'd have Suz and

Jenn spread the word among their colleagues. She'd be an even huger success than before. Who needed the stress of costume design? "Do you know how to iron?" Jasmine asked.

"No." Amy put Ken back on his shelf with elaborate care.

"Too bad. You owe me. It's time to learn." Jasmine held the iron out to Amy.

Amy accepted the iron as if it were fruitcake for Christmas. She ran the iron over the pants awkwardly. "There will be more interviews, hon."

"Nope. Done that. On to other things," Jasmine said. "Push the steam button or you'll burn them." Jasmine hadn't gone back for her portfolio, and she imagined Arturo had been spooked by the enormous, untended black box and the weirdo who left it. Maybe he had called the police and alerted the bomb squad. Maybe they'd evacuated the whole hotel. Maybe when all was clear, they blew her portfolio into millions of microscopic bits, just one more part of her forever joined with the hotel foliage.

"I can fix everything," Amy proclaimed. Well, everything but pants; despite a heroic struggle, she couldn't figure out how to arrange the legs on the ironing board, and they were a rumpled mess. "After all, Arturo's Italian, right? Italians are terrified of gypsies. Very superstitious. I could tell him something to get you another chance."

"Push the steam button. It's going to scorch." Jasmine reached over and pushed the button. "I didn't actually think I'd need to teach you to iron. How do you get through day-to-day life?"

"Wash and wear, baby."

Jasmine cringed.

"I could tell Arturo something about his One True Love."

"Steam. Button. Again. Good. Lay off Arturo." Jasmine smoothed the pants expertly on the board, demonstrating proper technique. The process soothed her.

"I'm just trying to help." Amy sighed and pushed the button, startling at the powerful hiss.

"Well, forget it. I'm really excited about making this business work." Jasmine ripped the threads of another seam with swift, sure strokes.

"You are so full of shit—" Amy began when the phone startled them both.

Jasmine jumped for it. It was surely Suz's boss, who was supposed to call with a moth-eaten vintage ballgown she wanted to wear to a fund-raiser this weekend. Rush job. Lots of detail work. Big money.

But Amy was quicker. Anything to get away from the hissing iron. "Hello. Yes. Who may I ask is calling?" Amy's eyes grew round and her mouth fell open. "Arturo Mastriani calling for Jasmine Burns? Certainly." She held out the phone to Jasmine.

Jasmine stared at the phone as if it were lime-green polyester.

Amy sighed. "Oh, for heaven's sake." She put the receiver back to her own ear. "Hello?" she said sweetly. "This is Jasmine."

Jasmine slammed herself back on the sofa in disbelief. Oh, this was bad. And good. No, this was completely bad. She watched Amy listen to Arturo's words, trying to divine meaning from the fake smile on Amy's face.

"Mmm-hmm. That was my plan." Amy nodded solemnly. "Weren't you clever to figure it out? I just love Italians."

Jasmine began to unravel, thread by thread. What was Amy talking about? If only her apartment were big enough to have an extension so that she could listen.

"Wait, let me write this down." Amy motioned to Jasmine for a pencil and paper. Jasmine pointed to the tiny drawer by the ministove. Amy got her supplies and scribbled something on the paper, which she then tossed to Jasmine.

It read, *Siddhartha, 6th Street, Thursday, 1:00.*

Chapter 5

Amy hung up the phone and beamed at Jasmine.

"What just happened?"

"You got the job."

Jasmine felt her limbs begin to loosen. She could move again. Breathe.

"He loved the drama of your presentation."

The puking? The trampling of the doorman in the mad dash to escape? "My presentation?"

"He thought you left your portfolio on purpose!" Amy snorted and threw her hands out in disbelief, brushing the iron with her pinky. She startled and stuck her burnt finger in her mouth.

"Go on!"

Amy took a deep breath and pointed her chin in the air. "He thought it was 'a daring and brave display of drama without words, exactly a costume designer's challenge.' Translated into English, I'm pretty sure that means you blew his mind, baby!" She returned her pinky to her grinning mouth.

Jasmine felt light-headed as she imagined Arturo with

her portfolio. Had she already barfed, or was she barfing while he was perusing?

"He thought the statement you were making about being all work, no talk was brilliant. 'You were your portfolio,' he said. Man, what a load of crap. Sucker, that one. Let me at him!"

Jasmine felt something strange in her abdomen. She felt—what was that?—happiness? Joy? No, it was more than that. Bigger. Rounder. Fuller. Bluer.

Bluer?

She closed her eyes and let the feeling wash over her. Swirls of royal Chinese blue purpled with a half-drop of red filled her soul with their vibrancy. They flowed and ebbed.

She knew that color. She had seen it once before. When she had graduated.

It was the color of success.

Amy was still talking. "He thought your work was, let me get this exactly right, 'smart, witty, and eloquent.'"

Jasmine let the color twirl and spin joyfully. She got the job. In a bizarro way, yes, but she got it nonetheless.

She couldn't wait to tell that blow-job sycophant Samantha. *Maybe I could put in a good word for you,* she'd tell her.

Amy flopped down on the bed, the iron forgotten. "This is the first time I've been a channeler for a spirit who says more than two words at a time. It's not easy remembering all this. . . ."

Jasmine forced her eyes open. The blue dispersed like a cloud. "You have to remember!" she cried. "Every single word."

"Oh, no. I have ironing to do."

That was it. A smile escaped Jasmine's lips and Amy smiled too. They remained frozen for a second; then they sprang together and hugged each other. Or, rather, Jasmine tried to hug Amy, but Amy was too enthusiastic and she squeezed the life out of Jasmine until she had to back off gasping for breath, knocking over the iron.

"Every word! Exactly!" Jasmine demanded as she righted the spilled iron before it could damage the exquisite wool. Wait, the pants could go up in flames! Her whole apartment could explode in an inferno! She got the job!

Amy grinned. "Right. Right. Well, he said that his next project is discreet."

Jasmine went to the window and looked out. Did she have a blue that matched the color in her head? She took Ken off his shelf and sat him on her lap. She covered his ears with her index fingers. "Go ahead."

"Oh, he can hear. After all, it was him and the kooky ideas in that idiotic book that failed you so utterly that you had to flee. Really, you have him to thank."

Jasmine uncovered his ears. "Okay. Talk to us." A thrill raced through her. She did have that blue-violet fabric. Third bin, second stack, toward the bottom. She had gotten it at an estate sale in Connecticut two years ago.

"He wants you to meet him and his associate at Siddhartha on Sixth Street to discuss the project."

Jasmine jumped up to find the fabric. She unstacked the bins. "Did he say what it was?"

"Only that you shouldn't tell anyone you're coming or that you got the job."

"Why hide out in a tiny dive of an Indian restaurant after sitting for a whole day in clear view of everyone in a trendy hotel bar in the theater district?" She got out the bin with the right fabric and rifled through it.

There it was. Four yards of Russian silk velvet with a tiny matching swatch folded carefully on top. She petted it.

"That's what the man said." A look of concern flashed over Amy's face. "Do you think you can do it?"

A second chance. Who ever got a second chance? She brought the swatch to the couch. She sat Ken next to her. It didn't match his eyes at all, too deep and leaning toward purple. The swatch was just enough fabric to make him a tiny shirt.

No. She didn't have to make him a shirt. She didn't need him at all. She folded the fabric carefully into a cube and put it gently into her pocket. Her lucky swatch.

"I'm doing it," she said, her voice strong. "With you two guys on my side to help, how can I go wrong?"

Josh sat in the subway-car-wide Indian restaurant at a back table. It was the middle of the day, but the place was dark, lit only by the Christmas lights strung on every surface, including the ceiling. Of course, it didn't help that Josh was wearing sunglasses. He had decided never to take them off. It was too risky, especially after his last overtipping adventure.

Where was Arturo? Josh loved the guy. They had met on the set of Josh's first movie sixteen years ago when Josh was only sixteen and Artie was twenty-six. They'd been fast friends ever since. But Artie was famous for his flighty escapades. Of course, he never let it interfere with work.

Yet.

Josh watched the door anxiously. The restaurant was almost empty except for six twentysomethings in Columbia sweatshirts finishing off the beers they had brought in brown paper bags.

Josh pulled his dark glasses down to the end of his nose and reread the article Mo had faxed him that morning from the *New York Post*. PASTRAMI PHILANTHROPIST STRIKES AGAIN! LEAVES WAITRESS $10,000 TIP. Damn. He'd really have to be more careful. Either he could do this play without anyone knowing he was in New York, or he could help people, but doing both was too dangerous.

The mysterious tipster strongly resembled People *magazine's Sexiest Man Alive Josh Toby, and the name on the American Express card read "J. Toby," the waitress reported. Toby's publicist, Maureen Reycroft, denies Josh is in New York. "He's researching his next Mitch Tank movie in Afghanistan," she reported. She issued a press release hinting that someone might be posing as Josh, although she didn't say why a person might do such a thing. Officials at American Express refused to comment.* Josh braced himself, then reread the last line of the article. *Bystander Wendy Straub who was in the restaurant at the time of the enormous tip commented that she was sure it was Josh Toby. "After all," she said, "if anyone is dumb enough to get a twenty-percent tip so wrong, he'd be the one."*

Josh let the attack stream through him, then out. *I am not reading celebrity nonsense while I'm here.*

He pulled out his worn book and tried to read in the dim light. But it was too dark to read the tiny, faded text.

A woman entered the restaurant, then fled as if she had rushed her cue.

Josh felt an absurd longing to chase after her and invite her to join him. *Whatever's the matter, I can help.* He shook off his ridiculous impulse. He was here to help himself, not strangers. Mo had given him hell for the big-tip fiasco. "Always doing for other people, Josh. New York this month is for you." He was going to blow his chance at doing this play anonymously if he wasn't careful.

He concentrated on his book. Romeo and Juliet *amplifies the age-old distinction between mind and body deconstructed . . . desire exceeds the language able to express it. . . .*

He slammed the book shut. *Impenetrable bullshit.* Romeo and Juliet were lovers. Did it have to be more complicated than that? Love and desire and women and men.

Or was it? He felt the familiar feeling of his body going rigid and cold. He was going to make a total fool of himself on that stage. No special effects. No reshoots. Why had he ever thought he could do this?

He opened the book again. His mother had given it to him for a twentieth birthday present, but he had never bothered with it. Now he had three weeks to figure this play out before rehearsals started. He had to nail his role. Prove to the world he wasn't just a pretty face but a real actor.

Finally, Arturo hustled into the restaurant, spotted Josh, and carefully made his way down the narrow aisle around the students. "Sorry, sorry. I had my monthly tarot card reading, and Madame Russo took longer than usual." He sank into the seat across from Josh. Josh felt so relieved to see him, his face went hot. Damn, this undercover nonsense was making him soft.

"So, did you find someone for the job?" Josh asked. He ignored the tarot nonsense. He and Artie had never seen eye-to-eye on that stuff.

"Yeah. I think so. You know, Madame Russo said I was going on a journey."

"*You think so?*" A cold dread iced Josh's veins. "I've got a journey for you—go get me an assistant who's for sure."

"Don't worry. I think she's on board. She's a phenom. Her use of color is visionary. I have no idea why she hasn't been snatched up."

"Awwww, Artie, what'd you get a *her* for? Costume designers are all gay men. Couldn't you have gotten me one of those? I'm already in enough trouble with Cleo over my East Coast disappearing act. I'm acting almost as flaky as you."

Arturo ignored the insult with good humor. "Don't think of Jasmine as female; think of her as genius. She'll put together some wow disguises for hiding you during rehearsals. Not that the dark glasses during the day aren't smooth."

Josh smiled and shrugged sheepishly. It was good to talk to an old friend.

Arturo went on. "Also, she'll be your dresser during the show so no one else gets near you." A dresser was the person backstage who helped an actor in and out of his costumes during quick scene changes.

"So where is she?"

"No idea." Arturo studied the menu, unconcerned.

Arturo was too laid back for his own good. His whole career was based on hunches and feelings. Granted, it had served him brilliantly. But still, Josh didn't like it. He liked relying on hard work and sweat and a great publicist.

Josh bounced his leg. He had gone for a seven-mile run at dawn, but now he felt like doing a few wind sprints. Maybe swing from the Christmas lights. Life in the city that never sleeps was one big snore when you were hiding out.

The waiter came, and Arturo ordered for the table—breads, dips, chutneys, curries.

Just then, the woman in black entered again. She stood stock-still at the front of the restaurant, her shoulders erect under her simple black leather jacket. She was thin, but nicely so. Not like some of those Hollywood starlets he was used to seeing. Her jet-black hair was shoulder length with bangs, blunt-cut, and bone-straight. Her eyes were lost behind huge black sunglasses.

She was the most poised, beautiful woman he had ever seen.

Wait.

What?

He was best friends with Cleo Chan, for God's sake. He had had lunch last week with Angelina Jolie. What was he thinking?

Yet he felt as if he knew this woman, had known her all his life. As if they were meant to meet in this crazy Christmas-in-October, darkness-in-the-daytime restaurant.

Arturo had his back to her and continued to talk about co-op boards and the size of his dog and something about a new seer Madame Russo told him about.

The woman coming toward him couldn't be the costume designer. Costume designers were flamboyant and colorful. This woman was the most contained human he'd ever seen. A closed-off personal space seemed to travel with her, an invisible bubble. An odd sense of calm overcame him. He wanted into that bubble. Out of his loneliness.

Arturo must have finally noticed that Josh had stopped listening, because he turned. When he saw Jasmine, he jumped up and stuck out an enormous hand. "Jasmine Burns! Arturo Mastriani. Gorgeous to meet you again."

The woman stared at the hand but didn't move. "Yes," she said after a long pause. At least Josh thought that was what she had said. He leaned forward to hear better.

Arturo pulled in his hand. "Right, well, please, sit down." He motioned to the chair next to Josh. "This is, well, we'll get to that. Please, sit."

The woman sat next to Josh as if she were wired with explosives, rigid in her seat, not granting him a glance.

"Let me lay it on the table," Arturo said. "Jasmine, this is Josh Toby."

Her lips fell open slightly, then closed. But she didn't turn to look at him, giving him the opportunity to continue studying her. Her lips were gorgeous. Pouty and pink with just a glimmer of gloss.

"I knew when I met you that I had found a person of few words," Arturo said. "I had a vision that you could handle a job like this. And my visions are *never* wrong. Right, Joshie?" Arturo reached over the table and smacked Josh on the shoulder. "Right. So I'll leave you two kids alone to figure out the details. Then, if it's simpatico with everyone, Jasmine, I'll have my assistant deliver the contract to your place tomorrow." Arturo popped a whole samosa into his mouth and held out his hand again.

She began to reach for it, then seemed to change her mind. She snatched her hand back, and it disappeared under the table.

"Right. Okay," Arturo enthused through his full mouth. "Josh, give me a call." He put his card in front of Jasmine. "You too. Great. Well, gotta get back to fittings. It was"—he paused—"interesting to meet you. Oh, and I'll FedEx you your portfolio back. It was amazing. The best I've seen in years. Really unique. What a feel you have for color! Unreal. You're going to be a star, kid."

He was down the aisle and out the door before Josh, or Jasmine, could do anything about it.

Chapter 6

Jasmine had to risk a glance at the man next to her. The ball her stomach had become was rolling in place like a hamster's wheel, picking up speed. She yanked down her sunglasses, peered at the man, then pushed them back into position.

Good God, it is Josh Toby. My possibly One True Love is next to me, dipping pakoras in chutney as if this was a normal situation.

Well, it was normal for him. He didn't know he might be her destiny. She gulped. *Me and my One True Love the movie star doing green curry. No biggie.*

No. She was being absurd. He had a girlfriend. A gorgeous, A-list girlfriend. She was letting her fantasy life get away from her. This was work. Her True Love could be any Josh Toby.

"Hi." Josh held out his hand.

Must shake hands. Jasmine commanded her right arm to lift. The bastard wouldn't budge. "Hi," she managed to get out. Her heart was racing so fast, she was sure he could hear it over the twang of Urdu ballads coming from the kitchen.

Josh put his hand down. "I make people a little nervous." He smiled a glistening, Hollywood smile. Dimples. Bleached, straight teeth. He was an amazing sight. The man even smelled famous, like money. "Relax. I won't bite. I'm really just a normal guy."

She jumped up. *Yeah, but I'm not a normal woman. I'm a disintegrating mass of nerve endings.* She was disgusted that she couldn't control her body enough to prove to this guy that she wasn't acting this way because he was famous. But what could she say? *Oh, I act like a moron around all attractive men. Nothing personal.* Maybe she'd have little cards printed up, the kind deaf people give to strangers. Only hers would say, *The woman who handed you this card just ran off to vomit in the ladies' room because she's a tad anxious. Please don't take it personally. Thanks.* "I've got to go."

He looked astonished. "Don't you want to hear about the project?"

Must not leave. Must sit back down and pretend to be a human being and not some small woodland creature controlled by instinct. She forced herself to lower into Arturo's vacated seat. There, at least, she wasn't as close to him as before. They waited in ear-splitting silence as the waiter rushed over to replace Arturo's plates and silverware with a clean setting.

She had to speak. *Oh, what a lovely coincidence. You know, you just might be my One True Love as destined by Fate. Can you pass the raita and some nan, please?*

"So," Josh began, "here's my problem." He leaned forward, looked around suspiciously, then took off his sunglasses.

Jasmine touched hers to assure herself they were still

covering her popping-with-terror eyes. His eyes, on the other hand, were practically glowing with calm intensity. And that color. She had never seen eyes exactly that color before—a blue that whispered purple.

A whole new kind of terror filled her: *His eyes were the color she had seen when she got the job with Arturo. The blue purple. His eyes matched her lucky swatch.* She touched her pocket lightly to check that it was still there.

"We're doing *Romeo and Juliet*," Josh said.

Romeo and Juliet? *What's in a name? That which we call a rose/By any other name would smell as sweet . . .* The whole play was about the curse of the young lovers' names—the one thing that kept them from happiness. And Jasmine's future, ruled by the name of her One True Love. Or not. Or yes. She had to concentrate on breathing. In. Out. In. Out. She had to get a hold of herself. *I have $835 in my bank account, and the rent's due. I need this job.*

"It's a secret that I'm doing the play. So what I need from you are disguises to get me around Manhattan and through rehearsals. Then I need you to be my dresser during the play. No one else can get close enough to know it's me. When I go onstage opening night, I need to be unrecognizable."

Jasmine tried to take in his words. "Why?" she managed to get out. *Impossible,* she thought, trying to avoid his unavoidable eyes.

"It's a long story."

I only have two minutes before I self-destruct, so you better get started, buddy. "You need a makeup artist," she said.

"No. We do the makeup part ourselves. I want as few

people involved as possible. We'll do the rest with your costumes and my acting."

Jasmine's jittery stomach stilled. *He believed in fabric.* He knew that colors and cloth and excellent design could achieve miracles. That she could make him anyone, anything. What if he *was* her soul mate? The color of his eyes matched exactly. Tap-dance music started up in her head, and a troupe of dancing elephants two-stepped into her stomach.

He ran his hand through his dirty-blond hair, and Jasmine tried not to look at the sculpted muscles that made this simple movement possible. To dress a man like this would be like draping silk—the less fuss the better. But to disguise him? It was almost a crime. Colors flashed in her mind, one replacing the next, all wrong. *He should be naked.*

Oh, bad thought. The elephants did cartwheels. "I'm not the person you want."

"That's funny, because I'm starting to think you might be perfect."

Perfect. Her head was spinning. Oh, no. She couldn't have a panic attack here. "Impossible to disguise you at rehearsals in a tiny theater," she said quickly. Hell, it wouldn't be possible to disguise this guy in a crowd of thousands. His teeth alone were otherworldly. He had more sex appeal in his right earlobe than most men had in their entire bodies. He shimmered with confidence. "The cast would know within two minutes. You'd have to be so totally not you that you'd have to be . . ." *Me.* She dared a look at his eyes and was startled again by their intensity. Why was he looking at her like that? Was there food between her teeth?

He probably looked at everyone that way. Probably had taken Female Seduction 101: How to Make a Woman Feel Like She's the Only Woman on Earth.

No, she knew in her heart there was no class that could make this man before her who he was. He was a natural. He was a sexual creature the way other men were athletes or mathematicians.

Jasmine sucked in her breath. "You can't hide when you're as famous as you are. I'm sorry. I can't do it."

Jasmine pushed back her chair too quickly, and it smashed into the chair behind it. Her heart was pounding, her legs jelly. Her breath quickened with each moment. She tried to say good-bye, but her throat was completely constricted, so she nodded, then turned.

Then ran.

"Jasmine!" Josh called after her.

But she didn't stop. She couldn't.

She was outside. She fell against the bricks of the restaurant façade clutching her chest. Where was Amy? Amy was supposed to be waiting for her with a cab. That was the deal they had made. She'd be ready if Jasmine needed an escape.

A hunched man with a small white dog stopped and stared, but she waved him away. She had to get out of there before Josh came out. But how was she going to get away when she couldn't breathe?

A cab screeched to a stop in front of her. The back door flew open.

"Jas! Hurry! Climb in!" Amy stuck her head out of the back of the cab.

Jasmine jumped in through the open door, and the cab

raced away just as Josh pushed onto the sidewalk, the waiter right behind him, insisting that he only took cash.

"Sorry I was late," Amy said as they sped away from the scene of the disaster.

Jasmine fell back in the seat. She was gasping for breath. "Josh. Josh. He was. Josh."

Amy sucked in her cheeks and tapped her fingernails on her armrest. "What are you sputtering about?"

Jasmine took an enormous calming breath. "Josh Toby was there. The job is for me to work for Josh Toby." The city was flying by. But why were they heading west?

"Stop the cab!" Amy yelled to the driver.

He pulled over in alarm, the cab lurching dangerously across three lanes. "You are not to be sick in my cab!" the driver commanded. His accent was thick, his eyes dark and flashing.

Jasmine was thrown into Amy by the driver's abrupt swerve.

"Turn around, go back!" Amy commanded the driver.

"No!" Jasmine said. "Don't you dare."

The driver rolled his eyes and muttered something in Hindi.

Jasmine replied in Hindi. Her words, roughly translated, meant, "Watch it, honored sir, I understand you." Growing up in India had a lot of pluses in Manhattan.

Amy took Jasmine's hand. "Whatever you did in that restaurant, we have to fix it."

"How do you know there's something to fix? Maybe I was great in there."

"You were practically doubled over in the fetal position when I picked you up. Remember? We have to go back. It's destiny out the wazoo!"

"Are we going to Fifth and Forty-fifth or no?" the driver asked. "I have business I run."

Jasmine squinted at Amy. "Fifth and Forty-fifth? The New York Public Library?"

Amy shrugged. She tossed her mane of hair. "I found a Josh Toby. Another Josh Toby. He's waiting to meet you. He's a librarian. I didn't want to tell you because I knew you'd say no. But now that you have *this* Josh Toby, let's ditch the bookworm."

Jasmine let her head fall into her hands. "I don't *have* anybody. I'm going home."

"Josh Toby, movie star, and my kid sister," Amy mused. "Hot damn."

The driver muttered in Hindi, "A librarian is a scholar and a gentleman. Josh Toby the movie star is a dumb hack."

"I didn't think he was dumb," Jasmine said in Hindi. In fact, she thought he had looked at her with an emotional expertise that reminded her of the way her older gypsy relatives, the ones who were supposed to be witches, looked at her, as if they could see through to her soul.

She shook herself free from her thoughts. The man's IQ was totally beside the point. The point was that meeting another man today, much less another possible True Love, would cause internal organ damage at the rate her body was rebelling. But then, a librarian? That sounded so quiet. A librarian sounded like a man who would understand her and bring her peace. "His name is Josh Toby?"

"Josh Toby, senior reference librarian at the New York Public Library. He's waiting for you by the left lion," Amy said. She meant one of the two impressive stone lions that flanked the grand stairs that led to the library. "We could do a drive-by."

The driver must have agreed. Without waiting for instructions, he swung the cab back into the flow of traffic.

Chapter 7

The cab rolled to a stop in front of the library. Jasmine pressed her nose against the cab window to survey the scene. The place was packed with a midday lunch crowd enjoying the sunny fall day. Graduate-student types dotted the steps with their brown-bag lunches staining their khaki pants. A woman roller skater jived through the crowd, her eyes closed as she listened to her iPod. A mime dressed in all black entertained the assemblage by following oblivious passersby, mimicking their absurd walks, and exaggerating their mannerisms. If his targets turned, he abruptly looked to the sky, pretending to whistle. Tourists threw money joyfully into his upturned hat.

Amy opened the door of the cab and pushed Jasmine out. She stumbled onto the sidewalk. "Hey—"

But the door slammed and the cab peeled away from the curb, the driver calling out in Hindi, "Your father will thank me!"

Jasmine took a few desperate steps after the fleeing cab, then stopped. She looked at the lions. Did Amy say the left lion or the right? And was left or right from her vantage point, looking *at* the library, or from the other direction, coming out of the library? Her hands felt clammy.

Both lions were swarming with people on this gorgeous, blue-skied fall afternoon. Teenagers leaned against the lions' bases, talking into cell phones. A pigtailed girl in a Catholic school uniform sat between one of the lions' mammoth paws reading Jane Austen. Japanese tourists posed under the lions, smiling into very expensive cameras.

Then, to the left of the left lion, there was a man. Red curly hair, reddened cheeks on pale skin. He stood awkwardly, shifting from foot to foot. He was thin—too thin—and tall. He squinted at people passing by, then turned even redder when they met his eye.

He sure looked like he was waiting for someone but wasn't sure who.

He had to be Josh Toby. But now what? Had Amy told him the whole True Love story? Or had Amy told him that Jasmine was a secret admirer, finally making her move after months of asking pointless reference questions: What's the population of Zaire? The average temperature in Peru? Could you point me to information regarding major American city reference librarians and their feelings and beliefs on psychics and the possibility of True Love?

Jasmine was still standing where Amy had dumped her. Okay. He looked quiet. Nice. She took a step toward him.

Then stopped in horror.

The mime was making fun of Josh. He was standing behind his back, shucking and smiling, shuffling his feet. The mime expertly caught his mannerisms: his ducked head, his stooped shoulders, his slow advance, then rapid retreat as he eyed passing strangers with hope, then chagrin.

Tourists and a few not-too-jaded (yet) members of the late lunch crowd laughed. The mime put his hand under his shirt and palpitated it rapidly, illustrating Josh's beating heart. With the retreat of every stranger, the mime let his heart stop. He hung his head in defeat.

A little girl put a bill in the mime's hat, then ran up to Josh and stared. Josh, realizing that he was the center of attention, turned to see the mime with his hand beating a ferocious heartbeat. The mime stopped mid-palpitation, smiled, then patted Josh on the top of his carrot top and waddled away, penguin style.

The crowd laughed uproariously.

Josh looked around him desperately, as if looking for a place to hide.

Jasmine turned away and pretended to look for a cab. She could feel Josh's embarrassment deep in her gut as if it were her own. Her face was hot. Her hands sweaty. To her amazement, a cab actually pulled over for her, and without a backward glance, she leapt inside.

I don't want to be with a man who's like me.

She told the driver her address, her heart beating madly. *My True Love can't make me smaller. My True Love is supposed to make me blossom. To thrive. Not to turn me further inward.*

He's not what I want.

I want more.

I want the movie star.

Chapter 8

*L*ater that night, Jasmine was on her way to Madeline's restaurant to meet her two best friends, Jenn and Suz, when she saw it.

Or rather, it saw her.

Josh Toby stared at her from the cover of the *People* magazine hanging from the newsstand. SEXIEST MAN ALIVE! the headline proclaimed. The words nestled next to Josh's soft dirty-blond curls like lovers.

He had won. Again. Twice in a row.

Jasmine wasn't sure how long she stood on that corner staring into Josh's eyes. Those purple-blue eyes, slight crinkles at the corners, evenly set around a straight, unobtrusive nose. He seemed to be smiling at her. Seemed to be saying, *You and me, together, baby.*

The Josh on the magazine would definitely use the word "baby."

Would the Josh Toby at the Indian restaurant have called her "baby" if she had given him the chance? She tried to reconcile the two Joshes. It had been five hours since she had fled from him, but his image was etched into her mind as clear as day.

She grabbed the magazine and thrust her money at the man in the booth, avoiding his eyes. "Keep the change." She clutched the magazine to her chest and hurried to Madeline's.

The façade of the restaurant was painted soft pink, with scattered yellow daffodils. Jasmine opened the pink-and-yellow polka-dot door with the rose-shaped handle. The overpowering odor of lily of the valley assaulted her.

"Jasmine!" Madeline ran to her. "It's so good to see you! Suz and Jenn are already here."

Jasmine waved to her friends, who waved her over to join them.

Madeline, dressed in a red skirt and shirt outfit worthy of Minnie Mouse, led Jasmine to their usual table, a small round table in the back with a single daffodil in a pot in the center. Suz and Jenn were already having iced tea and spinach salads. Madeline had introduced the three regulars two years ago, and they'd had this Thursday night ritual ever since.

Jasmine sat down. "Thanks, Mad."

"I'll bring the usual, hon?"

Jasmine nodded.

Madeline floated away, smiling, taking the menu with its flower-dotted i's with her. Madeline was still pleased every time they met up.

"Hey, gorgeous," Suz said. She was Korean-American, a hugely successful stockbroker, and weighed about ninety pounds. She stood five foot one in her three-inch heels. "Is your sister gone yet?"

"Nope." Jasmine looked around her happily.

No men.

Oh, once in a while, a stray guy pushed through the

door. But he always retreated quickly in the face of the swishy cupcake-motif tablecloths. The first brunch after Jasmine had discovered the restaurant, a group of gay brunch-seekers almost took a table. But one had thrown up his hands at the last minute and Jasmine caught him saying to his rouged boyfriend, "Too poufy even for *me*," before they pushed out the door.

Jasmine put the magazine at the center of the table.

Her second meal with Josh.

"I brought reading material," she said, nodding at the magazine. She tried to sound airy and light.

"Sexiest Man Semialive," Suz declared.

"Semi?"

"He's yummy, but I hear he's a bit of a zero in the brain department," Suz explained. She leaned in to look at the glossy magazine.

"Who cares?" Jenn commented, licking her lips. Jenn was forty-two, but with her freckles and straw-yellow hair, she didn't look a day over twenty-five. She was constantly trying to smother her Iowa-farm-girl beauty with tight buns and black clothes, but it never worked. She taught yoga and glowed accordingly.

"Remember what I told you about my sister being a psychic?" Jasmine tried to sound calm.

Jenn lit up. "Right. One True Love." Jenn believed in the supernatural and True Love, despite her now-empty love life.

Suz would have none of it. She shook her head and crossed her arms.

"Amy heard the name of my One True Love," Jasmine said. She nodded to the magazine. "Ta-da!"

They looked confused.

"Josh Toby is my One True Love."

She was greeted with a deafening silence.

Suz pushed her spinach aside and pulled her laptop out of her enormous bag. She tapped her fingers impatiently while she waited for it to boot up. "I'm finding another Josh Toby. It doesn't have to be this one, right? Isn't that what you told us? Your sister just gets a name?"

"But it could be this one!" Jenn rose to Jasmine's defense. "Why not?"

Suz raised her eyebrows.

The ponytailed bus-girl poured Jasmine's iced tea into the oversized daisy-covered goblet. Jasmine tried not to be upset at Suz. After all, her friend had grounds for doubt. She hadn't exactly done a stellar job with a single one of the twenty-two men Suz had tried to set her up with in the last two years.

Plus, it did sound absurd. Women all over the world were sitting with their *People* magazines, wishing for a piece of what was inside its glossy pages. If the magazine sent out a beam of light from its open spine, the night sky would be lit up from all the women lusting after this man. A camaraderie of longing.

But Jasmine had met him. Could work for him. She was busting to tell her friends. But discreet meant discreet. She loved her friends, but she'd never spill.

"I don't think he's the brightest bulb," Suz said carefully, her red fingernails tapping against the keys.

Jasmine flipped to the article. "You don't get to choose your One True Love."

"And why does Jasmine care if he's smart? " Jenn asked. "Hell, if he were my One True Love, I'd get past that dim-bulb detail quick. Move on to more important assests. Mmm . . . like those."

Jasmine cleared her throat. All three women leaned forward to stare at the glossy spread. Josh, in jeans, no shirt, and a cowboy hat. He lounged on a tattered couch. Jasmine read out loud: "'Josh Toby. He's sexy, passionate, *and* he cooks.'" Her heart sank. "Ugh. He's a foodie." Jasmine wasn't much of an eater. Early on she had learned the perils of food. If it was green, it could lodge in your teeth. If it was red, it could splatter on your shirt. Whatever its color, a likeable man could speak to you when it was in your mouth, and the shock of needing to reply could choke you. Death by shyness. Jasmine was sure it happened all the time.

Jasmine continued to read. "'Now this California charmer is taking over as Sex God Royalty. Let us all bow down.'"

"Let us all throw up," Suz said. "You're too good for him." She was tapping away again.

Jasmine flipped quickly past a few more seductive poses, her face heating with embarrassment. "I only read it for the articles," she told her friends.

Suz knitted her brows as she frowned at the screen. "There are 4,347,612 hits for Josh Toby. The official Josh Toby Web site. The unofficial Josh Toby Web site. Josh Toby for president. Josh Toby in Japanese. Josh Toby nude."

"That one," Jenn commanded.

They all leaned over the computer screen.

Oh. My.

Jasmine's heart fluttered to a dead stop. His face was chiseled; his jaw firm. That pretty much described the rest of him too. She gulped and buried her face back in the magazine. *The articles!* "'Josh Q and A,'" Jasmine read. "'He's insanely jealous of his women.'" She stopped. "How many women? Is he jealous of all of them at once? Or one at a time?"

"He's been steady with Cleo Chan for years," Jenn said. "So I'd guess one. Although there's something cold about the two of them together." She paused. "You think he's gay?"

"Nope. Says here that Cleo's a lesbian," Suz said with authority. "Oh. This is WeHateCleoChan.com."

"Could they both go the other way?" Jenn suggested.

Josh stared up at them from the magazine.

"He's not gay. It would betray my faith in a kind and good God." Jenn sighed.

"It says here on IWanttoHaveJoshToby'sBabies.com that he and Cleo are getting hitched," Suz reported.

Jasmine's heart sank, which was crazy. "Find me another Josh Toby on that thing. There's got to be one somewhere in those four million hits." Not the librarian. Not the movie star. But someone in between. "Josh Toby Plumbing. Josh Toby Pizza and Wings. Some *normal* person. Oh, and he has to be in New York."

"Okay, I'm on it," Suz said. She was happiest when she had a job to do.

Jenn had taken over the magazine. "He never sends flowers because he doesn't like things that can die."

"There, see. The guy's an idiot," Suz proclaimed, still typing. "Everything dies. Even all those women. You're way too good for this guy. If there's another Josh Toby in here, I'm never going to find him."

They were all silent. Jasmine drank her iced tea. Jenn picked at her salad in a daze.

Finally, Suz said, "It's hopeless. There's too much on Mr. Gorgeous."

"Type in 'Josh Toby' plus 'average,'" Jenn suggested.

"I tried that. I came up with over two thousand sites with some variation of the phrase, 'Josh Toby's above-average dick.'"

Jenn and Jasmine shuddered.

"Please get that image out of my head," Jasmine begged. "Now."

Jenn resumed her reading. "'In his fridge is canned Bud Light and foie gras.'"

"I'd rather think about his above-average—" Suz began.

"Cars," Jasmine interrupted. She grabbed the magazine. "It says he makes his own face cream."

Jasmine's two friends burst into laughter, but Jasmine was starting to feel bad for Josh. To have the whole world pick apart your every utterance—that must be the worst kind of hell.

She imagined what *People* magazine would say about her if they had to do a Jasmine Burns spread. *Shyest Woman Alive! Jasmine Burns loves quiet meals with friends in girly-girl restaurants where men fear to tread. She enjoys colors, especially blue with a touch of purple. Her idea of fun is shopping for fabric. She loves to stay in and watch DVDs.*

Jenn turned the page. "That's it?" she complained. "Where is the part that says he's seeking his One True Love? That there's a hole in his life that isn't filled?"

"Or maybe a hole in his pants that demands the attention of an expert tailor?" Suz suggested. She had gone back to one of the nude Josh Toby sites, and her voice was dreamy and distant.

Jasmine leaned over and pushed the BACK button on Suz's Web browser until she hit a tamer screen. "Where's the part that says what he really likes is staying home with a DVD for a quiet evening while his girlfriend sews?"

"Hey, more bad news." Suz read from the official Josh Toby Web site. "'Josh has gone for one month to Afghanistan to research his upcoming role as Freedom Fighter Mitch Tank in Steven Spielberg's *Tank Command*. He is embedded with rebel fighters in a war zone and cannot be reached. We all pray for his safe and quick return.'"

Jenn shrugged. "So? You go to Afghanistan. I had a yoga teacher from there once. I could hook you up."

Jasmine ate the last of her pickle. Sixth Street was no war zone. Was that really Josh Toby at the Indian restaurant?

She again considered telling her friends that she had already met Josh. But she couldn't.

After all, she was supposed to be discreet.

And while Jenn and Suz were a lot of things, discreet was not one of them.

Chapter 9

Amy's bag was packed. Mostly with Jasmine's stuff, but Jasmine was so glad to see her go, she looked the other way. "When's your train?"

"I've got an hour. Don't worry. I'm leaving."

Jasmine was pretty sure Amy's leaving meant that she had spent all Jasmine's money and now had just enough for the train ticket back to Baltimore. But she didn't care. She just needed Amy out of her space so she could think.

Amy sat on the edge of the brown suitcase she had borrowed from Jasmine and munched a sugared donut. Her lap looked like it had been blanketed by a freak indoor snowstorm. "I was reading one of your shy-people books last night. They said there could be a trigger that made you all crazy with men."

Jasmine doubted that was exactly what "they" said, but Amy's bluntness sucked all the moisture out of her mouth, and it was hard to reply. Jasmine went to the window and looked out at the early morning sun hitting the maple.

"So? Do you think there was a trigger? Like, maybe that last con we pulled when you were sixteen? The one when you freaked out on us and split?" Amy tapped her lizard-skin cowboy boot against the floor.

Jasmine checked her watch, trying not to think about that day. She hadn't freaked out; she had calmly left. She had had enough. She left a note, after all, explaining that she couldn't live with them anymore. "I think you better get going."

Amy looked like she had no intention of moving until she got an answer.

Jasmine sighed. "Shyness is a chemical thing. It's about brain structure—"

"So you're doomed?" Amy seemed genuinely appalled.

"Well, environmental factors can play a role—"

"I knew it. We fucked you up!"

Jasmine could never explain the complexities of why she was the way she was. She wished there was a quick fix, an easy answer. Reasons for her inability to talk to men jostled against each other for attention: being taken from her father at two; feeling as if it was her fault he was gone; feeling guilty for having her mother to herself; living in India, a culture where women were taught to be silent and docile; her terrible disaster at sixteen with her tutor, Raj . . .

Then there was the other way to look at it: Men really *were* scary. Hell, you'd be nuts not to be scared of the kind of intimacy required of an adult relationship. Maybe she was the sane one. Everyone else was mad with rash optimism and hope.

Amy was gazing at her expectantly.

If Jasmine was ever going to get her to go, she had to satisfy her. "It was in school."

Amy leaned forward like a little kid around a campfire, ready to be amazed and terrified.

"When I was sixteen and came back to Baltimore to live with you guys. I had to go to school for the first time in my life after always having a private tutor. I had to read out loud. The boys laughed."

Amy narrowed her eyes. "But you can read."

"I was nervous. I got all tripped up." Jasmine scanned her bookcase until she found a suitable book. "It was Greek myths. Sisyphus. I couldn't figure out that name."

Amy shook her head. "That's dull as dust, Jas."

Jasmine shrugged. *No one here but us dust bunnies.* "Sorry. But that's it. That's how it is sometimes, the stuff you least expect."

Amy shook her head and mumbled, "Even your neurosis is boring."

Jasmine tried not to smile.

The buzzer rang.

Amy and Jasmine both jumped.

"Did you call a cab?" Jasmine asked hopefully.

"No."

"Maybe it's that woman who's supposed to come at ten with the torn crepe dress. She's coming all the way from the Bronx. She might be early." Jasmine pushed the button on the ancient intercom. "Hello?"

"Jasmine? It's me. Josh Toby. Let me up."

Before Jasmine could stop her, Amy lunged over her shoulder and buzzed Josh into the building.

"What are you doing?" Jasmine's stomach curled into a ball. *Hide*, every cell in her body seemed to shout. Why did she live on the fifth floor? There was no way she could climb out the window, and if she went out the door, they'd *meet in the hall*. She felt sick.

"I gotta meet him!" Amy cried. "Imagine if the voice came back! I could read him! Imagine if we could find out right here and now if he's the right Josh Toby! Maybe he's giving off your name! How do I look?" Amy paused. "Jasmine? Where'd you go?"

"Don't let him in!" Jasmine's voice came out muffled from behind the curtains.

"Oh, for crying out loud! How old are you?"

A solid knock on the door echoed through the space.

"Don't you dare say a word about True Love to him!" Jasmine hissed from her hiding place.

"Good grief!" Amy's cowboy boots clumped across the hardwood floor. The locks clicked open one by one. Then the whoosh of the opening door stirred her curtain, chilling Jasmine to the bone. Maybe she *could* climb out the window. How much could two broken legs hurt?

"Well, *hello*," Amy cooed.

Jasmine peered around the corner of the curtain. Josh Toby, movie star extraordinaire, leaned against the doorjamb and gazed at Amy. He was so smooth in his Yankees cap, untucked blue Oxford, faded jeans, and brown leather jacket. Around his Nikes scurried a medium-sized black mutt. The dog jumped up on Josh's legs.

You couldn't blame it. Most females in America jumped around Josh like that, tongues lolling. The man looked like he stepped off a movie screen.

Scratch that. He looked as if he were *still on* a movie screen. Bigger than life. Glowing. An image of the Greek myths came to her: Apollo walking among the mortals, shimmering around the edges.

"I'm looking for Jasmine Burns," he said.

"What a coincidence!" Amy cried. "She just happens to be playing hide-and-seek!" Amy cheerfully stood back and let Josh, in all his glory, enter the room. She tapped his shoulder. "Tag. You're it."

Josh scanned the all-white apartment. There didn't appear to be anyone there but this queen of the gypsies. He appreciated her belly-baring, tight, glittering shirt, and yet, disappointment that Jasmine wasn't there spread through him. He patted Buster, Arturo's dog, and released him from his leash. The dog dashed to the curtain and sniffed furiously.

"What's up, Buster?" He hoped the little guy didn't need to pee again. He shouldn't need to pee after their six-mile morning run. But what did Josh know about dogs? When Arturo said he was leaving town for a few days, he had jumped at the chance to take care of the little guy, but Josh hadn't ever had a dog (his parents thought it was cruel to keep a dog in New York City—they even marched against it once), so his dog skills were limited. Not that Buster seemed to mind.

"I'm Jasmine's sister," the woman explained. "Amy." She held out a multiringed hand.

He reached out to shake it. "I'm—"

"I know who you are," Amy said. She tightened her hold on his hand.

Dread overcame him. He yanked his hand free and took a step back. *A groupie.*

She took a step forward.

Buster barked at the curtain and raced in tight, quick circles.

Josh backed up another step. The back of his knees hit the mattress. He fell onto the bed, then quickly jumped up and moved away again, around the bed. Amy continued to advance.

"C'mere, Buster." He called the dog. *Stop snarling at the curtain and snarl at this lady before I have to.* Buster came almost to him, then raced back to the curtain like Toto from *The Wizard of Oz*.

"Is Jasmine here?" he asked. Oh, boy. Amy was looking at him like he was fair game. Her eyes were on fire, boring into him like blowtorches. *I'm going to be gypsy breakfast if I don't get out of here.* Mo had warned him about traveling without a bodyguard. Maybe he should have listened. He looked to Buster, who was still obsessed by the curtain. If only Buster were a German shepherd.

Amy came closer.

No. A pit bull.

Josh bumped into the bedside table and caught the all-glass bubble lamp just before it crashed to the ground. Nice lamp. Despite the fact that he was being attacked, he couldn't help but notice how simple and comforting Jasmine's apartment was. So cozy, so simple, nothing extra.

Very unlike the woman before him now.

"I need to tell you something very, very important. Something that will change your life," Amy said, closing the gap between them until their noses almost touched. Josh was against the wall. He couldn't back up another inch.

"Sure." He tried to dart around her, but she caught his arm and yanked up the cuff of his jacket. Her long, red nails looked sinister against the bare skin of his wrist.

"It's about your One True Love."

"My what?" He tried to shake off Amy's hand, but she held tight.

Suddenly, there was a rustling from behind the curtains, and to his amazement, Jasmine stepped out.

"Oh, hello," she said. She bent down to let Buster sniff her hand. She scratched him behind his ears. "Just cleaning the windows. Had to finish up." Buster jumped up and down at her feet.

Josh scratched his head. Could this get any weirder? And yet, he was infinitely relieved to see Jasmine. She looked pretty much the way she had yesterday—simply dressed, clean, neat, and beautiful, especially for a woman doing household chores.

You didn't find classic women like her in Hollywood anymore. No pretensions. No plastic surgery. No makeup. Lines from *Romeo and Juliet* came clearly to him: *That all the world will be in love with night, And pay no worship to the garish sun.*

Jasmine stepped between him and the rabid sister, jolting Josh out of his reverie. Buster followed at her heels, as if he had found a new master. *You've got good taste, buddy.*

"Please excuse my sister. She—" Jasmine began.

"I'm a psychic," Amy said over her sister's shoulder. "I can hear the name of your—"

Jasmine put her hand firmly over her sister's mouth. Then, as if she did this sort of thing every day, she pried Amy's hand off his wrist. Josh was fascinated by this new side of her.

"Amy, don't you have a train to catch?" Jasmine asked sternly.

"I didn't get a reading."

A reading? Oh, right, the psychic.

Jasmine stared her sister down. He liked this firm, in-command Jasmine. He stepped back to watch. Buster watched, too, staring up in doggy awe.

"You're scaring him," Jasmine said.

"Baloney. He's used to being mauled. He's a sex symbol. And for good reason." Amy scanned him appreciatively.

Jasmine turned red, and Josh was touched by her sensitivity. He was used to dealing with women who whispered offers of blow jobs into his ear, not women who blushed at the mere mention of sexuality.

"Just let me at him one more time—"

"Amy! I'm going to sic . . ."

"Buster," Josh supplied.

"Thank you. I'm going to sic Buster on you," Jasmine finished. "Back off."

"Yeah, I saw what he could do to a curtain," Amy scoffed.

"Hey, no dissing the pooch. He can hear you," Josh said.

Amy faked a lunge toward the dog. Buster whimpered and darted behind Jasmine's legs. Then he peered out and growled.

Amy growled back.

"I see it's a bad time," Josh said. "Buster and I can come back later." He felt oddly distraught at the idea of leaving. Where would he go? What would he do? He had hoped Buster would help him shake his loneliness, but so far, it hadn't worked.

Buster, who had obviously forgotten his fear of Amy in a doggy heartbeat, was now rolling on his back at Jasmine's feet. *Good dog.* Cleo would have shooed him off her expensive clothes. Cleo was not a dog person. Or a cat person. Or even a fish person. Cleo was a three-hour-a-day gym rat, twice-a-week-blow-outs, daily-professional-facials kind of person. And yet, Jasmine shined with something other than the expensive lotions and creams Cleo bought at the spa. *All the world will be in love with night . . .*

The sisters had squared off, staring each other down.

Finally, Amy flinched. "I'll go," she said. She grasped her sister in a bear hug and whispered something Josh couldn't hear in her ear. Then she picked up her suitcase. "Call me," she commanded Jasmine. Then she pulled a card out of her pocket. "You call me too."

Hoping it would speed her departure, he accepted the card and slipped it into his pocket. He'd send it to Mo later so she could make sure the security detail knew to keep this woman away.

Then, to Josh's relief, she left, trailed by a cloud of cinnamon and clove.

Chapter 10

Jasmine was rooted to the floor. Her feet had sprouted a vast system of tendrils that went down five stories to root in the bedrock of Manhattan. *Don't mind me. No one here but us ficus trees.* She had been in serious crisis mode, with no time to think when Amy was there. But now that she was alone with Josh Toby, well, *she was alone with Josh Toby.*

Josh watched out the window until Amy appeared on the street below. He shuddered, then turned back to Jasmine. "So, your sister's a psychic?"

Speak. Must speak. Open mouth. Make words. "Yeah." More. Go. More. Now. He's looking at you. "Yep." *Brilliant conversation, that.*

He sat down on the side of her bed casually, as if he didn't notice she had turned into foliage. The dog jumped up next to him. *Lucky dog.*

"So, are you going to work with me or not? Arturo insists you're the best." He bounced a little on the bed, as if planning to buy it. Then he leaned back on his elbows and gazed at her.

It should be illegal to be so handsome.

Jasmine had to sit down. Her legs, however, were still joined to the floor. She breathed slowly and counted to ten. *So, the world's biggest movie star, possibly my One True Love, is leaning back on my bed like a . . . a . . . man.* Oh, things were bad when she stuttered in her mind.

She eyed the couch just a few feet away. She tore her legs free and scurried for it. Buster jumped off the bed, hopped onto the couch, and cuddled in next to her.

She pet the dog. It made her feel better to have something nonmale to concentrate on. Well, the dog was probably male. She was so *not* going to check. "Can't work for you. Sorry," she managed to get out before her throat closed up on her. *Water. She needed water.*

Josh strolled around her apartment as if he hadn't heard her. Come to think of it, he might not have heard her, her voice had come out so strained. She tried not to stare at him, but it was impossible. His face was so familiar; he didn't look entirely real in person. Her mind flitted between images she had seen of him and the real man before her. Same dirty-blond curls, same purple-blue eyes, same easy loose limbs. But now he was so, well, three-dimensional.

"So here's the deal," he said. "I don't get any respect as an actor." Josh wandered to her kitchen counter. He opened a cupboard, pulled out her black NYU mug, and filled it with tap water. He looked at it quizzically, as if he wasn't sure how it had gotten in his hand. Then he looked up at Jasmine, crossed the room, and handed her the mug. "I'm more than just a pretty face and six-pack abs."

She felt herself blush. She gulped the water, only choking a tiny bit.

"You have no idea what it's like to be trapped in a body

that stops people cold. It's like they can't see the *me* behind it." He sat down in the chair across from her, looking ready for his close-up. "I sound like a total ass."

Don't think about his ass.

Or his pretty face.

Or his six-pack abs.

She guzzled more water, stopped, and stared at the mug in her hands in horror.

Or the fact that he read my mind.

She stroked the dog, who looked up at her lovingly, his pink tongue lolling to the side.

You have no idea what it's like to be trapped in a body that stops people cold. But she *did* know. A body that betrayed her every thought was exactly what she knew so well. It was her curse too. Only with her, it wasn't ferocious beauty but devastating shyness that no one could see past. *They shared a curse. Perfect understanding. Perfect love.*

"I want to act. Really act," he said. "Prove that there's a talented, smart person in here." He reached into the back pocket of his jeans and pulled out a crumpled square of newspaper. He handed it to her.

She unfolded it against her knee so that he couldn't see her hands shaking. The article was taped along the seams with yellowed Scotch tape. The ink was smudged and unreadable in places, but she could make out the headline: HACK WITH A PRETTY FACE SCORES AGAIN. OF COURSE. She scanned the article, picking up the gist: "barely capable," "eye candy," "dumb as a tack," "male bimbo sets another box office record."

She stared at the paper dumbfounded. *Josh Toby is insecure?* She refolded it and thrust it back at him. "It's just one person's opinion," she managed. But she thought of Suz and Jenn. They were convinced that Josh wasn't the sharpest tool in the shed.

It was just like Amy said. He needed her help.

Jasmine's head spun with the growing realization that he might be The One.

"I suck but I'm pretty." He paced, which wasn't easy in the tiny space. "It's what everyone thinks. Face it, it's what you think, isn't it?"

She felt her face go through all seven shades of Pantone red #185. "Well, I—"

"Right. See?" He cut her off. "I want to do Shakespeare. On the stage. Be a serious actor without the retakes and stuntmen and special effects. Arturo set it up for me. But I need your help. If everyone knows it's me, I'll get an audience filled with screaming thirteen-year-olds. Maybe a few scattered critics poking fun. I need a serious audience and serious critics to say, 'Hey, who is that guy? He's good.' Then they find out it's me, and bingo, respect."

Jasmine carefully put her mug down on the coffee table. She tried to get her head around what he was saying. No one was happy with what they had. A man could be Josh Toby and still feel he had to prove himself.

"Oh, hell, I almost forgot." He pulled a small box out of his pocket. It looked suspiciously like a jewelry box. He handed it to her.

She didn't move. *He wants to get married. It's True Love and he knows it.*

"Well, open it, Jas." He sat down next to her.

Jas? Trying to hide the tremor in her hands, she lifted the lid. She gasped and snapped it shut. But the light from the diamond studs had been imprinted on her retinas. Every time she blinked, she was blinded by their twin sparkle. She thrust the box back at him. "Oh, no."

"It's no big deal. Try them on."

It's no big deal. Was that true? Did a man like Josh Toby buy $8,000 earrings for women who ran out on him during the curry course? Well, why not? The man was loaded. These to him *were* nothing.

But what if he thought pricey jewels were the way to get her to work for him?

"I bought them because Cleo once told me that diamonds take attention away from the face," he said. "That's why she never wears them. But after I met you yesterday, I thought that you'd *like* something that took attention away from your face. You know, so you could get your bearings. Feel more at ease."

Jasmine's stomach flipped. That was about the smartest, kindest, most insightful thing a stranger had ever said to her.

He was holding out the box.

Impossible man. "If we work together—*if!*—it's work." *It's not perfect gifts that demonstrate scary understanding combined with thoughtful, beautiful, expensive solutions.*

He smiled at her. "Deal." He jumped up and started around the apartment again. Did this guy ever stay still? His smile held a wicked twist.

She had the sinking feeling she'd been tricked. "I didn't say 'yes.' I said 'if.'"

He leaned against her bookcase, and the effect was magnificent.

Yes. She tried not to sigh. "Why are you smiling like that?"

"Because once during every time we talk, you forget you're terrified of me and you take control. I was waiting for it." He bound back to the couch and sat down next to her. *The man was right about her again.* If she hung around him, could her once-a-conversation go to twice? Three times? A whole chat? *A whole life?* The possibility filled her with a breezy, blue optimism.

He was still smiling and her dread returned.

Could you turn down the gorgeous, please? She blushed. "What role are you playing?" she asked quickly, trying to reclaim her ease.

"Romeo, of course." He slid the jewelry box into his jacket pocket.

An image of Josh as Romeo melted every last bit of resolve. *Romeo, oh, Romeo, wherefore art thou, Romeo?* "Mercutio is the scene stealer," she managed, naming Romeo's sex-crazed pal. She wished he'd get up off the couch. He was too close.

His face lit up. "I thought of that. But I think Mercutio would only reinforce what people already think of me. Romeo is the deep one. The one who loves truly and fully. From a deconstructionist perspective, he fully represents the mind-body duality." He was moving closer.

"The what?" She backed away.

"I read that in a book. It made sense at the time." He paused. "I'm playing Romeo because he's the one with the best lines. Plus, he gets the girl."

"For a while anyway." *Until he pretty much kills her with his unrestrained, impossible love.*

He smiled. "Will you really do it? Please? Say yes." He shot her a sheepishly sexy pout, like the one in the full-page spread in the *People* magazine article. Also, like the one in the third naked Web photo, which she was definitely *not* thinking about right now. *Please get off my couch.*

"I need your help," he said.

She closed her eyes and heard Amy's words from the day she showed up in New York. *Josh Toby is your One True Love. He might need your help. . . .* "Okay. I'll do it. Yes," she found herself saying. *He needed her help.* It was her shot to impress Arturo. She had no choice.

Josh leaned in. "Hot damn!" He grabbed her shoulders and kissed her smack on the lips. Then he pulled back and looked into her shocked eyes. "I'm sorry. I shouldn't have done that. I was so sure you'd say no, then you said yes."

Jasmine couldn't move. Had she really just agreed to work with Josh Toby? To *dress* him?

Had he really just kissed her?

"Are you sure about this?" he asked, sensing her hesitancy.

"No," she said. The shock of the kiss still radiated through her. "Definitely not sure."

They sat in silence. Then slowly, so slowly, he moved toward her. Or was she leaning toward him?

He is not going to kiss me again.

He kissed her again.

I am not going to kiss him back.

Seconds. Minutes. The warmth of his lips on hers. *I'm kissing him back.* The rough stubble on his face scraped her skin, sending electricity down to her toes. Texture, warmth.

I'm kissing someone else's boyfriend.

Just for one more minute.

I'm kissing fucking Josh Toby!

She pulled back all at once, and he almost fell into the space where she'd been.

They stared at each other.

"I'm sorry," he said. "This time I thought you'd say yes, and then you said no, and I . . . I guess I wanted to change your mind."

Her hand went to her lips. *Changed.*

"So now you probably don't want to work with me." He balled his hands into fists of frustration. "I'm screwing this up, aren't I?"

She could feel her hot cheeks, her head beginning to spin into the endless vortex of her embarrassment. How many women caved in to him after a kiss? How many women did he kiss? Forget her shyness being irrational fear. Fear of this man was completely rational because the truth was, she wanted to kiss him again and then some. "I'll work for you, but only if we never, ever do that again," Jasmine said.

"Right. Of course. It was a mistake."

"An accident." She was falling toward him again.

"Not right at all." He was inches from her lips.

A sharp bark from Buster made them jump apart.

Buster's feet skittered against the window as he clawed to get at a squirrel scampering through the maple outside her window.

They jumped up and went to the window, sticking closely to opposite walls. Jasmine pretended intense interest in the fate of the squirrel. Confusion clouded her brain. But there was nothing to be confused about. This was a simple situation. True Love or no True Love, she couldn't kiss Cleo Chan's boyfriend. She couldn't kiss *her new boss.* She patted Buster as if he had just scared off a bear.

Actually, in a way, he had.

Must not make out with employer/movie star/One True Love/sexiest man alive who has girlfriend who happens to be sexiest woman alive.

I made out with Josh Toby. Jasmine swallowed an emerging smile. What would Suz and Jenn make of this? Had she done that on purpose just to have the experience? Or was it his intense sexual energy? Or was it the mug of water and the earrings and the fact that he noticed how she felt around him?

It didn't matter. Just so long as she never, ever did it again.

Josh lost sight of the squirrel and turned to Jasmine. "I don't usually do things like that. Really. I've been so lonely in New York. I guess I didn't know how lonely."

"It's okay." She could feel the heat in her cheeks spread through her like fire. Working with him was not going to be easy. Not only was he a man, in every sense of the word, but he was also a puppy dog, hopping with energy. He had no boundaries. No restraint.

The heat of his lips still burned into hers. She was sure her skin was seared where he had touched her.

"This is business. I'm hooked up with Cleo and you're—"

"Working for you."

"Right. I just, I've been—"

"Alone in New York." She searched for the squirrel, avoiding his eyes.

"Right. Again." He looked at her strangely. "How did you know?"

Because I'm alone in New York too. "Let's get to work."

"Work," he said. "Good. Work is good. I need a disguise before the media finds me and this whole enterprise is blown."

Jasmine circled him, studying him. A simple cloak could transform the meekest actor into Hamlet. But to transform Josh Toby into a nobody on the streets of New York? It was reverse magic.

She sucked in her cheeks as she inventoried him. *Forget the kiss. Don't stare at the shoulders. Ignore the eyes.* She shivered and tried to shake off her terror. *Work.*

She was a professional.

I want to be one of his temporary floozies just this once for a little bit. Oh, Lord, this man is too much perfection. . . .

No. None of that. Concentrate.

Then it hit her. She knew exactly how to disguise Josh. And not only that, but in the process, she could also make him the *least* sexy man alive. At least, the least sexy man to her. Kill two birds with one stone.

She smiled.

He smiled at her smile, searching her face. "What?"

She tried not to feel the effect of his intense violet eyes all the way to the tips of her toes. "Okay, I know what to do. Only you have to say yes before you know what it is. You have to do exactly what I say."

"Ooh. There it is again. Twice in one day. I like this side of you, Jas."

Jasmine tried not to melt into a puddle of desire. "Do you agree?"

"Sure. You're the boss. I'm your willing servant."

Now *that* was an image she didn't want to contemplate too hard.

After all, she had work to do.

Chapter 11

Jasmine made her way through the prelunch crowds on Fifth Avenue. *Just because I'm an assistant, assigned only to Josh, doesn't mean that I'm not going to learn everything there is to know about* Romeo and Juliet. *If Arturo wants to know the heel height on women's sandals in fifteenth-century Verona, I'll be there with the answer.*

And if Josh Toby happened to be the reference librarian on duty, well, all the better. Two birds with one stone. Because while Jasmine was on her way to the New York Public Library to research Shakespeare, she was also going there to study Librarian Josh Toby. If she could understand what exactly it was about Librarian Josh's clothes that marked him as a shy, timid man, she could transform Movie Star Josh into him.

The perfect disguise.

Or was she there for more than that? She crossed the street and stood before the library's expansive façade. Red and black banners hung between the grand columns announcing a show on illuminated Hebrew manuscripts. Jasmine felt queasy. Had she come for more than studying Josh? Did she, deep down, want to meet him? Talk to him? After all, True Love with Josh the movie star was impossible. They had agreed: no more kissing. After all, there was his girlfriend, her job, his seeing into her soul, her mortification, his shoulders . . .

Maybe if she had a boyfriend, it would help her to stop thinking about things that were clearly impossible.

Jasmine had forgotten how spectacularly ornate the library was inside. Even the metal detectors and gruff, bag-searching guards couldn't take away from the templelike awe of the place. Twin grand stairways snaked up either side of the two-story lobby. Every surface was gilded and radiant.

She made her way past the plaques and statues, up the stairway, and into the reference room. She scanned the massive librarian's desk. No Josh. She spent twenty-five minutes at the computers, one eye looking up Shakespearean costume tomes, the other waiting for him to show.

He didn't. Was it his day off? She fought off disappointment.

She put in requests for three of the most promising books. Thankfully, there was a woman at the desk. "Do you know where I can find Josh Toby?" Jasmine asked, picking at her fingernails for what she hoped was a casual effect.

"He's at the information desk in the reading room." The woman pointed to the next room. "That's also where you pick up the books."

Jasmine's body went into panic mode.

Let the terror flow past. Let it rise, then melt away.

No such luck. *Okay, just don't trip over yourself.* Jasmine made her way to the cavernous reading room.

People at worn wooden tables pored over books or stared off into space. Jasmine had come to this place at least once a week as a student. The musty smell of books and the people who read them made her nostalgic.

Don't have to talk to him. Just study from afar. Breathe. In and out. In and out.

Behind the information desk stood Josh, directing an Asian woman somewhere complicated. Behind the vast desk, he looked more sure of himself than he had on the sidewalk.

Jasmine waited for her books to come, trying to soothe her nerves.

Fifteen minutes later, a pock-marked librarian handed her the three dusty, oversized books she had requested. No one was allowed to browse the stacks at this library, and no materials left its gilded walls. She took her books and found a seat that faced Josh. When she was settled, she pulled out her sketchbook and colored pencils.

He didn't look up.

She sketched his pale blue eyes, shaded his eyelashes orange to match the tint of his close-cropped hair. She dusted his face in orange-brown freckles. More freckles. More. There. He was at least six feet tall, weighed at most one hundred and sixty pounds. A gold badge over his right breast pocket read, "J. Toby, Reference Librarian."

She turned away from him, putting her pad on the table. She soft-penciled his cotton sweater-vest, concentrating on getting all the details. Purple and pink vertical stripes. Yellow shirt underneath. Pens in shirt pocket, pocket protector. Underneath his awful clothes, he was a nice-looking man. His eyes were gentle and kind. She erased a touch of the blue, making them paler. A wash of white. A hint of green. Perfect.

"He's mine."

Jasmine looked up to see an obese woman looming over her. She smelled like a sewer.

"You can't have him!" the woman hissed in an unsuccessful library whisper. Every person in the room looked up. Her hands rested on her enormous hips. She wore a housedress so faded, it looked like a nightgown. Jasmine could see the outline of her black-and-pink polka-dot bra underneath.

"Now, Eleanor, let's sit quietly with the others or I'll have to call security," Josh said.

Jasmine nearly jumped out of her chair. Her heart beat wildly. How had Josh gotten there so silently? Must be a librarian thing.

He took the woman lightly by the shoulders, turned her, and nudged her gently as if she were a paper boat he was setting sail.

Eleanor floated off, looking confused that she was in motion, as if her pink fuzzy slippers shuffled across the hardwood floor of their own volition.

Everyone looked back to their books with a mixture of disappointment and annoyance.

When Eleanor reached her table, she looked around for a long moment, then sat down. Two people were already at her table, surrounded with plastic shopping bags brimming with their worldly belongings: more plastic bags, empty cans, shreds of newspaper. *Homeless people.*

Josh shrugged at Jasmine. "Sorry." Then he saw her picture of him and turned such a bright red so quickly, Jasmine was afraid he might pass out.

She kicked out the empty chair next to hers, and he fell into it.

"Oh. I. Oh," he said. He pulled an inhaler from his front jeans pocket and sucked deeply.

He was kind of cute, if she could get him into a forest-green shirt. His limbs sprawled in the too-small chair. As he gathered one leg in, the other escaped.

I know how you feel. The thought hit her in the gut. "The picture's for a play. *Romeo and Juliet,*" she hurried to reassure him. *A man is sitting next to me.* She waited for the familiar sensation of her body curling in on itself. But it didn't. This was so odd. *I know how you feel, and I don't feel it.*

"Oh. I like to play. Like plays, I mean. That. One. Right, then." His body fumbled along with his sentences.

Jasmine's eyes went wide. *Is this what I look like?* An amazing thought occurred to her: *He's adorable.* Could she also be adorable? It had never occurred to her that her vulnerability could be attractive.

Was that a good thing? Embrace the fear? Work it?

She cleared her throat, testing it. It seemed to be fully functioning. But that wasn't possible. *He is adorable. Possibly my One True Love.*

She felt fine.

I repeat: this man could be my One True Love on this earth as destined by Fate.

She inventoried her body. No hot cheeks, so no blush. No sweats. No closing throat. No palpitating heart. No quickening breaths. *No fear.* Where was her terror? She rechecked herself. She felt so . . . normal.

Great, just when she was ready to use her shyness, it

was gone. She nodded to her books. "I'm working on a production of *Romeo and Juliet*."

"Romeo and Jasmine?" In an instant, the red drained from his face, and he became pure, sickly white.

"How do you know my name?" A hiccup of familiar terror returned to her.

"The note. You note a wrote. You . . ." He took an enormous breath. "You wrote a note."

She laughed. Actually laughed. God, she felt amazing. He was so charming, so fumbled. And she felt so unfumbled, so free! "Oh, Amy's note. But—"

He reached into his shirt pocket and pulled out Jasmine's picture. It was a shot of her and Amy on the carousel in Central Park last spring. Only it was ripped in half so only she remained. "Oh, no. You must think I'm a stalker. Let me explain. It's so silly. See, my sister is a psychic." Her words came out effortlessly. *Love is the escape from anxiety.* No. That didn't sound exactly right. Surely love freed her somehow. Love was . . . calmness?

Hmm. That wasn't right either. Plus, look how poor Josh was feeling, squirming in his undersized chair. If love was calmness, this guy hated her guts.

Other patrons were scowling at them, annoyed at the noise. She lowered her voice. "My sister wrote that note," she whispered. Then she went on to explain about Amy and how she hears voices, amazed as the words flowed. Nothing stopped them, tripped them, tangled them, leaving them mangled and torn. *I feel like a million bucks, and I'm talking to a man who might be my One True Love. Maybe I'll be this free around everyone. I'll march into the production meeting Monday morning with my buddy Arturo, my head held high.*

She felt giddy with normalcy. She couldn't remember the last time she had been this close to a straight, attractive man without feeling insane panic. This Josh was different. She was different. Full of gratefulness, so fluid she almost felt recklessly drunk, she leaned toward him and finished her story. "So, that's why she thought you were my One True Love as destined by prophecy. You know, I'm starting to think you might be The One too."

Something had changed in him while she was talking. He wasn't white—or red—anymore but had returned to a normal pale pink. His feet had stopped tapping. His hands had stopped wringing. He was sitting up straighter. "Do you hear voices too?" he asked.

"Oh. No. But they're there. I sometimes wish I did."

She watched a look of infinite relief flood his face. "Really?"

"You should meet Amy. Her power is legendary. I think you'd like her."

He seemed to have gained control of his limbs. What was happening to him? Had he realized that he loved her, too, and was feeling at ease? "I'd love to meet her," he said. But his words sounded fake.

"This True Love stuff can be a little frightening," Jasmine said. Confusion tugged at her. The problem with never talking to men was that once you talked to one, it was uncharted territory. She had to know. Had he lost his fear too? "Do you feel anything odd?" she asked, leaning in close.

"Well, gotta get back to work." He started to get up, but she grabbed his wrist in a sudden panic.

"Don't go."

The look in his eyes stopped her cold. *He thinks I'm nuts.*

She felt desperate to explain. "I've never felt this way around a—" She stopped herself from saying "man." It sounded too sexual. "A stranger. Ever. I guess that sounds kind of crazy."

"Oh, no. It sounds perfectly normal to me." He leaned in toward her, took her hand from his wrist, and placed it gently on the table. "You can stay here as long as you like, and you can sketch me all you like if you do it quietly. But I can't have you and Eleanor fighting."

Jasmine looked from Eleanor to Josh and then back to Eleanor. *Eleanor and her friends are bag people.* "You think I'm crazy."

Josh motioned to the table. "We don't say 'crazy' here. We're a public facility, and all are welcome if they sit quietly. That's Tony. He thinks he's Jesus Christ. Which is fine. Jesus was a very quiet man. Sometimes he thinks he's Elvis, though. That can be a problem. Next to him, the woman with the Indian headdress, that's Suzanne, but she likes to be called Crouching Panther. Eleanor, who you met earlier, thinks she's my wife. Which is okay so long as she's quiet." He raised one freckled finger at Jasmine to prevent her from replying. "If we have complaints about body odor, we have to ask you to leave."

"No, you don't understand! I'm not crazy! Let me explain. See, the voices that Amy hears are—"

He gave her a practiced librarian shush: one finger lightly against his lips, his lips pursed, no sound, but warning eyes. Maybe they taught that in library school. "Amy's welcome too. Whenever it's cold outside, we get lots of friends who come in to keep warm. The weather turned this morning, and I'm glad you found us!" He looked to Eleanor and waved. Then he said very seriously to Jasmine, "No fighting with Eleanor. If you want to be my wife, too, that's fine. So long as everyone gets along."

Jasmine threw up her hands. She wanted the shy Josh back. Why had she ever told him about True Love? Of course he thought she was nuts. Didn't every book and article and utterance about men scream that the worst crime was to mention commitment and love? She had just felt so free and loose.

Dumb. Dumb. Dumb.

"Free lunch in the basement of the Episcopal church around the corner starts in ten minutes if you're hungry. Dan from Social Services comes through every other Thursday. He's very nice. Good luck with the Shakespeare. I love *Romeo and Juliet.*" He nodded, then turned and walked back to his desk. He slipped behind it and lowered the divider behind him.

Jasmine watched him hopelessly. She sank deeper into her chair. The eerie feeling that someone was watching her sent a chill up her spine. She looked to Eleanor, who was grinning at her with a triumphant smile.

Chapter 12

Now that Amy was gone, Jasmine had her apartment back and it was blissfully silent, except for the early morning trash truck. And the never-ending salsa music. The car alarms. The barking dogs. The old men arguing in Croatian two floors down.

She lay back on her bed and stared at the white ceiling. Josh Toby the movie star was gorgeous, startlingly sexy, and she was going to be working with him every day— work that would involve various degrees of undress.

Josh Toby the librarian put her blissfully at ease in a way she'd never experienced before with a man. Of course, he thought she was a bag lady.

She rolled over onto her stomach. Josh the librarian took away her fear. Josh the movie star increased it tenfold. So did that make the librarian the right Josh Toby? Or was her Josh Toby a third man? One she hadn't yet met?

If only Amy could still hear the voice, she could come back and tell Jasmine what to do.

But shouldn't Jasmine know? Shouldn't True Love be shockingly clear? Eyes meeting across a crowded room and a bolt of lightning? It was like that with Movie Star Josh when they had kissed. Or was that pure fear that had shot through her? *Face it, for me fear and love feel like the same emotion.*

Or was True Love like being with Librarian Josh? Calmness and ease?

Jasmine rolled off the bed and pulled on her robe over her long T-shirt. She put the teakettle on one of the two burners and began to pace. If both Josh Tobys were standing before her right now, who would she pick? Both their faces flashed through her mind. With every pivot, she changed her mind. Librarian Josh. No, Movie Star Josh. No, the librarian.

Two minutes later, the teakettle began to whistle and she still hadn't made up her mind.

She poured herself a mug of green Tetley and went to her enormous window. *Get with reality: I can't have either Josh. One gave me a stern body odor warning and an invitation to a soup kitchen, and the other is dating the most perfect woman alive.*

Jasmine looked out at the early morning street below her and gasped. Her mug slipped from her hands and clunked to the floor, splashing hot tea over her ankles.

Not that she could feel it.

Movie Star Josh was on his way up her front steps.

Didn't that guy know anything about phones?

Josh stood before her grinning with pleasure at his plan.

Jasmine tried not to gape at its impossibility. *Why hadn't she hidden behind the drapes again and not let him in?* In her rush to clean the spilled tea and whip on a pair of jeans, she had forgotten to be as petrified as she should have been.

"C'mon. I've never been with a costume designer on Halloween! I can't let this opportunity pass! It'll be a blast." She tried to focus on Buster the dog and another, smaller dog who had joined Josh's crew. The two creatures were happily sniffing their way around her apartment.

Josh was wearing his usual Yankees baseball cap and jeans with an untucked button-down blue shirt with the two top buttons undone (Jasmine tried not to notice his Statue-of-David pecs beneath), and his leather jacket. Was everyone from California so perfectly tanned in October? He didn't even have tan lines. At least, he hadn't in that picture from the Internet that she had checked one more time last night just to, um, remind herself of his ass. . . .

. . . uh, his assets.

Which, by the way, had no tan lines.

Oh, God. She had to keep a hold of herself. *Stop thinking about the man naked.* She reached under the sink and pulled out two dog biscuits. She had bought a box of them last night on a whim, in case Josh and Buster returned.

"So why do you have Arturo's dog?" she asked as the two dogs devoured their treats. So long as she focused on the dogs, she felt just bearably on edge.

"Arturo had to split town for a few days. Besides, I needed a running partner. And then, I figured Buster needed a companion, and this beauty was for sale at this diner in Brooklyn where I was having lunch yesterday. The lady who owned her turned out to be allergic."

"I have mice in my apartment bigger than her."

"She's part Chihuahua, but she *could* be part mouse." He smiled. "Her name's Lassie. She's not such a good runner. I have to tuck her into my jacket by the time we get to the park. But she's sweet. And Buster's just crazy about her."

Jasmine was touched by the image of the smaller dog nestled against his chest while he and Buster ran.

"I'm worried how Lass'll do when Arturo comes back from Baltimore to get Buster back."

Jasmine flinched at the mention of Baltimore. No way was Arturo's presence in Baltimore anything more than a coincidence. Amy and Arturo didn't have any contact.

Josh tossed his black leather (more skin, but at least only indirectly *his* skin) jacket on the couch. Jasmine battled the urge to touch its sensuous surface. The thing must have cost a couple thousand dollars at least. She gripped her new tea mug tightly, then spotted the label on the jacket. Versace. Okay, make that $9,736—$8,000 on sale. And she didn't think Josh Toby bought things on sale.

"So," he asked. "Halloween?"

"I don't do Halloween." She put down her mug and sat on her hands so that she wouldn't touch the jacket. "In fact, I hadn't even remembered that it was Halloween." Buster jumped into her lap, and she was forced to set her hands free to pet him. Lassie tried to jump up, but she was too short. She settled on the floor by Josh's feet.

"A costume designer who doesn't live for Halloween? Jas, c'mon. It'll be a trial run for you disguising me." He rubbed the top of the little dog's head.

Jas. His familiarity zinged through her blood and turned it to fire. "I wasn't thinking of dressing you up as a mummy zombie for rehearsals."

He smiled. "I'm game for anything."

Yeah, that was what Hollywood Dirt *said last week*

when it claimed Cleo called you an "animal in bed." Not that Jasmine had been reading the *Dirt*—again. Of course, when she was on her way to the library, she *might* have read a few words at the newsstand.

There was also that article about a man who looked like Josh Toby who left a $5,000 tip for a waitress in Queens after she had been talking on her cell about how her kid needed dental work that she couldn't afford. The waitress swore it *was* Josh Toby, but his publicist denied it strenuously, claiming that he wasn't even in the country.

Jasmine wondered if the guy in the restaurant had two dogs with him.

Jasmine remembered the expensive earrings. Was Josh giving away money too? Was that how superstars like him related to ordinary people? He was staring at her with his "you're the only person in the world" intensity. No, he related with his eyes, his body, every inch of him.

He continued to watch her, and she could see the gears of his mind spinning, taking it all in, her every nuance, recording her, processing her. It was eerie. "The parade downtown is rowdy, and there are mobs of people." She shuddered.

"What's wrong with people?" he asked.

"*Mobs*," she stressed.

"So?" He sauntered to her worktable. She noticed that as he went, his face leapt through several expressions. Hey, they were *her* expressions. *He was silently acting her out*, as if he were trying her on for size, putting her on like a costume.

She dragged her eyes from his face a moment too late. Next to her sewing machine, her sketchbook lay open.

He was heading right toward it.

She leapt off the couch, dove past him, and tried to swipe it off the table.

But she tripped over Lassie, and Josh was faster. He whisked it off the table, then held it just out of her reach. "What's this? Costumes for *Romeo and Juliet*? Is that me?"

Jasmine felt her face flush. "Sketches," she mumbled. Why had she spent so much time sketching his eyes? And why was he so tall? Well, she wasn't going to jump up and down like Buster and Lassie to try getting her sketchbook back.

She sank back on the couch. Josh was paging through the book, nodding and making small noises of appreciation. She discreetly kicked his jacket onto the floor so that she wouldn't submit to the incredible urge to touch it. She didn't want him looking up to see her stroking his jacket, adding to her already significant humiliation. Lassie climbed inside the jacket, curled up, and went right to sleep.

"So are these the costumes for tomorrow's production meeting?" He hadn't looked up.

"No." She willed herself to speak. She felt like a little kid who had been caught drawing nudie pictures. "Arturo does the major designing. He's the boss. They're just what I would do if I wasn't the assistant. Which I am. So I don't design. I . . . you know . . . get coffee and stuff." Or she would, if she ever actually met with Arturo. Since the Indian restaurant, she hadn't heard from him at all. His secretary, a gruff, terse woman, had messengered her a contract, her portfolio, and a schedule of meetings. The woman had scrawled a warning in red marker on the meeting schedule to be at each meeting half an hour early, prepared for last-minute changes. And that was it. The whole situation was ruining what was left of her nerves.

Josh slammed the book shut, making both her and Buster jump. Lassie didn't budge. "That's just stupid. These are great. You should design the costumes. I'm going to call Arturo." He whipped the tiniest cell phone Jasmine had ever seen out of his jeans pocket, pushed a button, and pressed it to his ear. The phone looked like it was made of solid gold.

"I thought Arturo was in Baltimore."

"I have his cell."

Good God, the man was pure impulse. Did he ever stop to think about anything? Maybe Suz and Jenn were right about him. "Don't you dare!" She leapt off the couch, then froze. What was she going to do, attack him? Grab his phone and fling it out the window?

He smiled a wicked, sexy smile. "Then go to the Halloween parade with me."

She felt her eyes go wide. He wasn't impulsive: The phone call was part of a plan. He projected boyish impetuousness so fully that his astute understanding of the situation was hidden underneath. After all the insights he had already had into her, she ought to know to be more careful around him. "Are you blackmailing me?"

He shrugged. "It's for your own good. You're so pale. You need some moonshine." He turned his attention to his phone. "Arturo? Josh. You're doing what? A gy—"

"I'll do it!" she gasped. *Oh, God. I just agreed to spend the day and half the night with this man.*

He smiled another wicked smile. "Artie, you there? Listen, forget it. I'll get you when you come back to New York. Yeah, Buster's great. He's got a girlfriend.

You wanna say hi?" He put the phone to the dog's ear, then back to his own. "He says don't bother coming back; we're having a ball. Yeah, we. Well, I'm here with Jasmine and Lassie. I'll explain later. Yeah. It's cool. Okay. Bye." He clicked the phone shut, then strode three steps across her apartment and scooped his jacket off the floor. Lassie tumbled out. "Oh, sorry, girl."

Jasmine watched him, frozen. The idea of parading around Greenwich Village with Josh Toby and half of Manhattan (and a pretty good portion of New Jersey) was sickeningly impossible. The Greenwich Village Halloween parade was rowdy, huge, and drunken. And while most of the men were gay and she wasn't terrified of crowds in the same way she was of men, still, there was Josh. Plus, it wasn't her scene.

Josh smiled a smile so intimate, her heart crashed into her stomach. Then, in a deft motion, he draped the coat on her shoulders. "I had a wicked idea. You go as me."

She stuttered incoherently. The heavy jacket smelled like leather, man, and autumn air. Also, a touch like Lassie. She could feel the jewelry box still in the pocket. Had he forgotten it or brought it back on purpose? Finally, she managed, "Who will you be?"

"I'll be you."

"But I'm no one." It was becoming uncomfortably warm inside the jacket. She couldn't move under its weight.

He pursed his lips. "Well, not really. But I get your point. Hmm . . . I'll be your bodyguard, Mohammad." He drew himself to his full height and stuck out his chest in an Arnold Schwarzenegger pose.

He looked absurd and she couldn't hold back her smile.

"You're too thin to be a bodyguard." *You're too beautiful to be a bodyguard—who'd want the one you were protecting with you around?* In fact. No. Well, maybe, yes. He was beautiful enough to be a woman. She was mad at him for blackmailing her, and this would be satisfying revenge. She felt the weight of the jacket as if it were a second, tougher skin. A skin that fit.

"What?" he asked. His eyes lit up to match the spark in hers.

"I'll be you." She paused as she considered the implications of what she was about to say, then rushed ahead recklessly before she lost her nerve. She could do it. She could make the costume with her eyes closed. She could transform this man into whomever she liked. "And you be your girlfriend, Cleo. That's my final offer. Take it or leave it."

But instead of looking horrified, he grinned. "Oooh, yes! Very wicked, Jas. I'll have to back you into corners more often. I'm in. Definitely in."

Josh stood by Jasmine's window with his arms stuck out as she circled his waist with her tape measure. She smelled like roses and Ivory soap. Her closeness thrilled him no matter how much he tried to fight off the sensation. After all, he was just here because he didn't know another soul in New York. Well, he knew hundreds of souls, but he couldn't see them without risking the world finding out that he was in New York. So he had Jasmine.

I am not here because she smells like roses and Ivory soap.

Her neck was like a swan's.

I cannot have a relationship. First, it's against my

*agreement with Cleo. Second, it would mean entangle-
ments that would interfere with work. And work is everything. Especially this work. Real work. The stage!* His
stomach squeezed into a ball.

She continued to study him with intense, professional
interest. Did this woman not even notice him as a man?
She was so uptight, maybe she didn't. *She was so uptight,
maybe she did.*

For the hundreth time since he'd been with her, he considered telling Jasmine the truth about him and Cleo, just
to see how she responded. But he wasn't sure if he could
trust her with such an enormous secret. He and Cleo had
promised each other not to tell a soul that their relationship
was manufactured. One slip, and it could all unravel.

This had never been a problem. Most women couldn't
care less that he was supposedly already hooked up. But
did Jasmine care about that? A professional desire (*yes,
just professional, hot shot*) to figure her character out
overcame him. *What motivates you, Jasmine?* "Don't you
want the exact measurements?" he asked. He let his arms
fall, then lifted his shirt to expose his perfect, six-pack
abs. "Cleo does wear her outfits pretty tight."

Jasmine flinched, then returned to her stony resolute-
ness. "This is fine," she whispered.

Ah-ha. There was a woman in there, under those layers
of reserve. His urge to figure her out felt a little less professional now. *It's not about sex and flirting and loneliness,* he told himself. It was about reaching this closed-off
person who seemed to desperately want reaching. In one
motion, he pulled the shirt over his head and stood before
her in his jeans. "I like things to be exact."

Jasmine, who was already holding her breath, sucked

it in even further. But she diligently retook the measurement, not meeting his eyes.

"Jas," he said. The urge to break through to her was overwhelming. But in his clumsiness, he realized, he was making her fear worse.

"Hold still." She measured his arms from shoulder to wrist. Around the bicep. Across the back of the shoulders. Her birdlike touches made him aware how unfair he was being. There had to be another way to reach her.

"I'm sorry I make you so nervous," he said, truly sorry that he had taken off his shirt. He was so used to people who laid it on the line. She was so closed, yet at the same time, she couldn't hide any of her emotions. The duality intrigued him. Maybe more than was good.

"You don't make me nervous," she squeaked. Her hands were trembling.

He cocked his head and raised his eyebrows. "I think I do." He watched her carefully as she moved away from him and jotted down measurements. He peeked at the numbers. He had to lay off the pastrami sandwiches.

He watched Jasmine watch him.

There's a woman under there, and I want to meet her.

Only he wasn't so sure that she wanted to be found. Especially by him.

Chapter 13

Ten hours later, a beautiful, very tall woman in a red sparkling sleeveless gown, two-inch heels, and a push-up bra sauntered down the middle of a swarming Seventh Avenue on the arm of an exceedingly attractive but somewhat short man in full Mitch Tank regalia: the regulation Tank Command dark sunglasses, the ubiquitous cigarette pack tucked under his camouflage army shirt, the green-and-black painted face. The night was clear, the moon hovering full and orange on the horizon.

Jasmine was tingling with the joy of being disguised. Why hadn't her self-help books suggested this? If only every day could be Halloween.

She looked around them at their fellow marchers. *For most of these guys, every day is Halloween.* The drag queens had, as usual, outdone themselves. Wave after wave of them, tottering on impossible heels, sauntered past. Around them, bloodied ghouls frolicked with inebriated zombies. The obligatory drag-queen impersonators—Martha Stewart with a beard and dressed in jailhouse stripes, Richard Nixon in a lemon-chiffon ballgown, even a few Cleo Chans with remarkable biceps—romped and hooted. It was Halloween in Greenwich Village, and there was nothing like it in the world.

The night air was crisp under the full harvest moon, but the crowds that lined the avenue several layers deep didn't seem to mind. Of course, most of them were way too drunk to notice.

Jasmine, enjoying her combat boots and plastic Uzi, drew appreciative "oohs" and "aahs" from the rowdy crowd. Josh, dressed as Cleo Chan, however, drew more heartfelt sighs, as 80 percent of the paraders and a good portion of the spectators were gay. They knew a sensational set of cheekbones when they saw them.

Josh, in his gown, leaned down to Jasmine. "My heels are killing me! Let's duck into a quiet bar."

Jasmine looked up at him. In his heels, he towered over her by a good foot. Jasmine enjoyed being out in her Mitch Tank disguise—that is, not being herself. She didn't want to stop. "Quiet? We'd have to rent a car and drive to Vermont for quiet."

"Hey, Cleo Chan," a frat boy hooted. "I love you!"

Josh strong-armed his admirer, who had ducked the police barriers that lined the avenue, pushing him firmly back toward his pack of buddies, all in matching Sigma-Theta sweatshirts. "Okay. Quieter," he said to Jasmine.

"Right." Poor Josh. Maybe she shouldn't have put him in such tottering shoes.

They made their way toward the police barriers, but before they could scoot under them, a man with a professional-quality camera jumped into the street in front of them, blocking their escape route. "How 'bout a kiss for tomorrow's papers?" he asked, camera already poised. "The world's most famous couple?"

Jasmine blanched under her makeup.

The crowds around them howled, "Kiss! Kiss! Kiss!" and, "C'mon, Josh! Give her a wet one!"

Jasmine realized that Josh was looking down at her very seriously. In fact, he was leaning toward her that same way he had in her apartment the last time he kissed her. She considered pulling away, but the crowd was going wild, pushing in. Before she knew what was happening, Josh/Cleo had swept her into his arms, leaned her back, and hovered centimeters from her lips.

"Welcome to showbiz, baby," Josh crooned as his lips touched hers.

Those lips again. They had to stop this. Her lips opened into his—stupid, disobedient lips, traitors to the cause.

What was the cause again?

Something about a peaceful quiet life . . .

Her lips yielded under his. Her whole body swooned. *Kissed by Josh Toby. Again.* Well, Josh Toby in drag in front of a hooting crowd, but still. Her lips parted and his tongue tickled her teeth. His arm supported her, which was good, as her knees had gone weak with longing. The crowd melted away around her.

He pulled her closer. Kissed her more firmly, her ammunition belt pressing against his sequins.

He kissed down her neck.

Oh, God. She bit his ear.

The camera clicked.

The camera clicked?

She pulled away with a start. The photographer was down on one knee, getting the best angle.

Josh pulled back, too, his wig askew, his boobs misaligned.

They stared at each other for a long, intense moment.

Then Josh raised himself to full height, straightened his padding, and gave the crowd a million-dollar smile. "Okay, show's over!" he commanded.

The photographer looked at him closely, then shook his head. "I shouldn't have had that last Jell-O shot," he said. "For a minute there, *you* looked like Josh Toby."

Josh shrugged but turned quickly away.

They ducked out of the parade and pushed through the crowds, Cleo/Josh leading the way.

Was that an act? Jasmine's lips were swollen and on fire. She pulled her army hat as far down over her eyes as it would go.

Stay in reality. Jasmine shook the kiss out of her mind. *Josh is a showman.* She followed the blur of his red ballgown through the throng. It was, if she didn't say so herself, the perfect gown. They had found it at a thrift shop on Third Avenue—slinky, long, and what a red. She had spent two hours sewing padding in all the right places, lengthening, shortening. She cut the jet-black wig into Cleo's latest style and did his makeup from a picture they clipped from *People*. It was an awesome job. He looked like an Amazon-on-steroids Cleo.

Jasmine thought back to their day together, getting ready for the parade. It had been fun picking clothes out with him. She was in control and had something to focus on besides the fact that she was with a man. She even relaxed enough to kick around some ideas for Josh's disguise for rehearsals. She rejected her first idea that he should be shy and retiring. It felt disloyal to the kind man she had met at the library.

No, Josh's disguise should be over the top, a Josh Toby

wannabe gone terribly wrong. They had found a pair of supertight, black leather toreador pants in a bin outside a jeans shop on Canal Street that said it all in rivets and snakeskin embossing.

They fled the main crowd and skirted the secondary crowds spilling out of the bars. A man dressed as Steve Irwin stepped on her foot, and then the crocodile woman next to him did the same. Jasmine barely felt either stomp through her combat boots. *Of course, Josh's kiss was just a show. He kisses for a living. He can't help himself. He certainly didn't* want *to kiss me like that.*

They pushed toward the West Side, the streets growing quieter except for the occasional pack of stumbling drunks. They wove through the parked cars, enjoying the night air and the sense of freedom, until they came to a neon-lit deli on Eighth Avenue. "This?" Josh asked.

"Sure." Her stomach growled in agreement.

The overmuscled greeter didn't give them a second glance as he gave them a quiet booth by the window. The place was half-empty, its tables dotted with late-night eaters—an overflowing booth of club kids in their trampy vampire costumes, a pair of elderly men scowling at their newspapers while their meals cooled beside them.

The heady aroma of overcooked burgers and fries made Jasmine feel even more like Mitch Tank. Until she remembered she was sitting across from Josh Toby, the original Sergeant Tank. She could still feel his lips on hers. The waiter brought them water, and she gulped it gratefully.

Josh took off his heels and rubbed his feet. "Whose crazy idea was this?"

"Yours."

"Oh, right."

He should charge for that smile. Jasmine tried not to stare. *I guess he does charge for that smile.*

But this was her personal show.

They accepted menus from the waiter, but Josh didn't even glance at his.

"That was fun," he said.

The kiss? Or dressing up like your girlfriend? "Yeah. If you like screaming, inebriated crowds and pushy photographers." She was sorry she had brought up the photographer—*the kiss.* Her face went hot. But surely Josh couldn't see her blush under her green and brown camouflage makeup. A rush of bravery pulsed through her. It was the feeling she'd been relishing all night: *I'm not me tonight. He can't see the real me.*

Was that what let her kiss him back the way she had? Let her hands run down his back?

She hadn't gotten nauseous once.

He broke into her thoughts. "You're an amazing costume designer, Jas. Anyone could dress me up in drag, but you captured something about Cleo that's hard to put a finger on."

That she's so gorgeous, she should be taken out and shot? "*You* captured it," Jasmine reminded him. "That's what actors do."

Josh shook his head sadly. "That's what actors try to do. This Romeo thing . . ." He pulled off his Cleo Chan wig and rustled his real hair dejectedly. "I'll need more than a great costume to pull it off."

"You'll be great," she assured him, amazed at how helpless he looked; although, maybe that was just his geisha-rouged cheeks. She studied the menu, trying to concentrate on anything but the man across from her.

The waiter came and they ordered.

When the waiter left, Josh said, "How do you know I'll be great?"

"If you can act with Juliet like you acted with me, with that kiss, you'll be set." The instant the words left her mouth, she wished she could pull them back. Why not just tell him straight out that she was obsessing over the kiss?

He looked at her askance. "I wasn't acting." He pulled off his fake eyelashes, wincing. Then he dipped a napkin in his water and began rubbing off his makeup. Bit by bit, the real Josh emerged. "I don't act about things like that."

Jasmine sucked in her breath. She felt her face go hot under her makeup. *I'm not wiping off a drop of this stuff.* She touched her fake stubble and did her best Mitch Tank impersonation. "Sorry, sweetcakes. I'm hitched."

Okay, so her best Josh Toby impersonation was lame.

"Not bad, Burns. But maybe one day, I'll tell you about what it's really like to be me." He pulled out the foam padding that had formed his substantial Cleo Chan boobage. "Need this for later?" he asked, nodding to her flat, flak-jacketed chest.

"Watch it. I've got an Uzi." It was so easy to talk to him in this getup. Guess all she had to do was dress like a crazed infantryman her whole life.

"Just kidding." He put the boobs next to his plate. "I like you just the way you are."

Thankfully, the waiter took that humiliating moment of discussing her A cups to appear with two beers. While he poured them into icy glasses, Jasmine's brain ricocheted from fear to ecstasy. Despite that kiss, this Josh couldn't be her One True Love. After all, she could only speak to him when she was dressed up like someone else. The other Josh was so right for her—once she steered him past his bag-lady confusion. But this Josh—he was removing eyeliner while gazing into a compact he had taken out of his purse, the reflection of his violet eyes mesmerizing—he was so wrong.

"So, you have a boyfriend?" he asked.

Was this small talk, or did he really want to know? She gripped her Uzi. "I have a boyfriend," she surprised herself by saying. She was thinking of her librarian. She could overcome their initial misunderstanding. She crossed her arms over her chest.

He put his compact into his fake-diamond-studded purse, pulled out a baseball cap, and settled it low on his head. Now, from the neck up, he was his old self. "No kidding. What's his name?" He took a swig of beer. Jasmine wasn't sure, but she thought he looked disappointed. He had disappeared under his hat, and she couldn't see his eyes.

Josh Toby. Jasmine took a bigger swig of beer. She checked that the buttons of her flak jacket were done up to her neck. "His name is Josh also. Coincidence." *Not.*

"So, what's he like? C'mon. Spill. What kind of man can penetrate the defenses of the elusive Jasmine Burns?"

The waiter brought their appetizer—a messy Greek salad plunked between them. Jasmine went to spear a green olive, considering what to say. Josh went for the same olive. They each pulled back their forks.

"He . . ." *He thinks I'm a bag lady.*

"What?" Josh went for a ball of mozzarella.

"He's very nice. He's a librarian."

Josh sat back and downed a swig of beer. He swished it in his mouth, then swallowed. "Oh, come on, Jas. Give me more than that."

Why? Jasmine felt her insides tighten in a sort of excitement that just wasn't right. "You tell me something about Cleo Chan," she demanded, trying to change the subject while also making a point. The beer—how had she finished it so quickly?—was going to her head. There was no way Josh Toby was flirting with her.

"Okay." He leaned forward. He seemed to consider for a moment. Then he shrugged, as if making up his mind about something important. "We've never had sex."

Jasmine fell back in surprise. "Oh."

"We've been 'together' two years, but we haven't been together more than two weeks since our first fake date, except for photo ops. And during those two weeks, we were only together in the sense that we were together with twenty-seven invited reporters and photographers, three personal assistants, two stylists, and a macrobiotic chef."

"Macrobiotic?" Jasmine's head spun. *No sex?*

"Don't ask. We were on a 'private' island in the Caribbean. You're probably the only person in America who hasn't seen the two thousand pictures from our reclusive, romantic vacation."

Actually, she had seen the pictures during one of her late-night Web-search adventures. She remembered one in particular, Josh and Cleo, arm-in-arm, strolling down the deserted beach. She hadn't thought about the photographer who must have been behind them for that perfect picture to exist. "I'm not understanding this," she said. "Why are you two together if you don't, um, you know?" Her face felt so hot, she was afraid her makeup would melt away.

Josh shrugged. "Twenty-seven invited reporters and photographers, three personal assistants—"

"You're together for the press coverage?"

"Bingo." He flashed his million-dollar smile, but it faded in an instant. "We work constantly. Seven days a week. Sometimes eighteen hours a day. Tahiti. Rome. South Africa. Sometimes for months at a time. It's too hard to have a real relationship. Work. Travel. Demands. Our publicist—we have the same publicist—put it together after . . ." He paused. "After one too many lawsuits from disappointed lovers who just couldn't understand that work comes first. Always."

Jasmine tried to take this news in. *Cleo Chan wasn't his girlfriend.* At least, not in the normal sense of the word. It was kind of sad, really.

"This is, by the way, top secret."

"Of course." *It doesn't matter if Cleo is his girlfriend or not; what matters is that he has just very clearly told me that relationships are way out.*

"But enough about me. Tell me about a normal relationship," he said.

Normal. Jasmine signaled the waiter for another beer. Who was she to call Josh sad? She had never even had a fake relationship with a man. He was light years ahead of her with his pretend romance.

He looked so expectant, she had to come clean. "Okay. Josh isn't exactly my boyfriend. Yet. But I *think* he's The One."

Josh's eyes went wide. "I knew it!" He popped half a hard-boiled egg into his mouth. "When you said you had a boyfriend, I knew you were too shy to actually have one."

"Hey!" She aimed the Uzi at him. Josh's face had gone from stoic fortitude to playful animation so quickly, Jasmine wondered if he had made up all that stuff about not having a real relationship with Cleo just to get her to talk.

The waiter brought her a second beer and took the empty appetizer plate from between them. Jasmine was amazed: She had eaten in front of Josh. She felt a wave of absurd pride. *I ate in front of a man without choking even once! Without even thinking about it!*

Was she making progress with her anxiety? Did it count as progress if she was dressed up like a killer and the man wore spaghetti straps?

"So there's a guy you're hot for, but you're afraid to talk to him?" Josh leaned back in the booth as if he wasn't still in a sparkling evening gown. Two women in slutty cat costumes who had just arrived at the next table stared at him intently. He jammed his wig back over his baseball cap and sat up in a ladylike pose. He waved at them impishly. They looked away, giggling.

"It's worse," she admitted. She was enjoying his playful looseness. It must be the beer. None of this counted as progress—beer, disguise, man in pearls. She couldn't take her ease with him too seriously.

"He's married, huh?"

Well, as long as they were trading secrets. "He thinks I'm crazy."

"Well, so do I. But that doesn't bug me. Actually, I sort of like it." He patted her hand.

She yanked her hand away before she even realized he had touched her. *Stupid reflexes.*

He smiled. "You need lessons on how to be with a man."

Her mouth fell open. "I do not."

"You do. You're a mess." He leaned forward. "I could help you."

She let her eyes scan his bodice. "Be with a man?"

"Face it, Burns. This is the first conversation we've had that hasn't made you physically ill." He held up a hand to stop her protest. "I notice these things. You're only at ease right now because you're dressed up like a homicidal maniac."

"Not true. Mitch isn't crazy. He only kills for his country." She hoped her lame joke would put him off the subject.

It didn't work. "Put down the submachine gun, take off the dark glasses, and tell me you enjoyed our day together."

"No!" Her right index finger tensed on the trigger. "I mean, I could. If I wanted."

He was about to protest when the waiter brought their main courses.

"Lesson one," he said, not taking his eyes from hers. "Eating with a man."

Chapter 14

He turned his pastrami sandwich this way and that, deep in thought. He looked up at her, catching her eyeing his sandwich.

She tore her eyes away and looked down at her own grilled cheese on white. White on white on a white plate. Bleck. She always ordered the plainest thing on the menu and was always sorry.

"Lesson one . . . wait, lesson one is over. That was how to kiss. And we know you're good at that. A plus."

Jasmine drew her lips into what she hoped was a stern frown. *If kissing was lesson one, then lesson two . . .* Her body went cold. "I am not taking lessons—"

"Lesson two is how to accept a gift—and a compliment—graciously. Would you like a bite of my sandwich, gorgeous?" He pushed his plate toward her.

"I . . ." Jasmine hesitated. She was on the verge of saying no. But she did want a bite. It looked amazing—glistening and piled high with meat, a touch of grainy Dijon peeking out the sides. She hated that her shyness always made her say no when she meant yes. Made her order safe white cheese when she wanted messy red meat. She cleared her throat. "Okay."

He shook his head. "Not 'okay.' Try, 'Yes, I would *love* a bite.'"

"I'm not saying that."

He bit into the sandwich. "Mmm. Not too salty. Moist."

She scowled at him.

"You are a lousy student. This is method acting. You want it. I walked all over town with you today, and you hardly ate a thing. I know you're hungry. Hungrier than that." He nodded at her limp, flat sandwich. "So *show* me that you want it. C'mon." He sat back, crossed his arms, and waited.

She continued to scowl at him. There were so many things in this world she wanted. But to *say* that she wanted them to a person like him was impossible.

He pushed the sandwich toward her.

She deepened her look of displeasure. Sure, it was easy for a guy like him, with no boundaries, to do and say whatever he wanted. *Stupid normal people.*

He pulled the plate back and took an enormous bite. A dab of mustard was on his chin.

Exasperated, she set her shoulders. "I would *love* a bite."

"Ooooh. That was *good*. See, now I *want* to give you a bite." His eyes grew serious and slightly smoky. He pushed the plate toward her again.

She picked up the untouched half of the sandwich and took a tiny nibble. "Mmm . . ."

"No way, Burns. I'm not teaching you how to be with a Boy Scout. I'm teaching you how to be with a man."

"A man in drag."

"C'mon, Mitch Tank. Take a real bite."

She picked up her half of his sandwich defiantly and ripped off a chunk. *Oh, my.* This was excellent pastrami. Dry rub, tender. Just as she closed her eyes to savor it, he reached over and snatched off her dark glasses.

"Hey! Give me my shades back," she mumbled through her bite.

"Now take a bite like that as Jasmine Burns. Not as Mitch Tank."

No problem. She still had her makeup on, so he couldn't see her blush. She bit into the sandwich. "Ha!" she said, her mouth still full. "See, I don't need lessons."

"Good. Then give me the gun and hat."

"No one touches my gun."

"Fine." He leaned in, took a napkin out of the dispenser, and dipped it into his water. He held it out to her. "Take off the makeup."

"No." She felt absurdly childish. But if he took away her makeup, she was sure that she would dissolve away with it. And she wanted to finish her half of the sandwich. "I spent an hour putting this stuff on. And the night is young."

He leaned back. "Are you this way around all men or just me?"

She took another defiant bite. "I don't want to talk about it."

"Something happened. What?"

Jasmine put down the sandwich. She felt slightly ill. "For your information, some people just *are* shy."

"But not you. You've got something else going on." He leaned in close. "What happened?"

Jasmine looked up at the embossed-tin ceiling. She took a deep breath and told him all about brain chemicals and inherited traits.

"Yeah, yeah. But that's not it."

She told him the living-with-her-mom-in-Bombay-then-coming-to-America-when-she-was-sixteen saga. "I guess I never got used to this culture."

"No way. What else?"

She sighed exasperatedly. "Okay." She told him the reading-Greek-myths-in-school story she had told Amy.

He shook his head. "Bullshit." He had finished his half of the sandwich and was munching on the pickle. "You can't tell me that you grew up in Bombay with your mom, then when you were sixteen, she put you on a plane to Baltimore to be with your sisters and dad, *who you hadn't seen since you were two*, and your cataclysmic anxiety-inducing event was in school reading Greek myths out loud? Bullshit." He offered her half the pickle.

"It's true." Jasmine crossed her arms over her chest.

"Why did your mother put you on that plane?" He pointed the pickle at her. "Method acting. Search for motivation. Find it, Jas. Tell me."

The urge to bolt out of the restaurant and never look back overcame Jasmine. *Run. Now.* But he looked so absurd, in his dress, with his pickle, that she couldn't abandon him.

"Don't look at me. Just look at the table and say out loud what happened."

Why could this man see through her like she was made of chiffon? She had never told anyone about her tutor, Raj. About the crush she had had on him. About thinking he loved her too. Then that day in the madhavi bushes. He was kissing her. But that rustling in the trees above them. Later, Raj admitted that three of his friends had bet him he couldn't kiss her. He hadn't meant for word of the bet to spread. He hadn't meant for everyone to be so mean.

It seemed so stupid, now that she was an adult. But the shame of that one event had scarred her soul. She had begged her mother to let her leave Bombay. But even in Baltimore, whenever she looked at a man, her first emotion was shame. Wanting what she couldn't have. Wanting what she shouldn't have. It was ridiculous. One kiss. One boy. How could that ruin her whole life?

Randi—the Hindi word for "whore" the neighborhood boys had chanted at her every time she went out. The rumor spread through their neighborhood like wildfire, growing bigger, fiercer with every soul it consumed.

I thought he loved me. But there was something else. Something more complicated and harder to get at. Somehow, she had felt ready, after Raj, to face her sisters for the first time in her life. Her life until then had been a storybook fairy tale. Even her parents' divorce, which she had been too young to understand, had delivered her to a kinder, more loving stepfather than the real father she had left behind. She had become a veritable princess in India. She had it all. *A tutor,* for heaven's sake.

Meanwhile, her sisters struggled back home. The postcards they occasionally sent—then stopped—had been heartbreaking in their desperation. Her mother refused to leave her One True Love in India, and their father wouldn't permit them to be sent abroad. Although by Indian standards (two dollars a day hired Raj) they were wealthy, there wasn't enough to make a difference back in Baltimore.

After Raj, Jasmine's overdramatic, sixteen-year-old mind constructed a self-image in which she now had suffered like her sisters. They would see she was one of them, tough and worldly, and would forgive her for being with their mother, for living a carefree life.

Only it didn't work out that way.

She had been so young and stupid.

"I'm sorry. It's none of my business." Josh touched her arm, and she startled back into the present.

She felt his eyes on her, but she couldn't look up. She concentrated on stopping her feet from jiggling. Calm. It's over. Don't look back. Just move on.

They sat in silence.

"I can't imagine being shy," Josh said finally. "My whole life, I'm studied, observed, taken apart molecule by molecule."

She picked at her untouched grilled cheese, pale and limp and cold. "It must be awful to be hounded that way." She was grateful to him for steering the conversation away from her. She took calming breaths.

"It is and it isn't. It's part of the job."

"So what's not part of the job?" she asked. She felt oddly at ease with him after their almost-conversation. Calmer. As if it was okay to probe where she had refused him entry. "Is Cleo part of the job?"

He shrugged. "Yeah. She is."

Jasmine admired his honesty. She took a long sip of her beer. "That's the saddest thing I've ever heard."

"Well, when you're a star, you give things up."

"What else have you given up?"

"My parents." He looked surprised at what he had said.

Then he shrugged again. "They think my acting is dumb. They're kind of serious. You'd like them."

"Do they like Cleo?"

"They've never met her."

Jasmine's eyes went wide. "You've been together years."

He let bits of the beer label he was shredding fall through his fingers. "My parents and I have differences. They hate L.A. They hate the films I make."

"So? You're still their son."

He shrugged. "Well, they're sort of right. The stuff I do is pretty dumb." He let the waiter take his empty beer. "What are your parents like?"

"My mom's still in India. My dad's in Albuquerque. I don't see either of them." How could he think it was okay for his parents to judge his work that way?

"But you see your sister?"

"Sisters. They're both in Baltimore."

"You're lucky."

"Well, we're trying to work through the past." She looked across the table at the most famous man in the world. He looked so stark and lonely just then. "You need lessons in being normal," she blurted, instantly mortified at what she had said.

"Yeah," he agreed, playing with the strap of his evening gown. "Maybe it's your turn to teach me something."

Jasmine considered. "I have an idea. If you're up for it."

He leaned forward. "C'mon, Burns. You've known me almost a week now. You should know that I'm always up for anything."

*   *   *

Jasmine couldn't believe she and Josh Toby were sitting on her ratty couch, eating Ben & Jerry's New York Super Fudge Chunk out of the same pint, watching a DVD of *Singing in the Rain*. They had changed out of their costumes. Jasmine wore sweats. Josh had on his jeans and T-shirt.

Lesson one in being normal.

He was letting Lassie lick the discarded carton lid with her fingernail-sized tongue.

Jasmine hoped he wasn't bored. She felt anything but bored. She loved this movie. Could watch it forever.

"I think Buster wants to dance," Josh said. In the movie, the rain was just starting to fall.

"Shh. Watch. Eat."

Gene Kelly started his famous puddle dance. Josh jumped up and started to sing along. His voice was perfect, his moves choreographed. "Well, c'mon. Get with it. Don't just sit there."

"You're a natural." The way he had become Gene Kelly in an instant was unreal. The way he swung his hips was unfair.

"Nah. Just did the damn play two hundred and twenty-three times in my days of local youth theater." He tossed her a yardstick to use as an umbrella. "Sing!"

Jasmine reluctantly got up. He showed her a little two-step. The music was infectious. The dogs were poised in excitement, their tongues lolling. Josh hopped onto the couch. He pulled her up with him and took her around the waist.

He demonstrated another complicated step. With his hands firmly on her waist, she tried it.

"Hey, you're not bad, Ms. Burns."

"Call me Debbie Reynolds."

The song picked up. He jumped down from the couch, pulling her after him. He twirled her around and around the apartment.

"Watch the sewing machine," she warned over the music.

"I'll buy you a new one. I'll buy you ten!" He leapt onto her bed, and to her surprise, she followed, as did Buster. Lassie yapped from the floor. The three of them stepped off the edge as if into an enormous puddle. Lassie skittered under the bed to meet them on the other side. Jasmine couldn't help but grin. She picked up Lassie and twirled her around the room while Josh and Buster waltzed.

When it was over, they all four fell back onto the couch, exhausted, smiling or panting, depending on the species.

When the movie finished, Josh and the dogs got up to leave. Josh gave Jasmine a quick kiss on the cheek at the door. "You know," he said, "I think I could get used to this normal life."

Me too, Jasmine thought. But she only smiled.

And then he and the dogs were gone.

The next day, Jasmine paced up and down the aisles of the empty theater, waiting for Arturo. The first production meeting was happening backstage in an hour, and she had no idea what Arturo needed her to do. Most likely, his sketches would have to be brought to the copy shop down the street to make enlargements that would then have to be mounted on foam core. She looked at her watch anxiously. She didn't want to screw up her first in-person assignment. Up until now, everything she'd done for Arturo, research and busywork mostly, she'd faxed to his assistant.

Yesterday, his assistant faxed back: *Meet Arturo in the theater, in front of the orchestra pit. He'll bring the sketches for you to prepare.*

She sank her hand into the lush red velvet of the first-row seats, trying to draw some comfort from the fuzzy fabric. It was real silk velvet, not the usual rayon. A million silkworms had dedicated their lives to ensure theatergoers a soft spot to sit.

Oh, to be a silkworm. A production meeting with the whole crew was a very big deal. It was when all the tech people—the nonactors—got together for the first time to lay the foundation for the show. From the props master to the stage managers to the sound designers—everyone was going to be there.

Except, it seemed, Arturo.

She jumped up and paced up the aisle. A, B, C, D . . . XX, YY, ZZ . . . she had reached the top of the house and turned to go back down toward the stage. The lonely echo of her footsteps in the vast space was not reassuring. *Maybe I got it wrong about where to meet Arturo and I'm already fired.* She tried to quiet her racing thoughts: catastrophic thinking. She knew from her self-help books that thinking like this was what made her freak out in situations that involved men like Arturo. She couldn't just take a situation at face value, but instead spun it into an extreme disaster.

She took a deep breath and pulled her camel trench coat more tightly around her. She had dressed so carefully for this day, her first real day of work. It was the perfect theater outfit—a black camisole with delicate lace around the neck and a pair of loose black jeans. But, as usual, just before she left her apartment, she chickened out and threw a light black cardigan over the camisole, then her knee-length trench coat over that. No way she was taking a thread of it off—she was chilled to the bone with dread. But still, she looked good. Casual and chic, yet understated—the perfect assistant.

Arturo is just late. There is no reason to panic.

He's dead and I won't ever have to face him!

She shook off her evil thoughts.

She paced back toward the stage, then climbed up the steps onto it and sat down, letting her feet swing over the edge. She could hear members of the production team scurrying unseen, shadows in the wings. Behind her, toward the back of the stage, a man in a brown angora sweater and his two assistants were hovering nervously over their model of the set, talking in hushed voices. Three men, each more stylish than the next, came noisily into the auditorium, deep in a discussion about wattage. They sank into the front-row seats and began scribbling diagrams on a yellow pad of paper, unaware of Jasmine's presence.

Could there be more adorable, well-dressed men in this place?

Her cell phone buzzed, startling her. "Hello?"

"Jasmine, it's Arturo."

Jasmine could barely hear him. "Where are you?" She jumped up and scurried down the stage steps. She paced in front of the orchestra pit.

"About to get on a plane to Rome."

Jasmine almost dropped the phone. "But—!" The three men looked up, annoyed.

"Listen carefully," Arturo said. "I can't explain. It's too crazy. But you have to cover for me."

"The production meeting starts in fifty-seven minutes." She was equal parts thrilled that she wouldn't have to face him and terrified that she was on her own.

Arturo laughed deeply. "I know. I'm sorry. But there was nothing I could do. The gypsy was right! I am the happiest man alive!"

Gypsy? This time, Jasmine *did* drop the phone. It skidded across the waxed floor and under the seats where the lighting techs sat. Jasmine raced after it, fell to her knees, and scuttled under their seats. "Sorry. Um. Got it." She picked up the phone and glued it to her ear. "Did you say 'gypsy'?"

"A fortune-teller. Remarkable woman. She told me the name—"

"—of your One True Love." Jasmine felt as if someone had punched her in the gut. As if Amy had punched her in the gut. Which she had, in a metaphorical way. Jasmine let herself fall into a seat. Row A. *A* for "Arturo"? For "alone"? No, for "Amy." Of course she was behind this.

"Yes! How did you know? Madame Russo, my spiritual advisor, told me about a gypsy. A seer who had a message for me. What could I do? I went to Baltimore, and this beautiful woman told me that my One True Love was Antonia Bonaventura. From my grade school outside Rome! The minute she said it, I knew it was true. Antonia! My childhood fantasy! My plane boards in two minutes."

Jasmine stared at the metal "A" plate bolted to the armrest of her seat. A *for "Antonia."* A *for "Armed Assault" when she found Amy.*

But Amy lost her powers. How could she have known

the name of his One True Love? The only reason Amy knew my One True Love was that she had heard it two years ago, when her powers were still spotty. But this? Was Amy lying about losing her powers? Or had she lied to poor Arturo?

Arturo was still talking. "Handle the meeting, then? Can you? Good girl. I knew you could. You're gorgeous! Brilliant! A genius! I'll be in touch!"

"Don't trust Amy!" she shouted into the phone. The light techs swung their heads to stare. It was too late. The phone was dead. *Don't trust Amy.* She was the one who shouldn't have trusted Amy. Did Amy still have her powers? But why would she lie?

Amy was infamous for her lies.

Jasmine sat with the dead cell to her ear. Three twentysomething women in jeans (hopefully props assistants), carrying parts of a car engine, scurried down the aisle, then disappeared backstage. Jasmine couldn't scurry. She couldn't move. *Handle it.* How? She didn't have any sketches with her. She didn't have the slightest idea what costumes Arturo intended. Maybe she could pretend Arturo wanted the play done in the nude. Come to think of it, Josh in the nude—

"You look like shit, honey."

Jasmine looked up to see her old classmate, Samantha Olivia. She hadn't seen her since the day of the interview (noninterview), on the street, outside the hotel two weeks ago. Had that really only been two weeks ago? Jasmine counted the days—fifteen. A lifetime.

"Oh, don't look so shocked to see me," Samantha cooed. "I got hired on as second assistant to the lighting designer." She pantomimed a yawn and rolled her eyes at the three men who were still scribbling. Samantha bent over and hugged and not-quite-kissed Jasmine. "What an adorable bunch these lighting guys are. Watts and voltage and yada yada yada and they don't even realize what total cuties they are. If they could just stop talking about this geek-out lighting business. Anyway, I heard that you got the Arturo job. Yowzer. Did you blow him?"

The lighting techs looked up this time. If anyone knew how to knock them out of their "geek-out" lighting obsession, it was Samantha in those skintight jeans and three-inch heels. They didn't look away.

Jasmine blinked, but she was still too frozen by Arturo's abrupt heave-ho to respond. Amy had gotten to Arturo, obviously, but how did she know his True Love's name? Gypsies lie to nongypsies all the time. It was part of their culture, a way to keep their mystery and make a buck.

But why did she do it?

Did I blow him? "Excuse me," she said to Samantha. She turned her back and punched in Amy's number on her cell. Samantha happily plunked into the seat next to Jasmine and watched her like a hungry puma.

"Amy here." Amy's voice was distant and jumbled. She sounded like she was at a huge party. Which she probably was, despite the fact it was eleven-twenty-six in the morning.

"Amy! What did you do to . . . ?" Jasmine looked over her shoulder at Samantha's not-so-innocent blinking eyes. She lowered her voice. "My friend Ken."

Amy's laughter rang through the tiny phone. "Oh, *Ken*? Yes, well, I sent him on a little mission."

"But how did you know—?"

"I lied."

"Lied!"

"He's *gadje*," Amy said, using the term gypsies used for anyone nongypsy. It wasn't a very nice thing to call a person. "What's the problem?"

"But how did you come up with a . . . choice?" Jasmine smiled weakly at Samantha, who grinned back. The woman had no intention of even pretending that she wasn't listening to every word. Might as well buy popcorn.

"I did a little research. Remember Aunt Emilia in Rome? She ran that little palm-reading shop outside the Colosseum, and she looked into things for me. Knew a traveling band of gypsies that knew Artie's village."

Jasmine did not remember an Aunt Emilia in Rome, but this was neither the time nor the place. "But why, Amy? I got the job, remember?"

"You shy people are so self-obsessed. Maybe it wasn't about you. I knew he was a sucker after that whole portfolio nonsense, and I needed the cash. I knew he was good for it," Amy said simply.

"I gotta go." Jasmine clicked the phone shut. She jumped out of the seat and began to pace again. Samantha followed her. Forty-seven minutes to the production meeting. It was impossible. The idea of presenting in the first place to all these assembled men (and Samantha) was impossible—she'd vomit, she'd faint, she'd—

Oh. My. God.

"Hello, my pretties! Hola! Hola!" A man strode down the aisle, a black cape blowing behind him. He had black hair slicked to his head, a jaunty, close-trimmed mustache, and black toreador pants so tight that Samantha's eyes almost came unglued. He looked like Antonio Banderas if Antonio Banderas were a pimp. No, a gigolo. A gigolo on LSD.

The man approached Jasmine and Samantha. Without hesitation, he grabbed Samantha by both shoulders and kissed her heartily. He held her at arm's length while she regained her badly shaken equilibrium, then turned to Jasmine. "Señorita." He fell to one knee, took her hand, and kissed it deeply.

Chapter 15

Jasmine knew those lips. She knew those pants. "Hola, señor," she said to Josh.

Samantha was staring in shock at Josh. Jasmine grabbed his arm and led him a few steps away. She hissed, "What are you doing here? The costume isn't done. You look . . . undone." Frankly, he looked exotically beautiful. Only Josh Toby could pull off a hairline mustache. Especially a fake one.

"I'm trying out my persona," he whispered back.

"A cape wasn't part of the plan."

"I know, but I couldn't resist." He grinned and wagged his eyebrows at her.

"It's . . ." She fingered the elaborately adorned cape. It was pure black Georgette silk with exquisite red velvet lining. Black and gold braiding rimmed the edges.

He looked both ways, then lowered his voice. "I was so nervous for you, I had to come and make sure you were okay."

"If anyone recognizes you, your anonymous acting plan is shot." She stopped just short of adding, "dummy." She pulled him a few steps more away from Samantha, who seemed to have frozen in a seat in the front row. "I can't believe you walked through Manhattan like . . . like . . . a rabid porn star."

"Walk? You're such a commoner." Josh let Jasmine's hand go. He reruffled the ruffles on his white shirt. "I took a cab."

The lighting techs got up and disappeared backstage to find a quieter spot.

Jasmine huffed in mute frustration.

"Do I really look like a porn star?" Josh asked, amused.

"Button up that shirt." Jasmine looked around to see who was taking this in. Luckily Samantha was still too dazed to seem to notice. Her fingers touched her lips where Josh had kissed her.

Josh fastened the button at his navel. "Tell me what's going on. I'm not leaving until you spill. Something's wrong. I can see it in your eyes."

"More buttons. Your stomach is too famous." She knew that sounded absurd, but if she had to look at that flat, tanned stomach much longer, she was going to have to touch it, and then she'd fall apart and tell him everything.

He did one more button. "Where's Artie? I'll kill him if he did anything mean to you. C'mere." Josh hustled Jasmine up the front stage steps and into the wings. "Now tell me what's wrong."

Despite herself, she spilled. "Arturo bailed. He wants me to handle the production meeting."

Josh whipped his cape in a triumphant arc and stamped his black boot, scaring Jasmine half to death. "That's magnifico! You will be a star!" he boomed. A piece of plaster fell off the ancient wall behind him and smashed to the floor in a cloud of dust. "A star," he said more quietly, coughing away the dust. They moved another step into the shadows.

"Are you nuts?" Jasmine shook her elbow free of his hand. The head carpenter was staring at them intently from his perch on a ladder set up midstage. Josh winked at him, and he looked away. "I don't have any costumes to present."

"You do. I saw them. The ones in your notebook."

Jasmine gasped. "Oh, no. Those were not for showing. Those were my personal sketches."

"You know this play inside and out. You did the costume plot, right?"

"Of course. But for Arturo." The costume plot was an outline of all the costumes a play needed, scene by scene, moment by moment. "Look, even if I wanted to present my own work—which I don't—I don't have the sketches here."

Josh looked at her askance. "This sounds like a job for too-tight-pants-man!" He held out his arms as if he were going to fly off into the sunset.

"Are you drunk? Go home. Now. Before someone recognizes you." She pushed him toward the stage.

He thought a moment, then said, "No problem. I'm gone. But meet me later? I gotta hear how the meeting goes. Plus, you've got to finish my disguise."

"If I say yes, will you leave?" It didn't escape her that he had agreed to leave a bit too quickly, but she was losing precious time and couldn't worry about what he was up to.

"Sí, señorita."

"My place. Eight." *I'll be the one reduced to a puddle*

of shame and humiliation after barfing on the stage manager at the meeting.

Josh turned dramatically on his heel and strode onto the stage; then he diminished slightly, shrinking before her eyes. He staggered a step, then slowly, carefully, made his way down the steps to the orchestra seats like an old lady.

Strange. But no time to think about it. Jasmine felt her whole body go limp with relief. That was one problem out of the way. She peeked out from behind the curtain to make sure he was really gone.

Josh had stopped and was staring back at her. To her annoyance, he waved her to the side of the stage.

"What?" she asked.

"We just had a conversation," he whispered.

"So?"

"So? You didn't blush once. Or break out in a sweat."

Jasmine blushed and broke out in a sweat so furious, she felt as if she had just run a marathon. But Josh was right. She had had an entire conversation with him. And she wasn't even in a disguise.

"And you agreed to meet me later!" Josh smiled.

"Out," Jasmine commanded.

Samantha rose from her seat, muttering to herself.

"Here, take this. A good-luck charm." He handed her the jewelry box. The earrings.

"Oh, for heaven's sake!"

"Wear them. Look, don't think of them as an expensive present. Think of them as a great way to buy yourself time. Everyone will spend a few startled moments looking away from your face and staring at your incredible earrings. You can take those few moments to pull yourself together, then knock 'em dead."

Jasmine opened the box. Josh was right. No one would be able not to stare at these babies.

"It'll work," Josh assured her. "Take the minute to remember how good you are at all this costume stuff."

Jasmine stuffed the box into the pocket of her coat. Was he right? Could earrings help her get through a presentation to a pack of beautiful men? "Okay. I'll take them. For luck."

"Remember, if you can talk to me"—he lowered his voice and leaned in close so Samantha couldn't hear— "me, the sexiest man alive, what's so hard about a production meeting with a bunch of techies? You can do it, Jas." And then, with a flap of his cape, Super Josh dashed down the steps and out of sight.

Jasmine put on the earrings. She'd think about how thoughtful Josh was later.

Now she had to figure out how to handle the meeting. First, she had to find the stage manager and explain the situation. That was it. She'd just go and do that. No meeting with the whole crew. Just a one-on-one.

Except that she couldn't. She stood in the shadows, paralyzed by the impossibility.

It would be like her interview all over again—a disaster.

But she had to do something. And do it fast.

I'll just go and talk to him. Surely he's a reasonable guy. I'll just explain that Arturo is sick. It's not a big deal. Hey, I just had an entire conversation with a gorgeous, sexy, kiss-me-again-and-this-time-I'm-never-letting-go man. . . .

Okay. Find out who the stage manager is. She had read his name in Arturo's notes: Chick London. Whatever kind of name that was.

She addressed a woman carrying a tray of coffee from Starbucks. "Do you know where I can find Chick?"

"She's right there." The woman pointed with her chin and hurried past.

She! It was the break Jasmine needed. A woman emerged from the opposite wing, barking at her two assistants who followed her with yellow legal pads at the ready. Chick was stocky and short and remarkably loud. As she strode across the stage, she gestured wildly and growled. Her voice carried to the back of the theater as if she was a classically trained actor. *But she was female!* "What the hell are we going to do about a set model that has no forestage! You were supposed to talk to that little twerp—" She noticed the scenic designers with their model behind her. "Oh, hi, Chris. Good job. Good job."

The "twerp" turned gray.

Jasmine took a deep breath and strode across the stage. "Excuse me."

Chick and her entourage stopped. They were center stage. "Who are you?" The woman stared at her earrings.

"Jasmine Burns." Jasmine focused on the woman so the men behind her couldn't spook her. Chick's astonishingly direct gray eyes scanned Jasmine with approval. "I'm Arturo Mastriani's assistant. Arturo can't make it to the production meeting—"

"So? You handle it."

Jasmine hesitated. "But the plan—"

Chick cut her off. "Make a new plan. You look capable. Get it done. This is the chance of a lifetime, hon. Work it. You look like a woman who knows how to work it." She looked at her watch. "You've got forty-four minutes."

Before Jasmine could protest, Chick strode off, her assistants in tow.

From the silent house, applause echoed. She turned to see Josh, still in the theater, giving her a standing ovation.

"Bravo! That's my girl! Knock 'em dead!" he cried as he made his way out the door. "The show must go on! Focus on the stage manager. She loves you. I love you!"

Jasmine stood center stage in horror. *I love you?* No, that was the sort of thing Hollywood people said to each other all the time. *Love ya, babe!* It meant nothing.

Then, to Jasmine's horror, Samantha rose from the seat she had been hiding in—she was hiding, wasn't she? Why else would Samantha be still and quiet? Samantha slipped out the door behind Josh.

Jasmine made a move toward the door, then stopped.

She didn't have time for Josh now. She had the meeting to worry about.

Chapter 16

The entire production crew—sixty-four anxious, gorgeous people, about two-thirds of them men—converged on a windowless room not much bigger than Jasmine's apartment. These old Manhattan theaters were famous for having inadequate space for meetings, but this was ridiculous. Sure, what happened behind the scenes wasn't glamorous, but it wasn't supposed to be life-threatening.

Jasmine stood at the doorway to the room, clutching her trench coat and letting the people stream by her. One beautiful man, another, another . . .

Jasmine let herself fall back against the hallway wall as she tried to imagine being so blasé. *Nice day outside. Perfect weather for the end of my career . . .*

Calm down. Jasmine thought back to her *Good-bye Shy!* workbook. The catastrophic thinking again. It was wrong to imagine the worst.

She glanced into the rapidly filling room. Its walls were closing in. Jasmine blinked away her hallucination: *the walls are NOT closing in.*

Were they? She blinked hard.

A single fan perched on a dusty file cabinet in the back

corner droned to no effect. A narrow, two-foot space had been left clear in the front for presentations.

Get into that room.

She peered in again.

Samantha had the lighting designers and a few other equally stylish men howling over something obviously hilarious. The words "world's longest blow job" were the only four Jasmine could make out. Everyone involved in the show except the actors were there, and they all seemed like the best of friends. The air was buzzing with anticipation.

Jasmine ducked back into the hallway, her back pressed against the wall, and tried to breathe. She had to go in. She was a grown-up with responsibilities.

She was a grown-up with hives.

Just go in.

Jasmine took a step into the room, and the heat hit her like a warning. *Flee. Need air.* A small, faded sign by the door said, "Maximum capacity, 49."

She stepped back out. *I'm only complying with the building code. . . .*

A woman wearing a tiny tank top and equally small miniskirt paused on her way into the room to stare at her. "You okay?"

"Sure," Jasmine managed to squeak.

The woman looked slyly side to side, then pulled two purple pills out of a child-sized pocket in her child-sized skirt. "These'll help."

"Only if they're cyanide," Jasmine said.

The woman folded the pills into Jasmine's hand.

Jasmine stared down at her sweaty hand, now stained purple. She shoved the things into her bag. She had waited so long, now there was one empty folding chair left next to a grisly man with a white beard resting on his enormous gut. He ate from a sandwich weeping lettuce and unidentifiable greenish juices.

Jasmine felt ill.

She skittered into the room, then leaned against the back wall for support. Okay, she was in. That was good. She didn't need to sit. Someone had to hold the walls up. She felt the sweat dripping down her forehead and wiped it off, realizing too late that she probably had a stripe of purple on her forehead now. *Someone shoot me. Please.*

The director, Allen McMann, and his assistant, Eric Pugalizzi, strode into the room, which instantly fell silent. Eric puffed air out his broad nose like a phlegmatic dog. Now Jasmine knew who the crew had been calling "the Pugster" all morning.

Next to the Pugster, Mr. McMann looked like a sleek, polished greyhound. No one called Allen McMann anything but Mr. McMann. Thin and long with deep-chocolate skin, he was all bone and gleaming flesh. His outfit was exquisite, a deep brown suit with a brown, tight, thin cashmere sweater underneath. The guy must be burning up, but he sure didn't look it.

"Let's move it! We've got one hour!" the Pugster barked. "Scenic design. On it! Go!"

The scenic designer and his three assistants leapt out of their seats, carrying the set model. They arranged it carefully on a small table they had dragged out of the corner.

The model was hidden with a white sheet, although it wasn't a secret. Everyone in the room had already seen it, except for Jasmine, who had come so late to the show. Countless discussions had taken place about it. It had been priced out by the technical director, worried over by the director, discussed endlessly by the lighting designers. And yet, everyone acted as if this was the first time they had seen it. The reason was simple: This was where factions formed. Undercurrents of disagreement rose up at production meetings like tsunamis that could flood the whole show without warning. Usually, the director took a stand and the rest of the tech crew, anxious to earn brownie points, piled on. It could get ugly.

The scenic designer took a deep breath and nodded to the crowd, then to Mr. McMann; then with great aplomb, he threw back the sheet.

The model was of two façades of suburban ranch houses. Each was pushed into one back corner of the stage. A long, black shared driveway ran between them.

How could you have a balcony in a ranch house? Everyone knew that *Romeo and Juliet* needed a balcony. Jasmine tried to imagine Josh sneaking into his neighbor's trashy kegger lawn party and whispering, *"What lady's that which doth enrich the hand of yonder knight?"*

Mr. McMann crossed his legs at the knee, and Jasmine felt her eyes pop. He was wearing pink, yellow, green, and blue checked socks. The socks were so absurd, peeking out from under his impeccable suit, that she thought she was hallucinating. No, those were his socks. This elegant, sophisticated man had a weakness for silly socks. *Concentrate on the socks. Speak to the socks.*

All her fear washed away. She felt normal.

Mr. McMann peppered the scenic designer with questions. How did he plan on doing the sword fights on such a small forestage? Did he even consult with the choreographer? The set was low; what did he intend to do about the endless sky? Was this Nebraska, damn it? The actors would be too cramped.

The scenic designer answered valiantly, but in the end, he and his crew slunk back to their seats promising changes. Mr. McMann crossed his arms and nodded at the Pugster, who shouted, "Next! Costumes! Arturo!"

Jasmine's fear leapt back inside her like a frightened child who had momentarily strayed from its mother. It grasped on to her, strangling her. The crowd's eyes swept the room, looking for Arturo. Jasmine stood stock still.

Her nose began twitching like a rabbit's. She tried to stop it, but it wouldn't stop. *Oh, good, a new symptom of my anxiety. What great timing.* She put her hand over the offending body part. *Stop!* But she felt her nostrils rise and fall. She had to get out of there before people started offering her carrots. She edged toward the door.

Samantha's voice rang out over the murmurs. "Jasmine, honey, showtime!" Samantha pointed a long, red-nailed finger right at Jasmine, and every eye followed. "C'mon, honey, we won't eat you."

Please, eat me and have it done with.

Samantha jumped out of her seat. "I'll take over, if you like, Jas. I know exactly what Arturo wants."

That bitch is taking my spot. Jasmine's eyes met Chick's. The woman nodded at her, and something inside of Jasmine clicked.

Samantha crossed her arms over her chest. She wore a triumphant smile.

Jasmine cleared her throat. "No. I've got it." Her body was a ball of exploding fire, terror mingling with anger. But she was going to do it. Even if it was the most embarrassing five minutes of her life, she was going to get up there and impress someone, somehow.

Jasmine's legs propelled her toward the front of the room. Every eye followed her as she bumped and skitted through the crowd. The woman who had given her the purple pills winked.

Socks. Pink and yellow socks. Not all men here. Concentrate on the women. She cleared her throat. "Hi. I'm Jasmine Burns," she managed to get out.

"We can't hear you!" the man with the sandwich shouted from the back of the room in a teasing singsong.

"Right." She tried to raise her voice, but it cracked. She watched in dismay as Mr. McMann crossed his arms and scowled. The Pugster did the same. Then they both glanced longingly at Samantha. *Oh, hell.* "Arturo. He. Well. He's—"

A commotion in the back made everyone turn. A shrill, cracking voice called, "I have Arturo's sketches. Excuse me!" Josh, dressed in too-short black pants—he was wearing a pair of pants that Jasmine had just hemmed for her shortest client!—and a stained white shirt with a pocket protector, made his way into the room. His white socks glowed against his black shoes. He smashed into a chair and was forced to hop the last few feet to her, holding his shin in pain in one hand and Jasmine's sketchbook aloft with his other.

He looked like a very nervous, blond Buddy Holly.

Jasmine fell against the front wall in relief as every eye turned from her to Josh, her geeky knight in shining armor. Or rather, in untied, black, too-big, shiny dress shoes anyway. His nose held up a pair of fake prop black glasses, taped with masking tape in the center. He had something green stuck between his two front teeth. She could tell because his lips were scrunched, and the two teeth stuck out like a beaver's. A tiny wad of toilet paper stuck to his cheek, held on by what looked like a tiny splotch of blood from a shaving accident but was more likely ketchup. There was definitely mustard on his tucked-in shirt.

He had never looked better.

Jasmine wanted to hug him for coming to her rescue. As the audience's focus shifted, her dread floated away. She practiced standing taller. She cleared her throat. *She just needed a minute to get herself together.*

As Josh almost smashed the set to bits with his enormous shoes, Jasmine unbuttoned her trench coat. She looked at each member of the front row and found something vulnerable about them. The cutie with the lighting techs was starting a bald spot. The tech director who had given her the pills, well, she had given her the pills. Samantha . . . Jasmine shuddered and looked away. She focused on Josh.

Josh finally bungled to the front of the room and tried to present her with her sketchbook. He fumbled it. Picked it up. Dropped it again. The crowd snickered, but in an embarrassed, kind way. *Poor guy.*

They were softening.

"Knock 'em dead, Jas," Josh whispered as he finally got the book in her hands.

The relief drained out of her as she stared at her sketchbook. Wait. Jasmine couldn't knock them dead. Her sketches had nothing to do with present-day suburbia. She had sketches for a play set in fifteenth-century Verona. No way could she open this book and pretend it was Arturo's. Arturo knew the setting.

But every eye was on her. Including Josh's twitching ones behind his absurd glasses. She had to hand it to him—the eye twitch was a great touch. He *was* a great actor. Not a soul recognized the most famous man in the world. She opened the book slowly. "Well . . . Um . . ." She cleared her throat.

Josh glanced down at the model of the set that he had almost demolished with his dorky entrance. His eyes widened, and he stumbled back into the space that Jasmine so poorly occupied. "What's wrong, Ms. Burns?" His eyes met hers, and somehow he conveyed to her that this, right now, was a play. An act. She had to figure out her part—quickly.

"Did I mess up again?" Josh asked.

"Yes," Jasmine said, trying to summon her inner actress. She did have an inner actress, right? Everyone must. Somewhere. "You brought only one notebook," she said, too quietly for anyone not in the first row to hear.

Josh's hand flew to his heart as if he were in pain. *"I forgot the second notebook!"* he said loud enough to please even the sandwich man. "Oh. Oh. Goodness. Golly. Gosh. Cover for me? Please? Artie's going to fire me for messing up again." He turned to the crowd, who was mesmerized by the poor, pathetic bumbler before them. They were ready to forgive this sad guy anything. And their sympathy extended to Jasmine. "I'm going to get the other book."

Josh made his way back through the crowd, once more banging into everyone and everything in his path, giving Jasmine time to think. Finally, he left the room with a heavy sigh, and half the crowd sighed, too, so sorry for him. So sorry for Jasmine having to deal with him.

Jasmine gathered her courage. All eyes turned back to her, but this time, they were dreamy and mellow. These people knew her story. Okay, the story was a lie. But they felt bad for her. This audience was hers. Josh had handed it to her.

She looked out at her sixty-four new best friends. Well, maybe sixty-three—she really couldn't count Samantha, who was whispering into her cell phone. "I'm so sorry about Jo—Jeremy!" Jasmine said. The words were flowing, and she didn't dare stop them. She was just an actress playing the part of assistant costume designer. "Arturo envisions . . ."

She paused and everyone leaned forward in expectation. Mr. McMann's mouth hung slightly opened. *Socks, pink socks . . .*

Jasmine took a deep breath. She gathered every ounce of courage, which was draining out of her fast. How would you do present-day suburbia with theatricality? Juliet had to be young and innocent and pure. Romeo had to be the same, yet he lived in a ranch house. . . . Jasmine was lost. Her mind scanned all three hundred and twelve productions of *Romeo and Juliet* she had seen or studied. "Arturo means to . . ."

She looked at all the expectant faces.

". . . keep them in period costume."

Mr. McMann fell back in his seat, perplexed. Everyone followed his lead.

Oh, God, she had lost them. She needed Josh to stumble back in. But he was gone. She flipped through her sketchbook, searching for the image she needed to jumpstart her brain. And then it came to her. She knew exactly how to do Romeo. "Arturo envisions starting the play in modern costume. But as the action advances, he sees the modern dropping away. With the decay of the suburban landscape, the costumes begin to morph—"

Mr. McMann sat up and finished her sentence: "—into the past. Even the landscape fades away."

People shuffled in their seats. A few coughed. The scenic designer and his assistants gasped.

"It doesn't become the past," she corrected, dizzy with her crystal-clear vision of what the play should be. "It becomes anytime—"

"It becomes no time! Nowhere!" Mr. McMann jumped up.

"And therefore everywhere," Jasmine said.

"Every time." Mr. McMann strode to Jasmine. He stopped before her, eyes blazing, socks hidden. "Arturo, is, as usual, brilliant, um, what was your name?"

"Jasmine."

"Jasmine. Very good. Go on."

Jasmine felt as if anything were possible. *He asked my name. He liked my idea. He's finishing my sentences.* But she could sense that the crowd needed help to keep up. "The falling away of the modern, then the historical, is the journey to the universal," she explained.

Then, to Jasmine's horror, Mr. McMann snatched her sketchbook and whipped it open. Jasmine tried to get it back, but he turned his back and paged through it.

Mr. McMann is looking at my sketches.

He was scowling slightly.

Oh, God. He hates them.

Mr. McMann sucked in his breath.

Was that a "this is beyond awful" sucking in of breath? Of course it was. The jig was up.

"Yes, yes. Indeed. Indeed," Mr. McMann said. "Excellent sketches. Excellent. These are perfect for the end of the play." He held up the book to the audience. "Look at these. Finally, someone who knows what they're doing."

Jasmine felt a huge weight lift off her. She was standing in front of a crowd of mostly men, practically touching them, and she had survived. No, more than survived. Triumphed. She shook off her trench coat.

Mr. McMann handed her the sketchbook. "Brilliant. Excellent."

The crowd was buzzing.

"Bring me the present-day sketches for the opening act when that poor young man gets them from Arturo," Mr. McMann said. His voice held a touch of knowing irony. Did he know there were no sketches? No Arturo? If so, he certainly didn't care.

Jasmine felt the first real smile of the afternoon spread over her face. They had completely forgotten how pathetic she had been at the beginning of her presentation. *Mr. McMann knows my name. I did it.*

We did it. Josh and me.

The crowd continued to chatter.

Mr. McMann leaned toward Jasmine. He whispered, "Nice sketches, *Arturo*." He winked.

Jasmine's heart dropped into her stomach. "I. Arturo. He—"

Mr. McMann stopped her with an upheld hand. "Don't want to know. Don't care. Just get it done."

Jasmine made her way to the one empty chair next to the fat, bearded, sandwich-eating man. He offered her his bag of greasy chips.

"Thanks." She took a chip. She tried to place him. "Are you with the prop crew?" she asked.

"I'm the janitor." He took an enormous bite of his sandwich.

Jasmine studied the chip. Why was she always so afraid of nothing? She smiled to herself and crunched down on it.

And she didn't even barf.

Cleo Chan sat on the white couch in her immaculate, all-white Santa Monica living room while her publicist, Mo, paced on the ocean-view balcony.

Cleo frowned at a copy of Tuesday's *New York Tattle Tale* that she held carefully in her manicured hands, trying to avoid getting the messy newsprint on her white Prada jumpsuit. The newspaper was open to a spread of pictures from the Greenwich Village Halloween parade. One picture was circled in red ink: a man dressed up like her kissing a woman dressed up like the character Mitch Tank.

She'd recognize the curve of Josh's biceps anywhere, the nape of his neck, the distinct angle of his jawbone. But who was the woman?

A sickening, sinking feeling gripped her. *A kiss like that, for me, from Josh, just once.* Cleo shook off a twinge of pain. *He's never going to love you back, dummy.* Why couldn't she get that into her head?

Cleo had been in love with Josh since the day she met him at a casting call for James Bond movie extras. It was an instant, complete, but entirely one-sided love. No matter how hard she tried—and in the beginning, she had tried (another twinge of pain)—he wasn't interested in anything beyond friendship. Cleo thought for sure he'd have changed his mind about her by now. Seen she was *made* for him.

I should have told him straight out that I loved him. Now that their charade of pretending to be lovers was two years in, it seemed too late. She hadn't thought it would take this long to get his attention and change his mind. She hadn't thought it would be so hard to have him pretend to love her. Sometimes—she cringed, her whole body almost doubling up in pain—she pretended that he really did love her. That the two of them really were an item. God, she was getting pathetic.

And if there was one thing she hated, it was being pathetic.

I'm the one person on earth who understands his life. Why doesn't he notice me?

Cleo checked that Mo was still on the balcony. She didn't want anyone to see her flinch. Even Mo. Especially Mo. *Let a flash of weakness show and it's over. Patience.* She repeated the mantra her psychotherapist had taught her silently in her head: *He doesn't like me as anything more than a friend because I'm not what his parents would want for him. It's not me; it's him. I'm too beautiful, too Hollywood, too fun. But Josh will see that I'm his destiny when he resolves his issues with his parents and accepts himself for who he truly is. I must be strong. I must be patient.*

She looked back to the picture.

I must be nuts.

That kiss looked so real, a kiss that sealed something deep and passionate.

She paged through the two-inch-thick clipping file Mo had given her. Article after article about a man who looked like Josh Toby giving away ridiculous amounts of money to strangers. One article even rated the front page of the *New York Times* Style section, Saturday edition, above the crease. THE J. TOBY TIPPER STRIKES AGAIN. BUT IS IT *HIM?* the headline read.

Of course it was him.

Josh was incapable of not helping. Stinkbugs, stuck feet-up in the middle of downtown L.A. sidewalks, could count on Josh to relocate them to nearby palm trees. Every homeless person between their lawyer's office and the Ivy could count on not only a handout, but also Josh knowing them by name. The last time Josh went to New York three years ago, he fell in love with that woman Margo, who was so good it just made you ill.

Cleo waited while the pain of it flowed through her and out.

More ammunition for her theory that Josh was looking for a woman his mother could love.

But Josh didn't bargain on Margo being so bent out of shape by his life. That he was more or less unavailable ten months out of the year made Margo crazy with jealousy and misplaced concern. *I would have understood*, Cleo had wanted to shout at him.

Eventually, Josh saw that the relationship was untenable. He had to either commit to a different life or cut the woman free.

Cutting Margo loose had nearly destroyed the man. He was apoplectic with guilt and regret, unable to work for three weeks. He even started talking about becoming a schoolteacher in some godforsaken third-world country with her.

It was Cleo's job to make sure Josh never threw away everything he'd worked for.

Maureen, or Mo as anyone who was anyone called her, came in from the balcony smelling of sea air and salt. She let her 100 percent naturally platinum-blond, waist-length hair cascade over her face as she leaned in to study the newspaper. Her white cotton peasant's dress flowed to her ankles. Hollywood gossip had it that Cleo hired her on as a publicist because she matched the all-white décor. It wasn't true, of course, but it made good press. Cleo liked the world to think of her as a shallow and unapproachable perfectionist. It cut down on the people who asked her for things.

And *everyone* asked her for things. Referrals, jobs, money, love, information, roles, autographs—it made a person crazy.

But if the constant pressure to give, give, give was bad for her, it was worse for Josh, who couldn't say no. Their faked love affair helped keep most of the jackals at bay. But Josh was hopeless. Always looking to help. And here he was, at it again.

"Josh wanted to kick around with his old friend Artie," Mo said. "To take a rest. So I set it up for him to go quietly to New York. He needed a break, Clee. He hasn't had more than two days off in eleven months."

"Artie? The flaky Italian costume guy? You should have told me." *He should have told me.*

"You were wrapping up with the *Project Paris* shoot. I didn't want to bug you. It sounded harmless."

"Harmless? Josh tongue to tonsils with who knows who in the *Tattler*? Josh giving away oodles of dough to strangers? He's out of control, Mo."

"I'm monitoring it. I got him to stop using the credit cards. Now, if he really can't help himself, he's leaving cash. Smaller sums. Nothing over five hundred dollars. No one can trace it." Mo paused. "He's a big boy, Clee."

Cleo sighed. "Josh on his own in New York is like an addicted gambler loose in Vegas. He'll get spooked by his awful parents and hook up with a woman he thinks his mother will approve of." Cleo put aside the paper.

Mo held Cleo's gaze too long. Did she pick up on the real reason for Cleo's outrage? Mo was too smart for Cleo's taste sometimes. "Who's the woman?" Cleo asked, trying to take the edge off her voice.

"She's a costume designer. I'll know more in a few hours. The woman who sent the picture is named Samantha Olivia. She's a theater wannabe. I talked to her this morning. She said that Josh is doing *Romeo and Juliet*. Off Broadway. With Artie and this woman."

Cleo jumped up at this alarming piece of news. "He can't do the stage." This wasn't about her anymore. This was about Josh's career. She felt a little better. Now she could go to Josh without feeling guilty and helpless. "Remember the last time he got on a stage in front of a live audience? It was at that roast for Pacino. He fainted dead away. We said he was sick then, but they won't buy it again. We've got to stop him before he ruins his rep."

"He wants to try," Mo said. "It's his choice."

Cleo shook her head. "We're his friends, Mo. We've got to get to New York. Now. Before our sweet Romeo ends up like the poor sod in the play—dead on a slab."

Mo sighed. Then smiled. "I already have the tickets, babe. Our plane leaves in two hours."

Chapter 17

Jasmine huddled over her sketching table, a single lamp illuminating her notebook. She had come home from the theater, jumped in a quick shower, and was now in her bathrobe, unwilling to waste time getting dressed. All she was going to do tonight was work. Maybe, if she got enough done, sleep an hour or two.

The costume plot was taped to the window in front of her. She worked through it as quickly as she could, sketching furiously.

Her triumph at the production meeting had carried her through the rest of the day's encounters. Everyone was forced to rethink their ideas in light of "Arturo's" brilliant conception of the costumes. The techies weren't dumb. They saw that Mr. McMann was behind "Arturo" 100 percent. To fight it was futile. One by one, they cornered Jasmine for more information. Now, they were destined to spend their evenings like Jasmine, hard at work to make the ideas a reality.

Jasmine went back to her sketches of Romeo's clan. She put them in ultrahip three-piece suits with shiny yellow shoes. She was filling in Mercutio's accessories—a pair of yellow-framed glasses—when a voice floated up from the street.

"But soft! What light through yonder window breaks? It is the West, and Jasmine is the sun!"

Josh.

Jasmine jumped up, spilling papers in her wake. Of course, Josh was coming to work on his disguise tonight. Her mouth went dry. She raced to the window and peeked out.

Her heart shifted into overdrive as she flattened herself against the wall. *Pretend he's not there*. No. She owed him for rescuing her at the meeting. Plus, work. Stilling her shaking hands, she pushed open the enormous window. A blast of cold night air reassured her she was awake. Josh stood below, his arms outstretched. She couldn't suppress a smile. "East."

Josh's arms fell to his side. "Damn." He reestablished his dramatic pose and called out, "It is the East, and Jasmine is the sun."

"Shuddup! I'm *trying* to watch *American Idol* here!" Mrs. Little's raspy Brooklyn accent rang out from two floors down.

"Arise, fair sun, and kill the envious moon—"

"I'm going to kill *you*!" Mrs. Little shouted.

"It's okay, Mrs. Little," Jasmine called down. Her insides were a-flutter. Was it okay? Could she handle another one-on-one with Josh?

He smiled up at her.

Oh, my. Oh, my. That man was pure, well, man. And she owed him. She owed him big.

She waved Josh inside. "I'll buzz you up."

He leapt onto the stone steps. "She speaks! O, speak again, bright angel."

Jasmine was about to reply, but before she could, Mrs. Little dumped a bucket of water—oh, please let it be water—onto Josh's head. "Mrs. Little!"

"I told you to shut your trap!" Mrs. Little shouted at Josh.

Guess Mrs. Little was off her meds again.

Josh held his pose despite the dousing. He fountained a stream of water out of his mouth, then said, "I'll be new baptized. Henceforth I never will be Romeo."

Mrs. Little applauded that sentiment with heavy, arthritic hands.

Josh winked at Jasmine and disappeared into the building.

Josh sloshed up the five flights of stairs, each step leaving a soggy footprint behind on the worn pine planks. He had left the theater that afternoon hoping he had done the right thing to bring Jasmine the notebook. But seeing her again peering out of her window reminded him of just how closed in she was. She might be furious with him for breaking into her apartment to get her notebook. Maybe she had planned for that nut to soak him.

His mind traced back to the production meeting. The memory of Jasmine trembling in front of all those people made him resolute. She had needed his help, whether she appreciated his methods or not.

He stopped dead, a puddle forming at his feet.

Jasmine stood at the door to her apartment, wearing a white terry bathrobe pulled tightly around her waist.

Maybe he could go back outside and get another one of those cold showers.

She stood back to let him in. "I just got out of the shower." She flicked on the overhead lights. "Looks like you did too."

Urgent memo to Josh: Do not think about this woman in the shower. Water, skin, water on skin.

She grabbed some clothes and slipped into the bathroom.

He waited.

He checked his cell. Scanned the books on her shelf. He hadn't noticed how many games she had the last time he was there. Chess. Checkers. Backgammon. He loved backgammon. Hadn't played in years. He had a sudden urge to play. He checked his watch. "Jas? You okay?"

No answer.

Had she fallen? Or, more likely, jumped out the window? "Jas?"

She emerged in a pair of faded jeans and an "I love New York" T-shirt. She had a towel in her hand that she tried to toss him casually. But her hand retreated too quickly, and the yellow towel fell on the floor between them.

She was still a nervous wreck around him. After their amazing movie night and pretty decent interaction at the theater, he thought she had gotten past all this. It was like one step forward, two steps back with this woman.

She kicked the towel toward him.

He tried not to smile at the absurdity of her fear. What did she think he was going to do? He picked up the towel, as if trying not to startle a small animal. He ran it over his hair, then wrung out the bottom of his T-shirt. "That lady had good aim."

"Thanks for helping me out today," Jasmine said. She sat down on the couch. Then she got up. Then, abruptly, she sat down again. Only to jump right back up. "You want some dry clothes?"

At her every attempt to sit, Josh almost sat too. Then up. Then down. They both stood. *Please relax.* The other night, hanging in her apartment watching the movie, she'd been great, totally at ease. Then at the theater, she'd been too wound up to be nervous about him. Now, thanks to his presence, she wasn't even at home in her home. "Maybe a T-shirt. The rest of me is—"

"Soaked." She rooted around in one of the huge plastic containers that lined the wall. He had the sensation she was going to dive into one of them and pull the lid closed over her. Finally, she emerged with a purple T-shirt and a pair of worn black running pants with a triple white stripe down the side and a hole in the knee. She tossed the pants to him. "These'll have to do for now."

He wondered whose pants these were. That other Josh she had mentioned? He looked around the apartment at the stacks of clothes everywhere. Three lime-green bridesmaid dresses hung from the curtain rod. A woman's suit with cuffs undone hung from the door. Stacks of women's pants formed towers against the wall. It was as if her apartment were full of people, only without the actual people.

He hesitated. Should he strip here, in front of her? Not that it was a problem. He had stripped in front of enormous crews. But he knew it would send her into spasms of blushing and shame. He eyed the small bathroom but decided that was ridiculously prim. She had tossed him the pants; he was going to change into them.

He pulled off his loafers one by one with the toe of the opposite foot. He tucked his shoes under the couch, then risked a look at her.

She was involved in a detailed inspection of her cuticles.

He turned his back to her, unbuttoned his jeans quickly, and stripped them off his wet legs. "I'm sorry I busted into your apartment for your notebook." He had to keep her talking.

"How did you . . . ?" She was engrossed in her index finger's cuticle, her face bright red, and was unable to finish the sentence.

He pulled on the sweats as fast as he could. "I used to live in these kinds of brownstones when I was a boy. I'm an expert at fire escapes and eighty-year-old windows. Plus, I learn a lot from my war movies about how to do the things a man sometimes has to do." He caught a glimpse of himself in a mirror. For the first time in his life, he wished he looked like an ordinary Joe. A seventy-year-old man in polyester. Anything to calm her.

He could see her reflection peeking at him. "There's no way you could get in that window," she said. "And I have three dead-bolt locks." Her reflection in the mirror was rigid with anxiety.

He grinned sheepishly, hoping maybe the indirect contact in the mirror would be easier for her to take. He draped his wet jeans over the stack of plastic bins without losing eye contact. Being able to stare at her image in the mirror was a rare treat. He hadn't realized that her shyness had been causing him to avert his gaze too. She was gorgeous and vulnerable and incredibly sexy.

And she was smart.

But he had to be careful. His was not a life that could handle relationships. And she didn't seem like the kind of woman who took relationships lightly.

"Okay, I lifted your keys out of your purse when you were freaking out at the theater, raced uptown, got your sketchbook, then slipped the keys back before you knew they were gone."

She loosened slightly. Almost smiled.

He felt like a king. A thieving king. But whatever, it was worth it to see her light up like that and lose an ounce of her tension. He relaxed too. Maybe he could take off the wet shirt. She was still clutching the dry purple shirt in her fist. He shifted slightly to pull the wet material away from his skin. He moved cautiously to the rickety chair opposite her couch. He was going to have to buy her new furniture first thing tomorrow. "Did it go okay at the meeting after I left?"

"Okay? It was a triumph. Thank you. I'm designing the costumes for an off-Broadway play with Allen Mc-Mann. It's the chance of a lifetime." She met his eyes for a moment, and he caught the sparkle. *More, stay just like that,* he wanted to urge her, as if he were a director trying to help her over her stiff performance. *That's the Jasmine we want to see.*

Then she looked quickly away, her shyness returning.

Her fear would be charming, if it wasn't so maddening. He toyed with the hole in his sweats. He'd have to buy her new sweats too. "So what happened to Artie? He's not returning my calls."

A shadow crossed her face. She looked oddly guilty.

"*You* did something to Artie?" This woman never ceased to amaze him.

She shook her head, her mind far off. *Yes, hold that!* He felt as if he were talking to someone who was darting in and out of shadows.

She said, "He's in Rome—in love."

"Artie? In love? The man hasn't had a relationship in his life with anything but a bolt of imported silk. It's impossible!" He rubbed his bare feet, feeling sheepish as it occurred to him that the same might be true of Jasmine. *Had she ever been with a man?*

Oh, boy. Stay away, pretty boy. The last thing this woman needed was a man like him as a first lover. And yet, the possibility of introducing her to sensuality made his whole body come alive. *Slow, cowboy.*

She had retreated back into the shadow of her nervousness.

They were silent for a moment, his shirt growing clammy against his skin. He eyed the dry shirt still clenched in her fist.

She cleared her throat as if preparing to deliver a soliloquy. "Ready to work?" she asked in a cracking voice.

Well, for her, that was practically a soliloquy. She was changing the subject on him, but he let her. Maybe if she took the lead, she'd feel more at ease. Plus, maybe if they tried on his disguises, he could get out of his soggy shirt without alarming her. "Right. Work."

She stood up. "Okay. So the Latin lover over-the-top approach was working. But no cape! I made a shirt." She strode to her sewing table and picked up a midnight-blue silky shirt, way flouncier than he'd ever wear. "You want to try it on?"

He shrugged out of his wet shirt with relief and tried not to smile as her eyes went smoky. They scanned his bare torso unashamedly. *Hello in there*. Slowly, and with great care, he raised his arms over his head to put on the new shirt. She was good—it was something he would never wear in a million years. It made him *feel* like a different person.

He could sense her eyes boring into him. She couldn't hide a single emotion. Every thought in her head appeared in her skin as blush, in her eyes as hunger, in her body as rigid tension. He had an urge to break through the tension. If he did kiss her . . .

Go slow, Romeo. Remember Cleo. Remember work. Think . . .

He pulled the shirt down and looked in the floor-length mirror. "Well?"

She tugged the fabric this way and that. "A good start."

"No offense, but it's not quite straight through the shoulders." He noticed that her hands were shaking, and he regretted his criticism. Being with her was like being with his parents. He didn't know what to expect. How to get close. He shook the thoughts of his parents out of his head.

"I made it that way on purpose," she explained. Her voice wobbled. "One shoulder is padded so you look askew. It's important that you don't look so perfect—"

"You think I look perfect?"

She turned red and made several short, raspy gasping sounds.

Stop! It's not fair to get involved with Jasmine when I know I can't give her a normal life. My life would kill her.

He cleared his throat. "The shirt's great. The blue makes my skin look—"

"Darker and deeper. That's the idea. Latin. I need to take it in right here."

She was so near to him, he could smell her citrus shampoo, her cucumber soap, her skin mellow and warm. . . .

She pinched the fabric and pinned it up with tiny safety pins that appeared out of nowhere, and still, her hands were shaking. All at once he wanted so badly to stop that shaking, to let her know he wasn't scary. If she wanted him, he could be hers—for a little while anyway. *There's nothing to be nervous about,* he considered saying. But instead, he raised her chin with one finger and kissed her lips.

Chapter 18

His lips were on hers, and the safety pin she had been holding in her mouth fell with a tiny *clink* to the floor.

Josh Toby is kissing me.

Again.

Words from her self-help books flooded her mind: *Take baby steps toward the final goal. Moving too quickly will only cause you to increase and solidify the fear reaction.*

She nudged each of her feet forward. Left. Right. Left. Right. Baby steps and she was against him.

Solid.

Explore the situation thoroughly before you're in it so that there are no surprises.

She let her hand touch his back. Shock waves flashed through her. *Enough exploring for now, thanks.*

Always be wary of situations that take you by surprise. Excuse yourself gracefully . . .

Oh, hell. She didn't care what happened, so long as it happened and happened *now*, *with him.*

He pulled her closer to him, but his kiss remained a question she had to answer. But she wasn't sure of this language. She heard herself sigh and her lips opened. His whole body relaxed, and his smile pressed against hers.

Guess I do know this language. Oh, I like a language that doesn't involve words. . . .

She was outside of herself, lost in this world of warmth and desire. There was no hesitation, nothing but wanting. Needing. She let her tongue explore his mouth. He tasted of man and desire.

His mouth escaped hers and traveled down her neck. She protested the desertion with a moan, then forgot what she had lost as waves of hot desire radiated from each biting kiss he took of her neck. Her chest. Her shoulder.

He whispered, "I've wanted to kiss you again for so long." His voice was as thick as fog.

His hand snaked under her T-shirt, and the warmth of his touch spread through her. Her hand ventured under his shirt. Then withdrew. Then under again. A hesitation. Then contact on the small of his back. She was shocked at the softness of his skin and the hardness of his muscles. His skin was like silk. Warm silk, just spun. No. Not silk—better than silk. To hell with silk. *Skin.* Her hands flew over his back. Amazing.

For the first time in her life, she had found something more sensual than fabric.

There was no turning back.

She struggled out of her T-shirt. He ran his fingers over the lace of her bra.

Real Belgian silk, imported lace—gone.

I'm going to lose my virginity to Josh Toby. She knew it was insane, and yet she didn't care. Him against her bare chest was perfect and unstoppable.

Until he stopped.

He pulled back and let his eyes roam over her.

She closed her eyes and let him drink her in. Better not to watch him. *Let him guide me.*

He whipped the blue shirt over his head. She didn't even mind the slight ripping noise as it cleared his expansive shoulders. Well, she minded a little, but this was no time to quibble. She'd make him another, ten more.

She opened one eye.

Oh, my.

The other eye opened and widened and *oh, my, oh, my*. She couldn't take her eyes off him. She stood back to take in the god-man who stood before her. A tiny scratch rose on his arm where the last pin, still open on his sleeve, had scraped against him.

She'd never let this man wear a shirt again.

Her hands tentatively touched his sculpted abs, his tapering stomach; she let her hands brush over his crotch and he moaned. In that instant, she knew that this was it, and she didn't care. Fate, destiny, prophecy. Maybe he was her One True Love. Maybe not. Who cared if he felt this good?

He seemed to agree as he scooped her up and carried her five strides to the bed. She had never been more glad that her studio was so small, because she couldn't wait another moment.

But he, apparently, could.

He stood back and watched her on the bed. Looking at every inch of her as if he owned her, and now he was going to see just exactly what it was that he had acquired.

Struggling against the fire that was ready to explode inside her, but losing, she fumbled with the top button of her jeans.

But he stopped her with a firm hand and guided her hands above her head. He pinned her wrists together with one hand while slowly, so damn slowly, dear God, he undid the top button of her jeans.

Her chest expanded and contracted. She strained up toward him. One touch. One taste.

He leaned over her but didn't touch her. She closed her eyes. He was too beautiful for words. She couldn't look at him one more instant, or it would all be over.

I could come just from looking at him.

He undid the second button.

How many buttons are on these damn jeans? Good God, had those words really come out of her mouth or did she just moan incoherently? She peeked at him and saw that it didn't matter; he understood without words. He smiled a smile that said, *I'll take care of you. Relax.*

"Josh, please—"

Another button. "Shh . . ."

She raised her hips to let him slide the jeans down her thighs. Which the bastard did so slowly, every inch an eternity.

She gasped as she felt his hand brush her wetness through her panties. His hand was gone, and then it was on her breast, and she couldn't take the exquisite torture another moment.

His mouth was on her breast. His tongue circling.

He let her hands go, and they flew to his back, through his hair, pulling him closer, urging him forward. He was against her all at once, and she crushed her hips into him, begging for release.

Before she could succumb to the glorious pressure, he slipped out of her grasp.

He stood before the bed, damn him, and watched her. Then he stepped out of the sweats as if there wasn't any urgency at all and then out of his boxers and—*sweet heaven and earth, what a man.*

He smiled at her obvious appreciation.

It took every ounce of her energy to keep from throwing herself at his feet. The pictures she had seen on the Internet were nothing compared to seeing him in the flesh. It was him and he was here and he was—what was that?

"Did you say something?" she croaked.

"A condom?"

"Oh. No." *Oh, no.*

He found his wallet in his jeans and slipped out a foil packet. Then he was back.

"Jasmine, is this your first time?" he whispered.

She nodded and gulped. "Is it that obvious?"

He didn't answer. Instead, he smiled so gently, it took her breath away. "Are you sure this is what you want?"

"Shut up and make love to me," she groaned. "Now," she added, just in case he wasn't convinced.

He smiled again and eased her thighs apart with his thigh. "Tell me if it hurts."

"It only hurts to wait."

Inch by inch—oh, God he was amazing—by inch, he slipped inside her. With each easing, he studied her face.

"Quit the kid gloves and fuck me," she commanded.

With an appreciative moan, he filled her completely.

My life is never, ever going to be the same.

Her desperate longing was replaced with something deeper as she rocked with him, his hand running through her hair, his lips on her forehead.

He's mine.

The thought overtook her so thoroughly she didn't care that it wasn't true. It *felt* true. And right now, the feeling was everything.

They strained against each other slowly, so slowly, so deeply, neither wanting it to end, and yet desperate for the ending. Together, they increased the pace. His eyes met hers, and he stopped moving, holding his body stiff against her.

"Don't stop," she begged. She grasped him desperately and pushed against him, pulling him deeper inside her, willing him to thrust.

But he refused. "Don't stop," he urged her. "I want to watch you come."

Near delirious with sensation, she thrust against him, knowing the end was near. His hardness was too much, his eyes too smoky, his mouth too devouring—she exploded in a wave of sensation. It consumed her, ripped through her.

And then he was moving inside her again, and she thought she would die with the sensation. She collapsed back on the bed, spent. She claimed her place to watch him now. His remarkable arms that held him over her, the glorious planes of his chest expanding and contracting faster, faster, until the pleasurable agony of release gripped him. She thought, *This is better than the magazines, the Internet, the Josh the world knows. Now I know this man. Really know him. He's mine.*

And that was when his cell phone began to ring.

They smiled at each other sheepishly.

"Guess we skipped right to lesson twenty-seven." He

kissed the tip of her nose, then rolled to the side so that she had room to breathe.

"Can't wait for lesson twenty-eight," she purred. She was floating. Life was perfect.

Except for that still-ringing phone.

He lay on his back, his arms folded behind his head.

"Are you going to get that?"

"No. The only people with this number are my agent, my publicist, and my . . ."

"Your fake girlfriend?" Jasmine's floating body crashed down to earth. What had she done? Sure, his relationship with Cleo was fake, but the reality was stark and bold: He had a fake relationship because he didn't have time for real relationships. Which meant that this was just casual.

She didn't feel casual.

For all she knew, the guy made love to a different woman every day. What had she been thinking, making love to the sexiest man alive? *Losing her virginity to the sexiest man alive?*

Oh, right, thinking didn't have a thing to do with it.

She felt sick to her stomach. She leapt out of bed, threw on her terry robe, and scrambled to his discarded, still-wet jeans. She fumbled through the pockets, found his phone, and tossed it to him.

He caught it easily, flipped it open, and looked at the tiny screen. "It's Cleo. I better get it. She wouldn't call unless there was an emergency."

Jasmine tried not to flinch. *Repeat after me: Josh Toby is not interested in real relationships.*

God, she was such an idiot. A lifetime of no men and then she had to lose her virginity to the world's most desired man. She perched carefully on the edge of the bed, wishing it were a cliff.

He clicked on the phone. "Cleopatra?"

Jasmine watched as he listened. A shadow passed over his face. Sex was nothing to a man like him. She couldn't expect him to change his lifestyle for her. She knew what she was getting into.

And she hated it.

"Okay. Calm down." He listened. "Four-twenty West One-oh-ninth Street. Apartment Five-B. See you." He clicked the phone shut. "Cleo's in New York."

Jasmine toppled off the edge of the bed, catching herself, just barely, on her numb feet. Josh Toby had just told Cleo Chan her address. She had sex with the sexiest man alive, and now she had to chat with his fake girlfriend, the movie star? And who else? Would there be a bodyguard? An entourage? A lawyer with papers for her to sign?

He lay back on the bed. "Cleo and Mo are on their way from LaGuardia. They'll be here in half an hour."

Jasmine ran her fingers through her hair and began a frantic search for her underwear. *Mo? Who was that? His fake mother?*

Josh fished her panties out from under him.

She snatched them out of his hands.

"Relax," he said.

"Relax?" She tripped into her underwear, snagging her toes on the elastic. She caught herself on the side of the bed. A little visit with the fake girlfriend/movie idol and a dude named Mo was not such a great finish to her first-ever time making love to a man. She felt like a world-class bimbo.

"You'll like Cleo. She's funny. Smart." He still hadn't moved. *Sexy jerk.*

"I'd like her better if she was dumb and ugly." Jasmine frantically pulled on her jeans. Her fingers fumbled with the buttons.

Josh reclined deeper into the disheveled bed, naked as a buck. "Cleo's just a friend, remember? Not a real girlfriend."

"I know. I know. It's just that she's . . . I'm . . ." What was she? Besides freaking out. She pulled on her T-shirt. He was right: She knew about his life before. But now it was *after* and everything felt different.

Relax. Get a grip. Think about something else.

Bad idea.

Her mind swam with the memory of kissing Raj in the bushes. She felt the same way now as she did then: betrayed. Why was it so casual for men to mess around with women? Why did being with a man leave her feeling used? "Get up," she ordered. *Be less gorgeous. Turn down the charm. Be someone else.*

He reluctantly uncurled his langorous body from her bed.

She tried to ignore the expanse of him as she concentrated on straightening the bottom sheet. Her head was spinning as she beat the wrinkles out of the sheet. *Why did I sleep with this man?*

He took her hand. "Jasmine. Are you okay?"

She shook off his grasp. "Fine."

"What we just did was amazing," he said. "I don't know how it even happened. It was different. I mean, I've been with a lot of women—"

Jasmine held up her hands. "Read about it in *Cosmo*."

He went to the opposite side of the bed and took a corner of the comforter. "What I mean is—"

"Stop helping me and put on your clothes," she cried. She sounded hysterical. She had to calm down. *Pretend it doesn't matter.* "Please."

"I was thinking of a shower. LaGuardia's more than half an hour away. Right? You wanna join me?"

She tossed the sweats at him, a little harder than she meant to. *Lots of women.* His relationship of convenience. Strutting around her apartment like a peacock—with the emphasis on the second syllable. What did she expect, for a sex symbol to take sex seriously?

He pulled on the pants, then picked up the blue shirt and held it out to her. "I ripped it."

"I heard. You can put it on the machine and get another shirt on. Here." She tossed him the oversize purple T-shirt she had found earlier. Stupid T-shirt was going to set his violet eyes glowing. She huffed in defiance.

He tossed the T-shirt aside as if he couldn't be bothered with incidentals, like clothes.

She stared in distress at his otherworldly beauty. *I slept with him because I wanted to and now it's done. Back to the real world.* She tripped over his boxers on her way around the bed. "Why aren't you wearing these?" She picked them up and tossed them at his chest.

He laid them over his jeans drying on the bins. "Jasmine."

The perfect Josh is waiting for me at the public library. That Josh wouldn't take sex so casually. Maybe she could get back there once her costume sketches were done. That was a calming thought. She needed more calming thoughts. "I'm sorry. I'm flipping out. I just wasn't prepared for Cleo to be part of our postcoital group hug."

His face lost its playfulness. "What we just did was amazing. Forget Cleo."

Jasmine patted and smoothed the pristine bed. "It was *fine*."

"Fine?" He scowled at her. "Liar. It was mind-blowing and you know it."

She hurried away from him, toward the window, so she could hide her face. Okay, it had been amazing. Her nerve endings were still sizzling. They'd be sizzling till next Thursday. But that was hardly the point. *Stupid nerve endings.* The point was that his attitude toward love and life was impossible. Hell, his life was impossible. She gazed down at the street. She half expected Cleo to be there already, like it happened in the movies: *Cut to limo on street. Cut back to apartment where man with washboard stomach stubbornly refuses to put on his shirt . . .*

He came toward her, and she suppressed a yelp of panic. His unfettered sex appeal was so unfair. "Amazing," he repeated, more firmly.

She picked up the purple T-shirt and held it out like a shield.

"Say it was amazing, Jasmine." He cornered her against the window. "It was special. I felt it. I know you felt it."

Had she? Was this just part of what a man said afterward when the woman he had just slept with was going bananas? She had no experience with this sort of situation. What do you do after you fall into bed with a man who has told you he's a workaholic who takes extreme measures to avoid real relationships?

First, stop inhaling the warmth of him.

Then, avert your eyes from the way his tanned shoulders taper into his slim hips.

Then, work.

She pulled out the wooden spindle chair in front of her faithful sewing machine and slipped into it. "I have to fix this shirt and get the costume sketches done and get your disguise done. I'll be up all night at this rate."

He backed off. The insufferable, impossible man was reading her mind again and seemed to know that she needed space.

Jasmine clicked on the machine and centered the blue shirt under the needle. He understood work. That at least made sense to both of them. She pushed the pedal, and the needle went up and down, up and down. She calmed herself with its rhythm, which seemed to be chanting at her, "He can't be yours. He can't be yours. He can't be yours."

Josh watched out the window for Cleo's limo while Jasmine sketched, ignoring him as best she could. He couldn't blame her. He and Cleo had a deal that was hard for most people to understand. It seemed so cold on the surface. Especially after such an amazing, mind-blowing sexual experience with a woman so perfect it was like she was made exactly for him.

The insistent honk of a too-powerful horn jolted him out of his thoughts. Jasmine must have heard it, too, but she didn't look up.

Josh's cell phone rang, adding to the din. He hadn't realized how quiet being with Jasmine was.

Jasmine still didn't look up.

He flicked on his cell. "No. I'm coming down. We'll all have dinner some other time." He shut the cell.

"That's my cue. I'll be back in twenty minutes."

Jasmine continued to sketch.

He fought the urge to give her a good-bye kiss. Better for him to see what's up with Cleo first, give Jasmine time to think. He slipped out of the apartment, taking one long, hard look around. Because as much as he knew what he wanted as a man, he knew that Cleo was the voice of reason.

As soon as the door clicked shut, Jasmine jumped up and peered out from behind the curtain. A black-clad chauffer held open the back door of a white stretch limo. A pair of endless legs in three-inch black heels emerged. The legs lengthened and straightened as Cleo Chan unwound herself from the car like a baby ostrich from a shell.

The woman took Jasmine's breath away.

Her clothes were exactly the way Jasmine would have costumed her for this scene: *Best friend puts floozy in her place, take one.* Although Jasmine admitted even she might not have conceived the black scarf tied around Cleo's head like Jackie O. It was a very nice touch, a not-so-subtle reminder of the world's most famous woman in mourning. Her black wool Calvin Klein pencil skirt hugged her hips, then her knees. Very conservative, to go along with the mourning-widow theme, but still sexy. A collared, wraparound black Prada merino sweater finished off the outfit.

Jasmine looked down at her jeans. They were dusty with drawing charcoal.

Josh emerged from her building, and Jasmine was engulfed by a wave of jealousy. This was so stupid. *Josh and Cleo are just friends.*

She fell back into her chair. *What arrived in that limo was not Josh's fake girlfriend but his real life.* The life of Hollywood excitement, glamour, parties, and constant exposure. The life of a workaholic who lives in the limelight for his career. As much as she'd like to pretend that the blue-jean clad guy in a baseball cap who liked to watch movies on her couch was the real Josh Toby, she knew he wasn't.

The real Josh Toby lived a Hollywood life in which people pretended to be lovers because real relationships were impossible.

She had to look again. She got up and peered out. Would it be her last glimpse of him ever?

Josh and Cleo kissed each other's cheeks lightly. Two insanely perfect people together—how it should be, how the world wanted it to be. Then Cleo stood back to let him climb into the waiting car. She searched Jasmine's window. Her look wasn't unkind, but it was sharp, a woman in control.

Jasmine felt a shiver run through her. *That woman wants Josh.*

No. That was absurd. They were friends. If Cleo really did love Josh, she, of all people, could certainly have gotten him long ago.

Cleo climbed into the car, and the chauffer slammed the door behind them.

One tear fell, but Jasmine pushed it away angrily. She did not love that man. Lust. That was all. Josh Toby was not her stay-in-and-watch-DVDs One True Love. Maybe, after she scraped what was left of her self-esteem off the floor, she would go back to the library and try again with the other Josh Toby.

The one who hadn't just made love to her.

The one who wouldn't break her heart.

The one who thought she was a bag lady.

Chapter 19

"How's Afghanistan?" Cleo asked the moment the limo door slammed behind her.

Before Josh could answer, the car screeched away from the curb. The sudden motion was alarming after the stillness of Jasmine's world. A soft-jazz CD played in the background.

Sandwiched between Mo and Cleo, he had to swivel his head to take them both in. Good God, what women.

Cleo was exquisitely made up, as always. The woman would be exquisitely made up at 3:00 AM on the moon.

Mo radiated just-scrubbed freshness.

He realized how much he had missed his two best friends.

And yet, he already missed Jasmine.

Could he have it all? He conjured the image of Jasmine in this limo with them. It didn't work. You had to live this world 100 percent or it crushed you. Jasmine was too private, too restrained.

The city rushed by while the car's white interior glowed in the purple accent lights along the running boards. Jasmine's apartment was all white, too, but nothing glowed purple. Rough wood. Textured walls. Flannel sheets.

The worlds didn't mix. He knew it and he hated it.

"Nice pants." Mo handed him a flute of champagne, which he accepted gratefully. Dom Pérignon.

The liquid was cool down his throat. "They're a loaner," he said of his tattered sweats. He batted Mo's tickling finger out of the knee hole.

"He lost his pants already," Cleo said. She leaned away from him, against her side of the limo to better survey him, her lips drawn tight with what looked like disapproval. Her green cat eyes narrowed.

Mo took a fortifying sip of her wheatgrass cocktail. Mo never touched alcohol. Never touched anything that wasn't pure and organic.

Cleo, on the other hand, hadn't been pure since her fourteenth birthday and hadn't been organic since before her first breast implant at eighteen.

Josh checked his watch. "It's great to see you guys, but you've got twenty minutes. I'm busy."

"So we see," Mo deadpanned.

"We're doing an intervention." Cleo tapped her nail extensions against the armrest, then abruptly leaned forward, peering around him. She addressed Mo. "We're too late."

Mo leaned back and playfully pulled back the elastic of his sweatpants. "Oh, dear. No undies. You're right. He's a goner."

"Hello," Josh said, waving his hands between them. "I'm here. Talk to *me*."

"We can't talk to you when you think you're in love. *Again*," Cleo said.

In love? Josh tried the idea on for size. *In love with Jasmine?*

He looked from woman to woman, astonished at the joy he felt as the idea took root. "Am I in love?"

Both women rolled their eyes. Cleo threw up her hands. "That's *exactly* how he looked when he was with—what was that whale lover's name? Margo?"

"Margo Campos."

Josh's stomach sank. He thought he had loved Margo, and it had been a disaster. Although, now, after Jasmine, he wondered if he really had loved Margo.

"Mo, intervene."

Mo pulled a worn, cloth-covered notebook out of her hemp bag. "Jasmine Burns. Small-time tailor. Costume designer wannabe. American of one-quarter gypsy descent—Kalderash tribe. Grew up in Bombay, India, with her mother and stepfather, Emeril Livingstone. Moved to Baltimore to be with her sisters and father at the age of sixteen due to some sort of sex scandal back home. Disappeared for four years, then resurfaced at Parsons in New York City. BA in textiles. MA in costume design from NYU. One sister is a doctor in Baltimore. One is a semi-famous gypsy psychic." Mo paused for breath.

Sex scandal? Disappeared for four years? Josh tried to breathe, but the women were too close. "Just because I don't know everything about Jasmine doesn't mean that I don't know her." His heart was pounding.

"That's exactly what he said about Margo," Mo reported. "Word for word." She flipped back in her book and nodded. "Yep. Margo said—"

"It's not like Margo." Dread filled him. *It's worse, because this time, I'm not leaving her behind.*

"Josh." Mo lowered her notebook and took his hand. Her nails were short and buffed to a shine. "We're here to protect you."

Cleo took his other hand in her red talons. "Tell the truth. Do we know more about her than you do?"

"She's shy. She doesn't talk much." His voice rose louder than he intended. He pulled his hands away from them and poured himself more champagne while he tried to shake the cloud that was forming on the horizon of his consciousness. He wasn't about to admit to his two oldest friends that they knew more about Jasmine than he did. They only knew Jasmine's past. He knew her present. That was what mattered.

But a secret past was bad news. Everything would be exposed. Could Jasmine handle it?

Cleo drank deeply from what looked like water but was more likely straight Stoli. "Shy? Oh, no. It's another Margo. I love you, honey, but you've got a problem with wanting to help people too much. And when you do, you hurt yourself *and* them. Listen to me very, very carefully. You don't have to live your life trying to please your parents. Last time you came to New York, you found some nice, politically and morally respectable girl who you thought would make your folks happy. But you know what, hon? It didn't. Jasmine won't either. *Romeo and Juliet* won't. Your parents will never accept your life. So don't tell me you love this seamstress. You love the idea that your mother will love her and that you can help her with whatever her shyness hang-up is. *But you will hurt her. And you'll hurt yourself.*"

Josh shook his head. "How do you know about *Romeo*?"

"Josh, is Jasmine quiet and respectful?" Mo asked.

"Of course."

"Is she kind and sweet?" Mo was taking notes.

"Yes, but—"

Cleo cut in. "Is there something about her that is appealing to your need to help her? Like, maybe, that she's shy? Vulnerable?"

Mo went back to reading from her notebook. "She suffers from acute social anxiety around males. She's seen a Dr. Crater, a Dr. Renee Jones, PhD—"

Josh snatched Mo's notebook and tossed it into the champagne chiller. *If Mo knows this much, the papers will know more as soon as they spot him with Jasmine. I can't expose Jasmine to that. She never chose that kind of life.*

"We're not ordinary people, Josh. We can't make ordinary mistakes," Cleo said. "The stakes are too high. You have to really think about this. What it means to bring this woman into your life."

"I think I love her."

Cleo flinched.

Josh looked closely at his friend, but her eyes betrayed no further emotion. Just strength and resolve. For a minute he thought he'd seen something else in her eyes, read something more in her tone. Was it hurt? Had he hurt Cleo? Was that even possible? It was hard to tell, as the exquisite creature across from him had turned to alabaster.

In the beginning, he had suspected that Cleo might feel more toward him than friendship. She had hinted at the possibilities for more. But he had discouraged her from the start, and she seemed to accept her role as his friend. It wasn't that he didn't love her—he did. As a friend. But there was something missing from her that he couldn't put his finger on. Something that Jasmine had.

Tenderness?

He was being ridiculous. Cleo had a heart of stone when it came to romance. She didn't love him.

But Margo. That had been a mistake. He knew it after the initial rush of their relationship had slowed. "It's different with Jasmine. I'm sure of it."

"You better be sure, Josh. Really sure. Because if you bring her into your life, she's fair game. You can't protect her."

He intercepted a knowing look between the two women. "What?"

Cleo asked, "Do you know a Samantha?"

"Samantha Olivia. She told us about *Romeo and Juliet*, Josh. She sent us a clipping from the Halloween parade. She gave us all the info. That's why we're here. She could turn you in to the tabloids anytime for big bucks. Just think of the headlines: *Josh Toby Cheats on Cleo Chan with Shy Seamstress with Shady Past.*"

Josh's stomach coiled into a ball. He felt off-balance and braced himself against the seat.

"You can't pretend to be a nobody, Josh. You can't pretend your life is normal. You have to be careful. For Jasmine's sake. Think of her, honey, before it's too late," Mo pleaded.

"Think of yourself, too, Josh," Cleo added. "Think of what's happened before with Margo. Do you really love Jasmine, or do you just love the idea of a woman you can help?" Cleo paused. A shadow passed over her face. "Because no one wants to be helped when they think they're being loved."

Chapter 20

Jasmine stared at the street below. It had been forty-three minutes since Josh left with Cleo. Jasmine took a deep breath. *I slept with him because he's fiendishly sexy.* That was all. Tomorrow, as soon as she dropped off the sketches at the theater, she was heading back to the library. She couldn't mess around with a man who lived so casually.

A man who lived so publicly.

The white limo turned onto her street, then stopped in front of her building. Josh jumped out before the driver could get the door. The limo pulled slowly away, leaving Josh alone on the darkened sidewalk.

Jasmine yanked the curtain shut. She dove for her comb and wrestled it through her hair. Ran lipgloss over her lips. Grabbed . . . wait. What was she doing? She was not taking him back.

"But soft! What light through yonder window breaks? It is the East, and Jasmine is the sun!"

I want him back.

Oh, cripes. Mrs. Little was going to freak. Jasmine

opened the window and leaned out into the chilling air. Despite her misgivings, she waved him up.

He disappeared into the building.

Two minutes later, he was standing before her.

But something was different about him. His eyes were guarded, questioning.

Something had changed.

Jasmine, what happened in India to make you come back to America? Where were you for four years when you "disappeared"? If the world finds out, will you be able to bear it? The questions were on his lips, but face-to-face with her, he couldn't speak them. She'd feel stripped, exposed. He was used to strangers assaulting him for the private details of his life. *Boxers or briefs? Top or bottom?*

But he knew that kind of scrutiny would destroy her. *If she stays with me, her secrets will be on the front page of every tabloid in the world.*

He had to be sure she understood that the world was closing in.

Cleo's parting words echoed in his head: *Do you really love her or do you just love the idea of a woman you can help?* Facing Jasmine now, the contrast between the two women was shocking.

Jasmine moved into the apartment, and he followed. Being back in her warm, textured studio was so comforting after the sleek limo, he almost sighed. "Cleo was worried. She's looking out for me. And for you."

Jasmine sat on the couch, and Josh stood before her. "We need to talk about what we're getting into. If you're with me, you'll be scrutinized. If you have secrets, we need to talk about them." He knelt on the floor before her and took her hands.

Her face drained of all its color.

He felt sick to his stomach. "Tell me now. I can put Mo on it. We can spin it."

He could see the pain in her eyes. He took a deep breath. He had to tell her what he already knew. Maybe it would drive a wedge between them, but he had to take the risk. "What happened in India to make you leave? Mo found out something about a scandal."

Her eyes widened with surprise.

"It's Mo's job to know everything. She's there to protect us. To protect you."

A thousand emotions passed over Jasmine's face. Josh was forever fascinated at how she couldn't hide a single thought. He wondered if she was remembering something awful. Something that the tabloids would love to exploit. Something that would send her into a tailspin. "Jas, I don't give a damn what happened in India. But if someone wants to find out what happened there, can they? Who else is involved?"

She sat perfectly still for a long moment. Then she spoke, her voice barely audible. "There was a boy, in India. It was nothing, really. It's so dumb I can hardly say it. In fact, if it was in print, people would laugh." The thought seemed to send a chill through her. "It's embarrassing because it's so dumb, not because it's bad."

He fell onto the couch beside her. "I have stage fright," he blurted. "Terrible, awful, throw-up-in-the-wings stage fright. That's my secret. What's dumber than a superstar with stage fright? I don't know if I can do *Romeo*. It's so insane, I can't stand it. But there it is."

"But all those movies?"

He smiled at the shock in her eyes. "I can go in front of the cameras, but on stage, I'm toast. There. That's my dumb secret. See if you can top that. A superstar who passes out in the footlights."

She smiled for the first time in hours. "Mine's dumber. Raj, my tutor, kissed me for a bet. The other boys were watching. I was sixteen. They called me the Hindi word for 'whore' after that. It was like something clicked inside me, and I couldn't look at a man. I felt like they all knew my dirty secret. And that's all it was, a kiss. That's the thing about anxiety—it doesn't make sense. *An inappropriate fear response to a normal situation.*"

"I'll kill him. Kill them all." That was Josh's most famous line. It was in all his Mitch Tank movies. But for the first time in his life, Josh really meant it.

Jasmine took his hands. "I should be over it. It doesn't make sense for a grown woman to be scarred over something like that."

"Maybe you're not. Maybe it's something deeper and that just triggered it."

"Maybe." She thought of how the ordeal with Raj had made her feel ready to go and see her sisters and father, a trip that turned out truly awful. The wanting to be loved. The hope of being accepted. The realization that what happened to her in the bushes with Raj wasn't actually bad enough to have her sisters accept her. It was all connected.

"I should be over my stage fright too. I forgot my lines in a tenth-grade production of *Grease,* and I relive that moment every time I get near a stage. The fear is automatic. I'm completely out of control. My body goes on autopilot."

Jasmine nodded. "I blush. Stutter. Shake. Even though I know it's dumb. And normal people don't get it. They think it's insane. That's the worst part."

"Sometimes, I wish I had a gushing wound, something that would show," Josh said. "At least if you're visibly injured, people understand. No one understands how powerless I am against the fear unless they've felt it themselves."

Jasmine relaxed into him. "So why are you going back to the stage if it terrifies you?"

"I have to. I have to get over it to respect myself as an actor. And as a person. Plus, I was sick and tired of being known as a beautiful fool. The stage is the only way to prove myself."

"So the stage fright is why you wanted to hide your identity?"

"Yeah. In case I chickened out. But it's a little late for that now."

Jasmine twirled her fingers in his hair. "Why? Cleo won't tell, will she?"

He looked into her eyes. "Someone named Samantha knows about us. About me. About the play."

Jasmine sat bolt upright. "Samantha Olivia? The lighting assistant?"

"Yeah, I guess."

Jasmine's hands balled into fists. "That bitch. I'll kill her. Kill them all."

Josh smiled. She knew the movie line too. And it seemed like she meant it. "I knew deep down I couldn't do anything anonymously. It was dumb." He searched her eyes. "But this isn't dumb. It's serious. We need to really think about this. I can't protect you from the media, Jas. They're jackals. Relentless. We probably don't have much time left before the world comes after us. Do you understand? I need to know that you understand what being with me entails."

They sat like that, together, as the night grew deeper and more silent around them.

"I should go," he said finally. "Let you think."

"Yeah. You better walk the dogs."

"Nah. It's not them. I paid the kid downstairs to take them home with him tonight in case I was late. It's just . . . late."

Jasmine knew she should let him go. She had work to do. The night had already fried her. And yet, she said, "I wish you'd stay." She held her breath.

"Are you sure?"

No. Definitely not sure. "It's just like *Romeo and Juliet,*" Jasmine said.

"A tragedy?"

"A force that can't be stopped." She bit her tongue. What was she saying? She snuck a glance at him. His eyes bore into her.

Then he lowered his face to hers. "Even Romeo and Juliet had one whole night together."

"Then they died," she reminded him as his lips touched hers. She tried not to gasp at the pleasure of it.

"We won't," he promised.

I don't care either way. She wanted to be with him. At least one more time.

"The ending of this play isn't written yet." He let his

lips brush hers, and she shuddered in anticipation of more. "We write it."

Jasmine let the tremor race through her. *If I could only write my own ending,* she wished. But she knew she'd never be in complete control of her emotions, of her body—of Josh.

But at this moment, in his arms, she understood how Juliet felt when she gave herself to Romeo: There was every reason not to, and yet, it couldn't be any other way.

This time was different, less desperate, more intimate. She still needed him, but there was something she needed to communicate to him beyond her desire.

They walked hand in hand to the bed, faced each other, and dropped their hands to their sides.

We've left reason behind. She knew that as clearly as she knew each and every curl that framed his face.

He lifted his shirt over his head.

Her hands traced his shoulders, over his chest, down his stomach, then around his waist as he pulled her to him. She lay her head against him and listened to the pounding of his heart.

His hands moved down her spine, sending every nerve ending in her body alight.

She pulled off her T-shirt and released her bra.

The sensation of her skin against his, his arms around her, made her forget all her doubts. *I deserve this.* She understood what he had told her, that his real life had arrived and would have to be dealt with. *But not yet.*

He trailed a line of kisses down her neck. Down her breasts. He fell to his knees as he kissed down her stomach.

She let her fingers slide through his hair as he gripped her hips and rested his cheek on her stomach. He held her like that, and she let her fingers explore his hair. *This man. Here. Now. Nothing else matters.*

Then he rose and unbuttoned her jeans, and she slid out of them. The fire in his eyes showed his approval of her slim form.

She had never felt more beautiful than at that moment.

Maybe we can make this work.

He pushed back the covers on the bed, and she lay herself down as he watched her every move. He stood beside the bed, touching her gently. His fingers outlined her eyes, ran down her neck, across her collarbone. He touched every inch of her as if with his touch he were drawing her, creating her. A breast. The curve of her waist. Her thigh. Down her leg and around her calf. *I am creating you for my pleasure; you are exactly what I envision. What I desire.*

He helped her slip out of her panties.

Then she watched him strip, an almost unbearable pleasure. His beauty had become part of him, not something other, outside of him, a force that came between them. *He was Josh, and he was perfection, and there was nothing either of them could do about it.*

He lowered himself beside her and took her in his arms.

Neither one of them spoke. And then they both did, without words but with their eyes, their kisses, their bodies. Jasmine realized what it was she needed him to understand. *I want you. All of you. Always.*

I think I love you.

She knew she could never tell him in words that she had fallen. Completely, helplessly given herself over to him. She could barely form the words in her own mind, to herself.

But she could tell him with her body.

She lost herself in his masculine scent, surrounded herself with the strength of his arms, his legs, each individually defined muscle of his stomach.

And what a stomach. Every woman should once in their lives experience a stomach as taut and narrow, as sculpted and powerful. And then there were his shoulders, the curve of his thigh, his cheekbones.

Immersed in the heat of him, she told him with her lips, her teeth, her hands that she needed him.

When she came up for air, gasping, and caught her reflection in the mirror, her thoughts turned to the millions of reasons that this couldn't last.

But she didn't care. Not now.

She dove back under the cover of their passion to experience his earlobe, his forearm, the nape of his neck.

When they began to make love, it was as if they had done it a thousand times before. So familiar was the feel of him inside her.

If it lasted one more moment, that would be enough. No, not enough. One more. One more. Closer. Her body shuddered into his as they climaxed together.

She closed her eyes and laid her head on his shoulder and pretended that the Josh Toby who held her was all hers. Because for that moment, at least, she knew that he truly was.

Chapter 21

Shut up or I'll pour another bucket on you rascals! Do you know what time it is?"

Jasmine awoke to Mrs. Little's raspy growl from three stories below. Then she heard a splash and colorful curses from the sidewalk.

Josh stirred beside her. "What the hell?"

Jasmine leapt out of bed and threw on her white terry robe. The clock read 7:22 AM. My God, what a night they had had. She certainly hadn't finished any of her sketches, and she didn't care. Her whole body still tingled down to her toes.

"Josh! We know you're up there! Just give us one for the money, and we're out of your hair!" a voice called up.

Jasmine went toward the window.

"No!" Josh bolted up, instantly awake. "Don't go near the window!"

Another splash.

"Tabloids. Paparazzi. They're not human. They'll eat you alive." Josh had his cell phone to his ear and began speaking into it. "What the hell is going on?" He listened a few moments, then shut the phone with an angry snap.

"Cleo?"

He shook his head. "No. Samantha. She sold us out to the lions."

Jasmine went white. "What do we do?"

Josh ran his hand through his hair. "We make coffee. And think."

Jasmine couldn't help herself. She went to the window and peeked out. To her horror, one of her better clients, Lucy Rowright, a law student at Columbia who lived two floors down, was talking animatedly to the photographers. She pointed up at Jasmine's window, and Jasmine snapped the curtain closed. *I'll sew your pockets shut, Lucy*. Jasmine could feel a hundred eyes on her already. She felt ill.

Josh found the coffee and was measuring it into the filter. He looked grim.

Jasmine couldn't move. "Is it always like this?"

"No. Sometimes they're in the closet."

Jasmine's body went clammy.

"Kidding." He poured water into the carafe. "Not really."

She fell onto the couch and closed her eyes. Images of her beautiful, soulful tutor, Raj, assaulted her. *Me and Raj sneaking off to the bushes. Raj taking my hand. The kisses. The tender touch. The strange and terrifying ecstasy of his kiss. The click of a twig breaking behind them. Jasmine spinning around to see a pack of boys, watching, a hungry look in their eyes. The ultimate shame—thinking someone loves you and then . . .*

Here we go again. People watching her make a fool

of herself with a man. She held herself absolutely still, willing herself to control her body. This was not the same. Josh didn't betray her. The watchers were outside. She was hidden.

Plus, now I'm an adult. She willed herself into maturity. *Think, don't feel.*

Think.

Why would Samantha alert the media to her and Josh? Money? No. She had her daddy's money.

She wanted Jasmine's job. Samantha had seen Jasmine at the production meeting. Maybe she didn't understand the subtlety of Jasmine being fearful of men, but she clearly understood that crowds of onlookers and Jasmine didn't mix.

Jasmine was impressed with Samantha's insight. Who knew that woman even noticed anything outside her own mirror? But then, it was Jasmine who hadn't noticed how shrewd Samantha was.

The crowd continued to call out to Josh.

"Can't we call the cops?" Jasmine asked.

Josh watched the coffee drip into the carafe. "Believe it or not, this is completely legal."

"Okay. So, let's fall back into bed. Never come out. Order pizza and ignore the world." Even as she said it, she knew it would only delay the inevitable.

"One shot, Josh! Just you! No floozy!" a voice called.

Jasmine flinched at the insult. *Randi,* they had called her in Bombay. *Whore.*

"And no shirt!" another voice chimed in, to lusty agreement from the crowd.

Jasmine's phone began to ring.

"Don't get it," Josh warned.

Jasmine looked at the display. "It's my friend Suz." She picked it up.

Suz was hysterical. "Hon, you're on channel nine."

Jasmine couldn't speak.

"They have a picture of you from like, five years or so ago, and they're saying you're with Josh Toby. And that you're some kind of 'alleged' sex worker. They're showing your building."

Jasmine felt the blood drain from her face.

"Jas? Are you there? Are you with Josh Toby?"

"Yes," Jasmine managed to get out.

Suz let out a war whoop. "You go, girl!"

Josh raised his eyebrows at Jasmine.

"Hello? Jas? Sorry. It looks like a mob scene. You need some help?"

"No. I'm fine. We're fine. I gotta go. We'll talk later." She hung up. "We're on TV."

"Okay, we've gotta get out of here. Now," Josh said.

"For God's sake, why?" Jasmine had no intention of going anywhere with that mob outside.

"If we're on TV, the crowd will only grow. They won't leave until they get what they want. If we stay put, we'll be stuck in here for days. They'll get into the building. They'll worm their way into the hall. They'll pay someone on the fifth floor across the street to set up their high-power zooms in their living room. Believe me, it's best to get out quick." He took her hands. "We could put on dark glasses and hats and push through them. Just say, 'No comment, no comment' and we'll jump in a cab."

Jasmine shook her head, the pressure building in her skull. "I can't go out there." She couldn't stop thinking of Raj. She felt so stupid. She felt so sick.

The photographers' voices were now overpowered by the desperate shrieks of teenage girls. Josh was right; the mob was growing.

"Okay. You don't have to go through the crowd. I'll create a distraction while you sneak out," Josh said.

"I can't make you face that craziness alone."

"It's no big deal. It's my job. You sneak out and go to your friend's house."

"I'll go to work."

"No. It's not safe there. If Samantha alerted them to us, they probably know about the play too." He paused. "Wait. They might have scoped out your friends. You need somewhere totally safe." He thought. "Go to my parents."

"Your parents?"

"It's perfect. I'll call them and set it up. Then once these jerks are satisfied, I'll meet you there." He was obviously excited by this change in plans. "I want you to meet them." He looked so earnest, Jasmine felt a fluttering moment of hope.

Meet the parents.

Meet the parents to escape from a rabid mob.

"At seven in the morning? Chased by photographers?" It was so sweet and traditional, if it wasn't for the screaming, demanding nutcases out front.

"My parents will love you. Don't worry."

"You think I'm worried about meeting your parents? I sort of have more urgent issues on my mind."

He kissed her quickly. "Exactly. That's my plan. There really isn't a better time for either of us to see them than when our minds are focused on other problems. Okay? Now, listen, here's the plan."

*   *   *

Jasmine had never been in the alley that ran along the left side of her building, but she assumed it was like any other Manhattan alley: dark, smelly, and full of rats.

In the current circumstances, it sounded divine.

Josh and Jasmine paused in the dark hallway that led to the alley door. They had just slunk down the five flights of stairs from her apartment, but Jasmine's heart was thumping as if they had just run a marathon.

"Okay, this is your exit. I'm going out the front," Josh said. "Count to ninety, then go. If there's someone in the alley, put your head down and run."

Jasmine gulped. "Why do I feel like I'm in one of your movies?"

Josh squeezed her hand. "While they mob me, you go slowly and carefully down the alley, walk to Broadway, and hail a cab. Take it to 1832 Riverside Drive." He pressed a note with the address on it into her palm. "My cell phone number is on there too. I'll be there as soon as I can." He kissed Jasmine's forehead. "Okay?"

Jasmine tried to silence her chattering teeth.

He gave her hand another squeeze. The commotion outside was growing louder. "Don't worry. I'll make sure no one follows you."

"How?"

Josh met her eyes with a deep, intent gaze and drew her to him. *Just like the movies.* She tried not to swoon. *Maybe it could be happily-ever-after.* He waited a split second for his cue, then said, "I'm going out there in my boxers."

Jasmine drew back and stared. She realized with a start that Josh was enjoying this. "But won't that be like shouting out to them that we slept together?"

"Not when I tell them that you're the costume designer on the play and we worked late into the night. I just slept over. I love Cleo. In fact, she knows I'm here. Hell, she's here in New York. She's looking after my dogs. Blah, blah, blah. Look, they don't want the truth; they just want the photos. Mo'll spin it fine if I give them the skin shots to sell papers."

Josh stripped off his shoes, socks, shirt, and pants. He bundled them neatly into a little pile, as if stripping in darkened halls under the light of one bare, flickering bulb was perfectly natural. Of course, for him, it was perfectly natural. He mussed his hair. "How do I look?"

Edible. "I should stay with you," she said. She imagined the scene. "They could get a picture of me barfing."

He handed her his discarded clothing. "It's me they want. Besides, this doesn't bother me a bit. It's my job."

The thought chilled Jasmine to the bone. She handed him back his clothes. "Keep these. How will you get uptown to your parents' without your shoes?" She knew the answer: he'd be borne on the shoulders of a thousand willing women.

He shrugged. "I'll manage."

"Won't you be cold?" She was perfectly aware that she was stalling.

"In *Tank Command Three*, I had to swim across a fifty-two-degree river in November. Twenty-seven takes. This is a piece of cake." He did a few left-hand jabs. "Ready?" he asked.

"Never."

Josh kissed her again. Then he straightened to his full height and started down the hallway. "I know you can do it. Action!"

"Wait!"

He turned, half-naked in the dim light, the sexiest man alive. *Don't go. I'll go with you. You shouldn't have to face those maniacs alone.* Her insides churned. "Good luck."

She watched him recede down the hallway. He put his clothes down inside the vestibule. Then he stretched, mussed his hair again, opened the door, and was gone.

Chapter 22

$\mathcal{E}$ighty-eight, eighty-nine, eighty-nine and a half . . . three quarters . . .

Just get out there, you coward.

She opened the alley door cautiously. The stink of garbage assaulted her. Despite the bright, crisp, early morning sun, the alley was dark with the shadows of the two flanking brownstones.

Piece of cake.

She slunk through the dimness, her black Converse sneakers crunching broken glass. *Please don't let me see a rat.*

Please let a rat be the worst thing I see.

A footstep from behind the Dumpster and her escape was over before it began. A flash of blinding light lit up the alley. Behind the flash was a man. Or something like a man. She couldn't see his face, as it was obscured by a camera. The enormous lens protruded like a grotesque nose. The camera clicked and snapped, a live animal on the attack. "Great. There now. Smile. Good. One more for Fat Larry."

Jasmine held her hands in front of her face. *Must go*

back inside. She spun around and headed for the door, her insides swirling. *It's just like Raj and his friends— people watching.* The ground turned to quicksand. She could imagine the headlines already: *Josh Toby's New Alley Cat.*

She tugged on the doorknob. It was locked.

Bile rose in her throat. *I can do this. It's not like Raj. Josh is different. He—* Her thoughts stopped. Josh what? Loved her? He hadn't ever said that. Of course he hadn't; they hardly knew each other.

Metaphysical thoughtfest later, please; now just get out!

She dashed blindly by the man, flying past in a burst of adrenaline and fear.

"Wait!" He caught her arm.

She struggled free of his grip and raced toward the light of the street. But it was too late. He had gotten pictures of her that would be plastered in sleazy newspapers all over the world. Cruel, uncaring people would pick up those magazines and study her every flaw. Nothing private. Like that day in Bombay behind the bushes with Raj.

Her stomach lurched as she stood on the sidewalk, paralyzed by her thoughts and the crowd streaming past her.

You don't deserve to be with him, a little voice said inside her head. *You get all the good stuff, while we suffer.*

It was the voice of Amy.

Fat Larry was on his cell phone with one hand while clicking the shutter button with the other. She couldn't move.

Amy had never said those words.

But she thought them. And worse, Jasmine herself believed them. *I didn't deserve love. I had Mom. I had everything. Amy and Cecelia lived a desperate life while I sat under the Ashoka trees and read poetry with Raj.*

Jasmine shook the thoughts out of her head. Fat Larry had shut his phone and was at it full-force again with his camera.

She was losing it, that's all. Her usual habit of engaging in disastrous thinking. Ninety-nine out of a hundred people would have shrugged off Raj's prank. Would have joined their long-lost families with a joyful reunion. Why did she have to be the one who relived the past over and over? Who felt guilty for her mother's actions? Her thoughts rushed around her like the mob of people around Josh.

Click, click, click.

Get a hold of yourself and run.

She pushed onto the now-crowded street. It was a circus. *Josh's life is a circus.* Why had she ever thought she could do this? In the privacy of her apartment, it seemed possible. But the mayhem was worse than she imagined—both on the street and inside her head.

Her neighbors, in bathrobes and sweats, spilled onto the sidewalk to watch the spectacle Samantha had created. Josh was on the landing, twenty feet away from her, waving at the adoring crowd. Photographers mobbed him.

Was that Mrs. Little hanging out the window with her ancient Polaroid? Where were her buckets of cold water when Josh really needed them?

The professional photographers leaned at impossible

angles to get their best shots. Children half ready for
school stood on their landings, shoveling cold cereal and
milk into their gaping mouths from unsteady bowls.

And in the midst of the chaos, Josh waved. Smiled. He
was buried in people.

He was a movie star. This was his life. The fact hit her
fully for the first time. Sure, she'd known all along. But
seeing him there, waving, forced her to accept the extent
of his public life. *He may not have been Cleo's, but he* did
belong to the world.

And he loved it. He was made for it.

Jasmine turned toward Broadway.

Click. Click. "Are you Jasmine Burns? How long have
you known Josh? Have you met Cleo? What would you
like to say to her now that you're boffing her man?" *Click.
Click.*

She turned back for a last look at Josh. He smiled and
laughed and chatted as the crowd pushed him against the
building like a pack of rabid lovers. A police car rolled
slowly down the street. It stopped across from the mob.
Two policemen got out.

*Over here, boys! Fat man with bad comb-over hiding
behind his camera.* She wished the coward would show
his face.

One of the policemen began taking pictures of Josh
with a silver point-and-shoot while the other spoke into
his car radio, gesticulating excitedly, as if doing a sports
play-by-play.

Broadway. The street streamed with morning commuters rushing for the #1 train. There wasn't a cab in sight. A
dog walker pulled along by a cluster of his charges almost
ran her down.

Jasmine dashed across the street and made her way toward the subway. She stumbled down the stairs, wondering if Fat Larry would follow her all day. Her whole life.

But he didn't. He stood at the top of the stairs and waved. "Thanks, doll! I can just tell we're going to be the closest of friends!"

She paid the fare quickly as a local screeched into the station. She dashed through the turnstile and onto the train just before the doors slid shut. It was a downtown train, not uptown, but she didn't care. She wasn't going to Josh's parents'. How could she when all she could say to them was that she could never, ever survive a life with their only son?

"You slept with Josh Toby?" Jenn handed Jasmine a cup of chamomile tea and then sat on the red vinyl and chrome chair next to her. Jenn's Hell's Kitchen apartment was pure retro, down to the pink shag rugs.

"Sort of. Yeah."

"No. You can't 'sort of' sleep with a man like that." Jenn was trying not to let her excitement show, but it was leaking out her ears.

"Okay. I did. Twice." One of Jenn's four cats head-butted Jasmine's leg, and she leaned down to pet it, hiding her smile. She couldn't help but feel an ounce or two of Jenn's excitement, despite her rattled nerves. "Maybe more."

Jenn practically hit the ceiling. "Oh, my little Jasmine!"

"But it's over. You can't believe how nuts it was this morning. It was a zoo."

"And that matters why? He's your One True Love.

It wasn't just great sex. It was prophecy." Jenn checked the muffins that she had whipped up and popped in the oven when Jasmine called from her cell. She switched off the oven and let them cool in the pan. "It *was* great sex, right?"

Jasmine scooped up the cat and tried to hide her smile in its fur.

"Prophecy!" Jenn cried, giving Jasmine and the cat a hug. "And is he nice too? Not that it matters . . ."

The cat jumped away, indignant. "Yes. He's incredibly thoughtful. It's a little spooky how well he seems to know me. But, Jenn, this morning was awful—like a nightmare after the most perfect dream."

"But it wasn't a dream." Jenn tossed the still-steaming muffins into a basket. She put the basket on the table between them. They smelled, well, healthy.

Jasmine sighed. Jenn never let sugar pass her lips. "It was a dream. The dream that he was an ordinary guy. The dream that we could be together without mobs."

"Cleo!" Jenn whispered under her breath. "I forgot about her. Oh, my God. What are you going to do about her?" Jenn's half-hidden smile belied her delight at the situation. "I could teach you some karate."

Jasmine considered telling Jenn about Josh's fake relationship with Cleo but didn't. She couldn't give away Josh's secrets. Even to Jenn. "The whole world is going to hate me for ruining the perfect couple."

Jenn bit into a muffin. Jasmine took one from the basket, then moved it around on her plate, pretending to let it cool. *Josh and Cleo's fake relationship has to stay secret. I'll be reviled all over the world.* "Can I stay here?"

"As long as you need to, hon. Don't worry about a thing. We'll watch movies. And I'll cook."

Jasmine managed a weak smile. "I'll get us take-out. Putting me up will be enough stress for you."

"But shouldn't you call Josh? Won't he be worried if you don't show up at his parents' place?"

Chapter 23

Josh leaned on his parents' buzzer until the intercom crackled to life. "Huh? Hello?" His father's voice emerged from the static. "Who's there?"

"Dad. It's me. Josh." Had he woken his father? But shouldn't Jasmine have woken him ages ago? If Jasmine wasn't already upstairs, where was she? The last time he had seen her, moving slowly toward Broadway, she had looked mad with terror. Had she gotten cold feet? Run off to hide?

Relax. Maybe he hadn't woken his father. He was letting his thoughts get away from him.

A pause. Then the buzzer signaled the unlocked door. Josh pushed through the pre-war wooden and glass door. He took the stairs two at a time.

His unshaven father stood in his bathrobe and sweat socks at the hallway door. "Joshie?"

Josh's heart sank. "Dad. Is she here?"

"Who?"

"I'm right here." His mother appeared in a gray Columbia sweatshirt pulled over a pink striped cotton nightgown that came down to her ankles. "Joshie? Are you back from Afghanistan? What's going on?"

His parents had aged, shrunk, and grayed since he'd last seen them four years ago, on December 23, when they had agreed to come to the opening of the first *Mitch Tank: Tank Command* movie. They were coming west anyway for a conference at UCLA on dissenters and Dostoyevsky. Halfway through the movie, he spotted his father in the lobby, reading a dog-eared paperback.

They hadn't stayed for the holidays.

"Don't you remember I called you? About Jasmine coming?" Panic rose and Josh's voice wobbled.

"Oh, yes, your, ah, friend. She didn't show up," his father said. "*Jasmine*. I bet there hasn't been anyone named Jasmine in this building since the twenties."

"There was that girl Lilac, honey. In the studio downstairs," his mother reminded him.

His parents receded into their apartment. Josh followed dutifully as they catalogued all the women they had known in the past seventy-two years named after flowers. "So many in the sixties! Remember Dandelion?"

Josh threw open his cell phone, then realized he didn't know Jasmine's number. He was used to shouting up to her from the street. How could he find out what had happened to Jasmine? Dread streamed through him. He fell into a chair. His body was ice. She had left him, hadn't she? She had told him she couldn't live his life, and he hadn't listened. Cleo and Mo were right.

"Did you have breakfast, Joshie?" his mother asked. She sat down heavily at the Formica table that inexplicably stood in the middle of the living room between the frayed couches like an overgrown coffee table. It was piled with books and stacks of unbound manuscripts. It killed Josh that his parents wouldn't take any of his money so they could move to a bigger place.

Josh stood and walked to her. He planted a kiss on her forehead. "Mom. Dad." He nodded at his father, who stared at him as if he were a ghost. "I have to go."

"But you just came."

Josh peered down twelve stories to the street. There were no photographers there. And no Jasmine. Worry clogged his veins. The Hudson River flowed by, ominous and gray.

His cell phone rang.

"Jas?"

"Honey. It's Mo. She's not coming."

"What? Where are you?"

"I'm on my way uptown to get you. I'm sorry. She went to her friend Jenn's apartment in Hell's Kitchen. I'll be there in three minutes to pick you up."

Josh felt his parents' stony stares. They hadn't accepted the existence of cell phones, which struck them as an inexcusable rudeness.

"He accepts a phone call in our house like it's his office," his mother whispered to his father, loud enough for Josh to hear.

"There's no sacred space anymore," his father whispered back. "What's next? Dinner on the toilet?"

Josh clicked his phone shut.

"Don't you have time for coffee?" his mother asked. "We haven't seen you in ages."

Josh tried not to react to the fact that his mother didn't know how long it had been since she'd seen him. *One thousand, four hundred, and ninety-one days.* "I'll be

back. And I'm bringing someone. I want you to meet her."
A nagging thought in the form of Cleo's voice filled his
head: *You're with Jasmine to please your parents.*

Their eyes widened under their unruly eyebrows.

"Cleo?" his mother asked, as if confused as to why she
would ever want to meet such a woman.

"Cleo and I are just friends," he told his parents.

They stared at him, slack-jawed.

"I knew he couldn't love a woman like that," his father
said.

"No, it's not that," Josh insisted. "Cleo's great. The
coldness is an act. She's an actress. She's good. She's
very nice underneath."

"Is this new one . . . ?" His mother stopped, not wanting to tempt fate.

"Ruth, her name's *Jasmine,*" his father warned.

"She's a gypsy," Josh said.

"Another despised, exiled people!" his dad said happily. He clapped his hands. "I'll go buy bagels."

Josh climbed into the white limousine. "Take me to
her. Now. I'm not messing around, Mo."

Mo nodded at the driver, who U-turned across four
lanes of Riverside Drive as if there weren't speeding taxis
and lumbering buses crashing across every inch of as-
phalt. "Josh, I don't think you should pursue her."

"I'm not asking what you think. This isn't showbiz.
It's my life."

"That's the problem," Mo said. "She can't live your
life. It'll kill her."

"Are you still talking?" he asked, irritated that Mo
might be right. He had to hear it from Jasmine.

Mo crossed her arms and leaned back. "I'm not saying a word."

Josh's cell phone rang. "Jas?"

"Josh. I'm fine. I'm at my friend's."

"I know. I'm on my way." He realized how creepy that must sound. "Mo was making sure you were okay. It's—"

"I know. It's her job. Josh, don't come here."

"Jas—"

"I need time to think about all this. Just give me some time, okay?"

Josh held the phone loosely. "I need to see you."

Silence. He could hear her breathe. "I don't think that's such a good idea. I'm sorry. I don't think I can do this." Her voice caught.

Josh felt like he had been punched in the gut. "Listen, I'm going to take care of all this."

"I'll call you soon. I need time to think," Jasmine said. Then she hung up the phone.

Josh held the dead cell phone to his ear, hoping she might come back.

"It's for the best, hon," Mo said. "You don't have the time or energy for a relationship. Especially with someone who can't handle the exposure. If you back off now, you're sparing her agony."

Josh fell back against the seat. Would it have been better for everyone if Juliet had spared Romeo the agony? Told him she needed time? Told him to beat it? He glanced at Mo. Romeo's publicist would have been pleased.

Josh felt exhausted. Beaten.

Lucky for Romeo, Juliet didn't have a cell phone, Josh thought, staring out the window as New York sped by.

*   *   *

Jenn set Jasmine up on her sofa in a nest of blankets with an unlimited supply of energy bars, fortified muffins, and a thermos of tea. "Now don't go anywhere. I'll be back from work around seven at the latest. I'll send Suz to check on you."

"I'm fine. This is great. I just need to think," Jasmine said. *And order a pizza.* Her stomach was rumbling.

"Good. Think. I have lots of chanting tapes and meditation aids in the bookcase if you need them. Help yourself."

Jasmine nodded politely. She loved Jenn, but she was dying to be alone.

When Jenn finally left for her yoga studio, Jasmine let the full weight of what had happened settle over her.

But what had happened?

I'm in love with a movie star.

Now that was catastrophic thinking.

I had a brief affair with Josh Toby, and now I'm ending it.

There, that was better. She tossed and turned on the lumpy sofa, and before she knew it, she fell asleep.

When Jasmine woke up, the autumn sun had begun to set. The night sky, at least the square of it she could see from Jenn's kitchen window, was orange and hazy with the coming night.

Guess she had been pretty worn-out.

She moved around Jenn's orderly apartment, trying to collect her thoughts. Jenn's message machine was blinking. Jasmine hadn't answered any calls or even checked her cell phone.

I did the right thing. I can't be with him.

She broke off a piece of muffin, tasted it, then tossed it in the trash. No wonder Jenn was so thin.

Josh and I barely know each other. The natural progression of a relationship—time to explore antique shops together, have brunch, go away for long weekends to romantic bed-and-breakfasts—was impossible. By tomorrow, everyone would know her name. She'd have to commit to Josh and he to her before they had time to be sure.

Maybe that was why Hollywood relationships never worked. In the glare of the cameras, you had to deliver your lines. Even if you weren't sure they were true.

How can I miss so badly a man I barely know?

By the time she heard Jenn's key in the lock an hour later, she had decided exactly nothing.

Chapter 24

Suz brought the tabloids the next day. They were worse than Jasmine had feared. On the coffee table in front of her lay the top five rags. She and Josh were on only three of the covers (Oprah had lost ten pounds that week and beat them out for the other two covers; Jasmine had a newfound love for Oprah). But Jasmine's picture was inside all of them in a double-page spread: her in the alley looking pale; her dashing into the subway looking desperate; her, in every shot, looking as alone and miserable as she felt.

She inhaled, trying to drive away the terror of those five minutes. The panic of being cornered in the alley came back to her in a rush. Looking at the pictures made her queasy.

But I miss Josh.

And yet, there it was, proof in four-color, 35-mm focus that they could never be together. She picked up *Holly-wood Dirt* and read from it, trying to quell the quaking that overtook her. A "reporter" had dug through her past and found out she had been "missing" for four years. He ate that up, suggesting that she had been in jail. Plus, he wrote, there were "reports" of a harem in India. A neighbor was quoted as "confirming" that she sold drugs out of her apartment, all those strangers coming and going. TAILORING BUSINESS FLIMSY FRONT FOR FILTH, the headline screamed.

It was only a matter of time before they found Amy and started a whole new hullabaloo about Jasmine's kooky belief in a psychic who professed to know about One True Loves. Jasmine had tried calling Amy all day to beg her not to talk to the press. Cecelia, their oldest sister, had called Jasmine immediately, full of sisterly concern and already sick with the knowledge that it was never smart to trust Amy to do the right thing. Cecelia promised Jasmine she'd hunt Amy down and talk some sense into her, with big-sister force, if necessary.

But Amy not talking to the press was like a fish not swimming in water.

"This is the only one that bugs me," Suz said, holding up the *New York Post*. "The rest are obvious nonsense. But this one's odd."

Jasmine took the paper. It was the gossip page, just a paragraph of type, with names in bold and a stock picture of Josh. *This reporter has heard rumors of Toby's difficult relationship with his parents and his lifelong desire to bring home a girl they'd respect. Could Jasmine Burns be the good little girl that Cleo could never be? Last time Toby came to New York without Chan, he ended up with a woman out to save the whales. We'll keep an eye on this new Girl Scout!*

Jasmine felt the blood drain out of her. "Josh wanted us to go to his parents'."

Suz banged her fist on the table. "Either you're a

druggy slut ex-con or a Girl Scout, but they can't have it both ways."

"I could be a slutty Girl Scout," Jasmine suggested.

"Couldn't she just be a normal woman, in love?" Jenn asked.

Suz shook her head at her friend sadly. "What fun is there in that? No one to hate."

Jasmine held her head in her hands. "I can't stand this anymore. Can we talk about something else?"

"Good! You have to get your mind onto other things," Suz declared. "Go back to work. Get a hobby."

Jasmine tried to clear her head. Of all the nonsense that was written about her, the *Post* article really was strange. "I could search out the other Josh Toby."

"The librarian?" Jenn asked. "Didn't you say he thought you were nuts?"

"Hey! Now there's something. Action. I like it." Suz was already pacing, making a plan.

"I don't understand why Josh doesn't come out and say something to these vultures," Jenn complained, unwilling to disconnect from the issue that interested her most. "He should tell the world that he loves you and that you're great and he's done with Cleo." She paused. "And then you should get married." A deep, dreamy breath. "And introduce me to George Clooney."

Jasmine tried to clear her mind of the complicating secrets that she couldn't tell her friends. "The thought had occurred to me. I mean, that Josh should go public," Jasmine admitted. "But it's not so simple."

"Of course it is," Jenn proclaimed. "'I love Jasmine!' He should scream it from the rooftops."

"Have you spoken to him?" Suz asked.

"He should call *her*," Jenn insisted.

"He does. Every hour on the hour. She doesn't answer."

While they argued, Jasmine drifted to the window. What if Josh did declare that he and Cleo were done? Was that what Jasmine wanted? To strangers, it mattered. But to the three of them, it meant nothing. The right thing to do was tell Josh she didn't care what the world thought. She'd be his secret lover and endure the wrath.

The mere thought of enduring the consequences of that made her insides twist. True Love was not a life of lies.

She thought of Cleo. Flying out to New York. Unwinding herself from the limo. The way she looked up at Jasmine's window.

And all at once Jasmine understood: Cleo loved Josh. She had planted that article in the *Post* about Josh wanting to please his parents. She wasn't going to let him go without a fight. And she had just fired the first shot.

Josh threw down the *Post* in anger. "Who placed this?" he demanded of Mo. Josh knew enough about the press to know that nothing made the papers unless someone wanted it to. Especially something like this. It was a subtle message, just for him.

And for Jasmine.

Mo shrugged.

Josh caught her averted eye. "Oh, no."

Mo shrugged again. "It was bound to happen, Josh. I think it was always in the cards; we were just too preoccupied to see it."

Josh sank as deep as possible into the hotel couch.

Buster and Lassie leapt into his lap. "I'm an idiot," Josh said. "How long have you known?"

"I realized it somewhere over Kansas. Cleo seemed manic. More manic than usual. Then when you got in the limo, it was clear there was something different about you. I think she panicked."

"This just got really complicated, didn't it?" Josh's stomach hit the floor. *Oh, Cleo.* "Where is she? I have to talk to her."

"I think it's about to get more complicated." Mo looked pained.

Josh waited, his eyes closed.

"Cleo found out about Jasmine's sister Amy," Mo said.

"The gypsy?"

"She's a psychic."

"I know. I met her."

"Good. Then you know her special power?"

Josh opened his eyes. "Uh-oh. What?"

"She can tell a person the name of their One True Love."

Josh tried to get his head around that. He didn't believe in psychics, but he didn't *not* believe in them either. Did he believe in One True Love?

Why didn't Jasmine tell me about this?

"According to the sister, Jasmine's One True Love is named Josh Toby."

Josh stopped cold. *Oh. Maybe that was why.* He tried on the idea for size. *One True Love. Jasmine. Fate. Destiny.* "Wait. I think Artie talked to this woman. She sent him to Italy after a childhood sweetheart." Josh felt like he had been hit in the gut. Could the psychic be right?

Were he and Jasmine fated to be together? He had thought so the minute he had seen her in that Indian restaurant, but it was too absurd a thought to contemplate.

But he had felt it.

Mo eyed him warily. "Cleo left two hours ago for Baltimore to see this gypsy. She wants to know once and for all if she should let you go or make her move, and she thinks this Amy can tell her."

The next morning, Josh went to the address Mo had given him. He hadn't enjoyed threatening to fire her for the information, but they both knew she would cave. She was, after all, on his side.

He hoped.

He rang the buzzer. Someone buzzed him up, and he took the stairs two at a time. By the time he reached the sixth floor, he was panting and insanely nervous. What if Jasmine wouldn't open the door? What if she wouldn't speak to him?

The woman who opened the door had strawberry-blond hair and soft blue eyes. She tried not to stare at him but didn't succeed. "Hi. I'm Jenn."

"I have to talk to Jasmine. Please. Is she here?" But he knew the answer before he even finished asking.

Jenn shook her head. "She left half an hour ago. To work."

"She's at the theater?" He had already turned and was halfway down the stairs. He had to see her. Now.

"No." The woman hesitated just enough to let Josh know there was something she wanted to tell him.

He felt sick. He came back to the door.

"I can't tell you where she is. I promised."

Josh felt his world closing in on him.

He didn't like to do this, but he didn't have a choice. He sized up Jenn with an expert appraisal, then drew himself up to full height, shook himself free of the desperate man he was, and let himself become Mitch Tank. His eyelids grew heavy and his voice deepened. He leaned against the wall, letting his head drop and his bangs fall over his face. He counted to five.

This has got to be the best performance of your life, buddy. He turned his face to Jenn. "Break your promise." He looked at her and then looked harder, squinting, putting all his desire for Jasmine into his stare. He held the rest of his body completely still so she could take in the image he hoped he projected—a dangerous man so desperately in love, he might do anything, with anyone, to get the info he needed.

Jenn sighed.

Thanks, Mitch. Josh held the pose. One, two, three—

"Okay!" Jenn cried. She bit her lip, not quite suppressing a smile. "She went to the library. New York Public. It's on Fifth and Forty-fifth. She's going to kill me."

"The library?" Josh became himself again, his body stiff with anxiety. "The librarian?"

Jenn nodded. She looked confused, as if half of her was aware that she'd betrayed her friend while the other half was still drunk with the pure pleasure of letting herself be seduced by Mitch Tank.

"Is his name . . . ?" Josh paused. He already knew the answer. A darkness flooded his veins.

"Josh Toby," Jenn confirmed.

Josh felt like he'd been punched in the gut again. *Another Josh Toby. Jasmine's One True Love?* He turned to go. Then turned back. He took Jenn's hand, truly grateful.

Jenn gulped, her eyes dreamy and unfocused.

He raised her hand to his lips and kissed it. *This one's from the real Josh.* "Thank you."

"Thank *you*," she said, somewhat breathless.

But Josh was halfway down the stairs, cell phone pressed to his ear.

Jasmine sat in the morning chill on the granite steps of the library, reliving the nightmare of the last few days. She studied the library's grand entrance. The early morning sun had disappeared, and gray clouds moved in, making the November chill more severe. People in suits stood in line for bagels from the street vendor on the corner, rubbing their hands together to keep warm.

Jasmine looked forward to winter. She imagined snow covering the streets, burying the grime, making the endless streams of people scurry inside for cover. She liked the quiet life. Silence sustained her.

Reason number 457 I can't be with Josh.

Maybe she could go back to India. The thought had occurred to her more and more frequently over the last two days. She could almost hear the cuckoos that pecked at the dust and sang in the early morning coolness. The hot sun. The barefoot children. The smell of curry in the air by nine in the morning. And the fabric that draped the women. Reds and oranges, blues and greens, flashing silks.

Raj. His friends. Her humiliation.

Her memories of Raj melted into memories of her sisters. Was Raj a way for her to focus away from what really bugged her? That her sisters had rejected her? Hated her? Their life was one of small-time cons, a struggle to survive. She could still feel her sisters' disapproval of her softer, quieter ways. She had wanted so badly to prove she was tough like them. But they hadn't fallen for it. So she went to seek out toughness.

She had left her sisters a note and disappeared.

But a hard life wasn't in her cards. The four years she spent in Ohio still filled her with nostalgia. She had hooked up with a local theater company. Mrs. Engelton, the old woman who ran the costume shop, didn't ask questions about the girl who slept on the rusty cot in the back corner, because she was kind and because Jasmine could sew. When Jasmine was four, her Indian nanny, her aya Amita, had taught her to use a needle, to understand fabric as a living, flowing force. The four years Jasmine spent at the theater under Mrs. Engelton's wing had solidified her skills in turning fabric into language.

And turning herself invisible.

She was a master at both.

Until now.

Jasmine watched the sidewalk for Josh Toby, reference librarian. Josh Toby, her One True Love? With the other Josh having gone so terribly wrong, she had to give this Josh another chance.

"Jasmine?"

Jasmine turned, startled.

It was a blond woman. A blond woman who knew her name.

Chapter 25

The woman was striking, in a pale blue linen dress under a black wool coat. Both designer. The curve of the lapel was the signature of Valentino. This season. Not cheap. Her hair was endless and so blond, it seemed possible that it had sucked up all the sunshine that had once belonged to the day. Jasmine watched the woman open the lid of her coffee, inhale, then close it again.

Now what? Was she a reporter? A stalker?

"I'm Maureen." The woman was suddenly next to Jasmine.

"Doing a little before-breakfast stalking?" Jasmine asked. The crush of commuters streaming past was thickening as nine o'clock approached. *Wait, that name rings a bell.*

The woman inched closer. "People call me Mo. I'm Cleo and Josh's publicist."

Mo. Jasmine went pale. She preferred to be followed by the paparazzi rather than by this otherworldly being. What could Josh and Cleo's publicist want with her other than to warn her to bug off? Jasmine looked around. "Is Cleo here?"

"No." Mo opened the lid again, letting a cloud of steam escape her coffee. "I don't actually drink the coffee. I just inhale it. My system can't abide caffeine." She put her nose close to the Styrofoam and breathed deeply.

Jasmine didn't know what to say. *So, how's today's stalking, you Hollywood weirdo coffee inhaler?*

"You want it?" Mo held out the cup to Jasmine. "I've had my fill."

Jasmine did want the coffee. Badly. All Jenn had in her kitchen was chai and herbal tea. But did you accept gifts from stalkers who were about to tell you to scram? Maybe from stalkers with hair made of sunshine who could pull off light blue linen in November. She wanted to touch the fabric, test its weight. "Sure."

Mo handed her the cup as if she were handing her something sacred and ancient.

It was a mochaccino skinny latte. Guess when your bosses were multimillionaires, you could afford pricey coffee you never intended to drink. *Hope it's not poisoned.* Scenes from *Romeo and Juliet* came to Jasmine. *The friar gives Juliet a "death" potion; Juliet must appear to die in order to live.*

Please return to the real world! It's Starbucks, for crying out loud.

"Cleo's not here," Mo said after watching Jasmine drink the coffee. "It's hard for her to come out. She gets recognized, mobbed." Mo scanned Jasmine's face, as if trying to read how she was taking that tidbit of info on the miserable lives of the rich and famous.

"Can't imagine what that's like," Jasmine said finally.

Mo smiled so gently, Jasmine was afraid the woman

was going to reach out and touch her. "Welcome to their world."

"It's quite a world," Jasmine said. Part of her wanted to inch away, but part of her resisted. Maybe she was desperate to talk to someone who understood Josh. But this would be the scene where Mo tried to scare Jasmine away. *Not necessary,* Jasmine wanted to tell her. *I'm already gone.*

"I know about your sister Amy. I know about your One True Love. I know about the librarian."

Jasmine's mouth fell open.

"It's my job. If you know Josh, I know you. I have to. There are too many crazies who want a piece of him."

"Did you tell Josh?" Jasmine's body had turned to ice. *Mo must think I'm one of the crazies. Wait, she sniffs coffee fumes. We're even.*

"He knows."

Jasmine tried not to jump up and strangle the woman for information: W*hat did he say when he found out I think he's my fate, my destiny?* Now Jasmine wished the coffee *were* a death potion. Actually, she didn't need it. She could die right there on the steps from embarrassment.

Mo sat calmly, contemplating the cloudy sky. "So, is that how you feel about Josh? Is he your One True Love? I can help make it work if you want it to work. I'm not your enemy. We just have to get the spin right."

"The spin?"

"For the press. We can't have what we had at your apartment. I usually handle that. I didn't expect Samantha to reject our offer."

"Your offer?"

"To keep quiet. We offered her a quarter million."

"I don't think she cares about money."

"I misread her." Mo shook her head sadly.

Jasmine was relieved that Mo's scary know-everything aura had broken down at least once. She struggled to find words for the nagging discomfort she felt ever since seeing Josh on the steps of her apartment surrounded by the mob. Maybe this woman could explain Josh. Make it all better. "It's not the cameras so much as the way he is in front of the cameras."

"He has a dual life. He wants to please his fans. He wants to please his parents. The two don't mix, so he's in constant conflict."

"What about pleasing himself?"

"There's one thing you need to understand about Josh, about any star: He lives to please others. That's what pleases him. He's a very public person."

Who is he pleasing when he's with me? In bed? Jasmine shuddered at the thought.

"Look, there's your librarian," Mo said.

God, this woman was worse than Amy with the know-it-all business. Only Amy used spirit guides. This woman must have an army of private detectives at her disposal.

"Quick, tell me what you want," Mo said.

"I want to be a normal person."

Mo nodded.

"Wait, I didn't mean normal like not famous. I meant normal as in not afraid of stupid things that normal people—" Jasmine stopped, frozen. Josh Toby, librarian, had spotted Jasmine. He waved and headed toward her.

"Hi, Jasmine. How've you been?" Josh Toby, librarian, stood before her, smiling sweetly. He wore black jeans and a ratty off-brand overcoat. His scarf was polyester. "I was worried about you."

"Hello." There it was again—pure ease. Jasmine tried not to react to the joy of it. "Josh, this is my friend Mo." Jasmine gestured to her right.

But Mo was gone.

"Hello, Mo," Josh said politely to the space where Mo had been. "It's nice to meet you." Then he turned back to Jasmine. "I was wondering how you were. It's been weeks since you've come to visit us."

Jasmine looked around for Mo, aware that her distraction was making her look even nuttier. "She was right there. Really. She's Cleo Chan's assistant. I guess that sounds sort of odd. This has been the oddest week."

Josh startled slightly at the mention of Cleo Chan. "You look tired. What happened to your pants?"

Jasmine looked at a rip in her jeans that she hadn't noticed before. She had been wearing the same jeans for days. "Oh, a guy with a camera was chasing me down an alley a few days ago . . ." She stopped at Josh's alarmed look. "He just wanted a picture. You know, they hide in alleys."

"Do they?" he asked politely.

"They were really after my friend. He's sort of famous." Why was it that the one man in the universe she could speak to was also the one man she really ought to shut up around?

"Hey, I have something for you," Josh said, sparing himself a response to what he obviously thought was a grand delusion. "I've been carrying it around forever." He opened his brown leather bag.

He pulled out a small, red leather book. "*Romeo and*

Juliet, pocket edition. I found it at The Strand, and I thought of you."

Jasmine accepted the book. "Thanks. This is . . . *perfect.*" Jasmine thought of the other Josh at the center of the mob. *Not perfect.* She flipped through the book.

Josh looked at his Timex, then jumped up. "I've got to get to work. I'm glad to see you're well." He turned to the empty space beside her. "Nice to meet you, too, Mo. Come in and get warm, okay?" Then he turned and hustled up the stairs. Jasmine watched him show his ID, slip into the building, and disappear.

She waited a few moments to see if Mo would reappear in a burst of sky-blue smoke. Maybe she had never been there. Maybe Jasmine had imagined the whole conversation.

No, she couldn't imagine shimmering, pale-blue linen that looked good in November.

When she was sure Mo wasn't going to reappear, she considered her options. She could go to the theater and work. Even though she had been working at Jenn's, she was still falling behind on the sketches. She should be starting muslin mock-ups of the main pieces by now. She drank the last drop of Mo's coffee. A cold wind had started to blow. The street was emptying of the get-to-work crowd, and the remaining stragglers walked slower, often in pairs.

Pairs.

Jasmine tried to contain the aching sorrow that was overtaking her. If Librarian Josh was so right, why was she still sitting here? She was calm and at ease around him. But it didn't feel like love.

If it *was* love, did she even want it?

Maybe Movie Star Josh was her One True Love, and she had experienced him, and now she had to let him go. Amy never promised that True Love would bring happiness. You were lucky if you got a taste.

Jasmine's head ached. A church bell tolled in the distance, and the guards threw open the library doors for the waiting crowd. A crowd of readers. This was so much more her speed.

Jasmine watched the people stream inside. *I believe that love brings happiness.* How could True Love bring only misery? Maybe Librarian Josh was the One after all.

She was going into that library to explain her sanity to him once and for all.

At this point, what did she have to lose?

Josh wasn't the least bit surprised to see his publicist sitting on the steps of the library. He sat down next to her on the cold granite and nodded.

"Nice day," Mo said.

"Not bad," he remarked.

They sat in silence.

"Okay, fill me in," he said finally.

"Jasmine is here to see another Josh Toby. He's a librarian."

"I'm way ahead of you. What else?"

"He's not a bad guy," Mo reported, trying to hold her voice neutral.

The words struck Josh solid in the gut. "You're trying to say that maybe this Josh Toby is the right one? That I'm not the knight in shining armor, coming to rescue her?"

"It's not the movies, hon."

Josh sat back on his elbows. "Maybe I'm the wrong guy for the part. I should leave her alone. Let her get on with her life. Let her decide." He tried to keep the building fear out of his voice. A librarian? It was perfect for her. Was it fate? Did he believe in fate?

"She did decide, honey. She's here."

Josh let Mo's words sink in like jagged glass. Why hadn't Jasmine told him about the prophecy? Maybe she thought he'd think she was nuts too. But who says that spirits don't exist? No one knows for sure.

Jasmine believes in a prophecy that says she is destined to love a man named Josh Toby. Okay, fine. He could believe that. Hell, he had friends who believed carbohydrates were the work of the devil. True Love made sense at least. *There is one person on this earth meant for me.*

But which Josh Toby was meant for Jasmine?

Me.

He felt it as surely as he felt the cold, hard step under him. "You're wrong, Mo. I'm the one."

"Josh, when you were with the paparazzi, I watched Jasmine sneak out the back alley. Fat Larry was there, waiting. She looked like death, like she was being tortured. She could barely make it down the street."

Josh winced. "Fat Larry. That bastard. I should have known it was him from the awful look in Jasmine's eyes in those shots." Josh watched a pigeon land on the head of one of the stone lions. He imagined Jasmine in the alley with that rat of a photographer. He was one of the most aggressive of the bunch. Josh felt ill.

"You have to let her go, Josh. She might make you happy, but your life makes her miserable."

"Unless I give it up." His words surprised him.

"Give up Hollywood?" Mo raised her eyebrows.

Josh turned to Mo. Who was she really working for? Him or Cleo? Or playing both sides for herself? "I need one more chance. I really love her, Mo. You're my friend. Help me."

Mo didn't miss a beat. "Jasmine's in the third-floor reading room, center door. I'll wait here in case you need backup."

Josh went to the room Mo described, and there was Jasmine, reading a tiny red book at the center of an enormous mahogany table. Readers sat scattered around the room, deep in concentration. The silence echoed off the twenty-foot ceiling.

Josh stepped into the room as if entering a church. He pulled off his Yankees cap and stuffed it into his back pocket. But before he got close enough to speak, he stopped.

Chapter 26

A tall man with orange hair entered the room from a hidden door built into the back wall. He sat down next to Jasmine.

Her face brightened at the sight of him, and they leaned their heads together. They seemed to be discussing something in the book.

Josh moved farther into the room, but away from Jasmine. He wished he had a book to hide behind. Instead, he slipped into a seat and lowered his head to watch.

The man whispered something in Jasmine's ear, and she responded with an open, easy face. She pointed to something in the text and the man nodded; then she smiled again. Josh's heart sank.

It had taken him days to get her to smile at him like that.

Why wasn't she nervous around this guy? A rioting surge of jealousy rose in his gut.

Prophecy?

Maybe he's her brother.

A librarian passed his table, pushing a cart stacked with ancient-looking dusty books. "Hey," Josh said as quietly as he could while still getting the librarian's attention. "Is that Josh Toby?"

The woman glanced where Josh pointed. "Yep. Head reference librarian. On break, I suppose." She continued on, her cart's right front wheel squeaking. When she was a few feet away, she stopped again and looked back at Josh quizzically.

He ducked his head.

She continued to stare, open-mouthed.

He pulled out his baseball cap and yanked it down over his eyes.

She shook her head, as if shaking away a ghost, and went on her way.

Josh concentrated on Jasmine.

He thought of what Mo had said to him. *You have to let her go, Josh. She might make you happy, but your life makes her miserable.*

Was it true? Was he being selfish wanting Jasmine? He had to talk to her. But he hesitated. Something was stopping him from intruding on the conversation she was having with the other Josh Toby.

I love her. Why was he hesitating breaking up a conversation she was having with another man? It didn't make any sense.

He stood.

Then sank back into his chair.

I will mess up her life.

He had so much. So much money. So much fame. And she was struggling for . . . for what? Had he ever even asked her what she wanted? The job, of course. He had helped her with that, helped her to shine at the production meeting.

But this wasn't about a career. It was about what really mattered.

She wanted to be a normal person without her debilitating shyness around men. She didn't have to tell him that. He saw it in her eyes, always. It was her constant struggle. He'd have to be an idiot not to have seen that.

But here she was, in public, with a man, relaxed.

Wasn't that what he had promised her on Halloween?

She was okay with me in the bedroom, just us together. She was better than okay.

But maybe being okay in bed wasn't enough. They couldn't spend their whole lives in bed. *Too bad about that.*

Josh stood and began making his way out of the library. It was best. It was right. He got to the doorway and took one last look back.

The man took Jasmine's hand. The hand that had slid down his back, making him mad with desire.

No way, Mr. Toby!

Josh strode back into the room.

Jasmine loves me and I love her. That was all that mattered. The rest would follow. To hell with being at ease. Love wasn't about ease and not being afraid. Love was about being terrified. Just look at Romeo and Juliet. Hell, *he* was terrified. He'd be nuts not to be terrified of a connection as strong as the one they had experienced.

Maybe letting her go was the right thing.

But if there was one thing he was determined to change about his life, it was that from now on, he wasn't going to choose the right thing.

He was, for the first time in his life, going to choose love.

Chapter 27

"Hi." Josh nodded at the other Josh and sat down next to Jasmine. "How are you?"

Jasmine sucked in her breath. *Both Joshes at once.* Her throat began to close. She forced out introductions. "Oh. Um. Right. Ah. Josh, this is Josh."

Josh held out his hand. "Josh Toby, head reference librarian."

Josh shook it. "Josh Toby, movie star."

Librarian Josh didn't blink. "Nice to meet you."

Jasmine choked on whatever ridiculous words her mouth was conspiring to disgorge. Was Librarian Josh going to offer Movie Star Josh the soup kitchen and counseling with Dan from Human Services? She glanced up at Elvis and his friends at the far table. Elvis waved happily.

"We have to talk." Movie Star Josh took Jasmine's hand.

"Where are the photographers?" Jasmine looked around the vast room.

Librarian Josh raised his eyebrows. He scanned the room for the invisible photographers. "No cameras in the library," Librarian Josh warned. His gaze stopped on Josh. "You look so much like him."

"Like who?" Josh looked up at him.

"The movie star. Josh Toby."

"I am the movie star Josh Toby."

"Right. And that's Elvis. And that's Jesus."

The two men waved from their seats across the room. Jesus was doing a word search.

"And," Librarian Josh added, "Jasmine here is my One True Love. You can be whoever you like here as long as you're quiet and respectful."

Jasmine made a small, animal-like sound. Mo had already told Movie Star Josh about the prophecy. Yet, she felt her face go hot as the fact sunk in. That was all she needed, another man thinking she was nuts.

"Mo told me about the prophecy," Josh confirmed. "Why didn't you tell me?"

She was frozen with embarrassment. Why didn't she tell the sexiest man alive that she believed a gypsy prophecy ordained that she was his One True Love? Jasmine felt herself slip down the hard wooden chair. *Oh, please, let me slide under the table and disappear.*

"Jas?" Movie Star Josh stopped her escape with a solid hand on her shoulder. "Talk to me."

Librarian Josh was on one side of her. "I *am* a huge fan of Cleo Chan," he said. His eyes had lost their focus, and he wasn't speaking to anyone in particular. "We went to high school together."

Breathe. In. Out. Breathe. Jasmine turned to look first at one Josh, then the other. As long as Jasmine kept her eyes on Librarian Josh, she could inhale the air in the room. The moment she looked at Movie Star Josh, the oxygen sucked out of the room like a giant vacuum. It was like bobbing underwater, then coming up for air.

Librarian Josh seemed to come out of his trance. "I think you're upsetting Jasmine. I'll have to ask you not to bother the patrons, sir."

"I'm not backing down, Jas," Movie Star Josh said, ignoring the librarian.

She looked from man to man. Underwater. Above. Under. Above.

Both Joshes watched her with growing concern.

Josh took Jasmine's hand in his. "Please? Can we go somewhere private? I have something I need to say."

Jasmine fixed her eyes on the spine of the small red book. Librarian Josh had carried around the book for weeks. It was so touching, it made her heart ache.

Movie Star Josh was staring at her as if she had two heads.

Right. She had to focus. He was asking her to talk about the possibility of enduring a life of madmen chasing them. *He was asking her to choose him.*

The terror of the paparazzi came back to her. The flashing cameras. The fat man's sweaty hand on her arm. She had to end this now, in person. It was only fair not to dump the world's biggest movie star by cell phone. "Okay. We'll talk." She turned to Librarian Josh. "Is there somewhere private?"

Librarian Josh hesitated, then led them to the invisible door in the wall. He clicked a hidden notch that served as the handle and opened the door. Jasmine and Movie Star Josh stepped in through the doorway.

"There's a box of old clothes in the staff room. Lots

of winter stuff. Take what you need. But no stealing from the staff fridge!" Librarian Josh warned them sternly just before the door clicked closed behind them.

Jasmine and Josh found themselves alone in a dark hallway, lit by a single, bare, overhead bulb. Déjà vu flooded her as she thought of their last hallway encounter at 109th Street, before Josh had faced the paparazzi. At least Josh was going to keep his clothes on this time.

Hopefully.

An orange glow from a small room off the hallway drew them both to it.

It could have been a sitting room in a Jane Austen novel. In fact, Jasmine had the distinct impression that Tolstoy or Edgar Allan Poe or even Austen herself might join them at any moment. This was, after all, the bowels of the New York Public Library. Who knew what ghosts found a home here? If Shakespeare showed up, she'd like to show him what she did with Juliet's dress in the balcony scene. He'd know exactly the mood she had been after and approve.

A carved, mahogany coatrack held several overcoats. She recognized Josh's ragged coat from earlier that morning when she met him on the steps. Sure enough, there was an oven-sized box of used clothing, overflowing with parkas and ski hats. The only sound in the room was the humming of a small refrigerator in the corner.

They sank onto the overstuffed couch. Jasmine wished the room had a window to distract her. There was nothing but her and Josh in this room. She had to face him.

"Spooky," Josh said. "I feel like Willie Shakespeare's

about to come and tell me a thing or two about my pathetic Romeo."

"Your Romeo isn't pathetic." Jasmine couldn't believe how much she had missed him in just a few short days. She could feel her body pulling toward him as if he were magnetic. But her mind was shouting, *Run!*

"You haven't seen me onstage," Josh protested. "Rehearsals start next week."

Jasmine was grateful for the change of subject, but she had to hurry and say what she needed to say before she dove into the box of coats to hide. "Josh. We can't be together. I'm sorry."

If Josh was surprised, he didn't show it. "Wait—"

But Jasmine rushed on. "Seeing you with those photographers was like seeing a stranger. You were great up there. They loved you. You looked so at home and natural." Jasmine paused. Her heart was beating wildly. "But meanwhile, I was trying not to barf in the alley while that photographer attacked me."

A shadow passed over Josh's face. "I'm so sorry." He scooted closer to her.

"No. Stop." She pushed him away. "I don't want you to be sorry. Don't you see? When you're with me, you're diminished. You can't be you. And when I'm with you . . ."

Josh pulled himself back up on the couch. "You're barfing in an alley." He let his elbows rest on his knees. He combed his fingers through his hair. "I don't love the attention. It doesn't bother me, but I never loved it. It's part of the job. But I can change that. I can cut back on work. Even take a few years off."

Jasmine's head swirled. She closed her eyes to fight

the vertigo. "You need to act, Josh. I can't be responsible for you walking away from what you love."

"I don't care about it. I care about us."

"But you do, Josh. And that's okay. Who hasn't dreamed of being the center of things, being loved, admired?"

"Have you?"

The question stopped Jasmine cold. Did she want to hide, or was it only her nerves that forced her into hiding? She hadn't thought about it before.

Josh spared her an answer. "What do you want, Jasmine? To go on being the same old you? Or do you want to change? To be more? To brave it?"

Jasmine took his hands. "Josh, I can't go out there and be with you. I thought I could, but I just can't. The idea of being in the public eye with you—even just for a day—makes me physically ill."

"Is it the librarian?" Josh asked.

"No. Not him. Really. He still thinks I'm nuts. Actually, now he thinks you're nuts too. But this isn't about him."

"The prophecy. You believe it, don't you?"

"Yes, I do believe it. Amy has amazing powers. I've seen them in action. But all she gets is a name. My One True Love could be either of you. Or neither one of you. He could be some mechanic in Iowa named Josh Toby."

"So, couldn't Amy do more voodoo and know if my True Love is Jasmine Burns? Wouldn't that confirm it?"

"It's not so simple. She lost her powers. She doesn't hear the names anymore."

"So the only way to know if I'm the right Josh Toby—"

"Is to know." Jasmine stood up. She paced the tiny room.

"What we have—" Josh tried to catch her arm.

"What we *had* was impossible. I can't live with the chaos, and you can't live without it. You and me out of the bedroom doesn't work."

"I don't have a problem with that." Josh took her in his arms, but she shook him off, trying not to smile at his lame joke.

"What we had wasn't a life. I can't expect you to live in my world any more than you can expect me to live in yours. I saw you up there, Josh. You were glowing. You were alive."

Josh shook his head. "I don't accept this. I know you can do it."

"It's not yours to accept, Josh. It's my decision. I can't be with you. Don't you see that? I just can't."

Chapter 28

Five days later, the costume shop buzzed with four-weeks-to-curtain frenzy. The milliner, the infamous Lola Barracuda, a three-hundred-pound black woman with an impenetrable Jamaican accent, sat between two impossibly skinny and pale blond assistants. Jasmine sat across from them, taking them one by one through her sketches of thirty-three hats. And those were just the hats for Juliet.

They leaned over the sketches, Lola emitting the occasional grunt. Jasmine wished she cared more, but she couldn't get her mind off Fat Larry, who was sitting at a coffee shop down the street from the theater. At least worrying about Fat Larry was a welcome break from the endless days of being unable to take her mind off Josh. He had disappeared since they had spoken at the library.

Vanished.

She missed his smile. Missed his jumpy dogs. Missed talking to him about nothing. Missed making love.

But rehearsals started today. Act I, Scene I, onstage at 10:00 AM. Josh would have to show—unless he bailed.

And he might bail. Ever since Samantha leaked to the

papers that Josh was doing Romeo, the buzz began. The articles, the fans, the camera crews.

And Fat Larry.

Fat Larry had offered Jasmine a quarter-million dollars to do an insider exposé on Josh's "previously suspected" drug problem. He laughed and accepted full credit for making up the original story about Jasmine being a drug dealer when she accused him of it. He kept shoving the contract at her, telling her that her side of the story to go with the alley pictures would make her a star. When she refused to take the contract, he slipped it under Jenn's door. She shuddered to think how he had gotten into the building. The papers outlined that she'd have to offer up at least three original "facts" about Josh's sexual preferences, three "facts" about his drug preferences, and three photographs of them together.

Well, that last one was certainly a deal killer.

Jasmine flipped the page to hat #34, the first of Romeo's hats. The first sketch was more a hood, for his secret wedding to Juliet. Lola grunted and took undecipherable notes.

Without Josh around, Jasmine had hoped the attention would go away. Instead, besides the growing crowd outside the theater, she was getting a whole new kind of attention—from her family. Amy vowed to come up and fend off the worst of the press, but Jasmine was sure Amy wanted to come to get her slice of the action. Jasmine was even a little worried that Amy wasn't here already. It struck her as suspicious that Amy hadn't hopped on the first train. After all, Amy and Fat Larry were made for each other. *True Love or True Flake?* the headlines would ask with a picture of Jasmine below. Jasmine hoped she wouldn't have to find out if it was better to be considered crazy or a drug dealer.

Cecelia, Jasmine's other sister, begged Jasmine to come to Baltimore. She warned that Amy was up to something, although she admitted she didn't know what. But the costumes were being stitched now, so Jasmine couldn't leave. Especially since Arturo still hadn't shown up from Rome.

Jasmine glanced at the clock. Rehearsals were starting in twenty minutes. She had no idea if Josh would show up or not. She'd ask the stage manager if he was expected, but everyone gave her a wide berth now that she was a semifamous drug dealer. Either that, or they smothered her with attention, fishing for an invitation to her and Josh's first drug-dealer/sex-star dinner party.

Samantha was firmly in the latter category. Not that Jasmine had spoken to her since the paparazzi incident. What was there to say?

So what if Josh did come back for rehearsals? Jasmine stood by what she had said; she couldn't live his life. She had hate mail from Josh's fans all over the world to prove it. Her mail was now delivered in plastic U.S. Post Office bins that Suz picked up every day and threatened to dump in the trash. But Jasmine *wanted* to see them, to solidify the rightness of her decision. Nothing like strangers ranting against her evil plan to pull Josh into the lurid underworld of sex and drugs to convince her she had done the right thing. Plus, she had to turn the death threats over to the police, even if she didn't take them seriously herself.

She did miss the feel of Josh's hand running through her hair.

The way he looked at her like she was the only woman on earth.

The way—

"So, you get that for me by the end of today, sugar?" Lola asked in her heavy Jamaican lilt.

Jasmine broke out of her reverie. "Hmm?"

The enormous woman shook her head sadly. "I thought the drugs was just tabloid lies."

"It was! I mean, is."

The woman sighed. "I need Romeo's hat size. By the end of today. I have to make him eight hats, sugar."

"I'll have the costume shop manager get it for you."

"Good." Lola covered Jasmine's hand with her own. She leaned in close, her nose almost touching Jasmine's. "I've seen genius and I've seen genius destroyed, sugar. You have the gift. I know these aren't Artie's designs. Artie could never have done these. They are yours and they are magical." The woman opened her eyes wide, showing the whites all around her pupils. She lowered her voice and practically growled, "So get off the drugs and get your man, sugar. If anyone deserves the sexiest man alive, it's a woman who can design hats like this."

Josh waited outside the door to his Santa Monica house, praying Cleo was home. He held a bouquet of calla lilies and a two-pound box of Godivas. He hadn't shaved in days, and his eyes felt heavy. He jingled the keys in his pocket. He could just go in, but it didn't feel right. He had been calling Cleo for days, but she wouldn't answer his calls. The only way was to come to L.A. and see her, even though he longed for New York. He rang the bell again.

Maybe she wasn't here. Relief flooded through him.

Coward. He peered in the window and saw a familiar-looking brown suitcase. So beat up, it couldn't possibly be Cleo's. Déjà vu flooded him, but he shook it off. *I'm just spooked.*

He unlocked the door and pushed it open. "Cleo?" His voice echoed off the bare floors. There was the unusual smell of cinnamon and clove in the air. Herbal tea, maybe.

Mo had assured him Cleo was back in L.A. In fact, he had spoken to Mo ten minutes ago, and she had checked for him by cell phone—Cleo was in the house. Mo wouldn't lie. Josh understood that Mo hoped he would fall in love with Cleo now that he knew she loved him. Solve all their problems.

If it was true.

A tiny part of Josh wished it was true.

What if it was true and he just had never realized it?

His practiced speech ran through his head. *You should have told me, Cleo. I never would have agreed to this arrangement if I had known. I do love you, you know. Just not in that way. I wish I could say why. You're a beautiful woman. A beautiful person. Who knows what makes a person fall in love?*

Voices emerged from the back screening room. Music too. A soundtrack. Cleo must be in there watching a movie. Probably dailies from her current project. Josh moved through the familiar house with a deep sense of emptiness. *This has never been my home.* There was too much travel, too much shooting on location. This place was bare, cold, white—a set for a made-up life.

He pushed open the door of the screening room.

Cleo sat in the first row.

"Cleo?" He could only see the back of her head. Even in the darkness, her hair shone. She didn't turn around.

"I love you," he said. Or rather, an image of him, ten years younger, said on the screen. Cleo was watching the last movie they had done together. Of course, he should have recognized the soundtrack.

"I love you too," the screen version of Cleo answered as she fell into his arms.

Josh clenched his teeth as his heart twisted in pain. Cleo in the dark, watching their old love scenes. How long had she been at this?

A close-up kiss filled the six-foot screen.

Josh moved down the four rows to the front of their private theater. He sat down next to Cleo. There was a basket full of wadded-up tissues at her feet.

She didn't acknowledge him.

He couldn't be sure in the dark, but it seemed as if she wasn't wearing makeup. He couldn't remember the last time he'd seen her without makeup. She looked like a child.

On the screen, her eyes drifted shut. Her hands moved through his hair. He pulled her closer. They had shot this scene four times before the director was satisfied. "The endless kiss," the crew had grumbled. "What we suffer through for money," he had joked.

The memory shot fresh jolts of pain through him.

He put his hand on hers. "Cleo. It wasn't real."

Cleo shook her head. Her voice was a whisper. "It was real for me."

The lovers on the screen had fallen into bed. They removed each other's clothes with reverence and incredible lighting. "I do love you, Cleo. I've always loved you. Just not like that. It can't ever be."

She looked at him for the first time. Her eyes were moist with hurt and shame.

"You're my best friend. Don't do this," he said.

"Shhh." She looked back to the screen.

The two people on the screen looked like strangers to Josh. The movie had been a huge hit. Their fans had gone wild, thrilled by the chemistry and the fire they swore they witnessed between them.

Josh braced himself for the end of the scene. Their perfect bodies moved together, both of them fully greased with baby oil. He could still conjure the smell. The camera caressed her thigh. His shoulders. A close-up of his hand running down her arching back. A quick cut of a body double's breast. Then the climax. Cleo's head thrown back in mock ecstasy.

God, he hoped it was mock ecstasy.

He looked at the real Cleo and winced as a single tear rolled down her cheek.

He realized then with terrible clarity what he should have realized before: She wasn't that good an actor. *It was real.*

"I've been an idiot."

She nodded as the screen went to black.

His mind raced with all the things he should say. Then, before he could speak, another scene started. From his cameo appearance on her *Agent X* HBO show. Another kiss. Another bedroom.

Another tear following the first.

"I'm sorry," he said softly. And he was sorry, because even at that moment, he was thinking of Jasmine.

So he did the only kind thing he could think to do.

He got up quietly and left.

Jasmine, Suz, and Jenn sat around a small table at Madeline's. The two friends ate while Jasmine stared at her sandwich.

Josh hadn't shown up for the first day of rehearsal, and Jasmine couldn't believe how empty she felt.

Her friends watched her with concern, shooting each other worried looks.

She had spent the whole day yesterday in a state of agitation. The costume shop was in the back of the theater, on the second floor, in a corner that looked out over a dingy alley, so it wasn't easy to check the stage all afternoon without seeming anxious. After her third trip in the shadows to the stage, she overheard the prop master suggest to one of his assistants that she was probably looking for drugs.

"Jas?" Jenn ventured. "Why don't you come and take my masters 6:00 AM. Ashtanga class before work tomorrow? It might loosen you up."

Jasmine shrugged. "No, thanks."

"Jas?" Suz leaned in. "Let's get some of those cheap tickets to Cancun this weekend. It's still hurricane season, so they're dirt cheap. Margaritas on the beach. Maybe some emergency tsunami drills with the cute pool boys."

Jasmine poked at her sandwich. "Gotta work."

"I don't get it," Jenn ventured. "If you're so miserable, why don't you talk to him?"

"There's nothing to say."

"How about, 'I'm an idiot. Let's try again,'" Jenn suggested.

Suz straightened in her chair. She nudged Jenn. They both turned white.

"What?" Jasmine asked.

They were both silent.

"Is there food between my teeth?" Jasmine ran her tongue along her top teeth.

"That's too bad you don't want to talk to him, Jas," Suz said breathlessly. "Because guess who just walked in."

Chapter 29

Jasmine looked up and her heart—the traitor—filled with hope.

Josh stood in the front of the restaurant in blue jeans and an untucked blue shirt. The bag slung over his shoulder still had an American Airline security tag plastered on its side. He wasn't wearing his usual Yankees cap, and Jasmine could see his eyes clearly.

Looking right at her.

She froze. Her stomach backflipped in joy. Then frontflipped in despair. He had been on a plane. Which probably meant he had been in L.A. Which probably meant he had been with Cleo.

Geez, what did she care? She had dumped him, after all.

Jenn raised herself into perfect posture. "Oh, my. Oh, my."

"I have banished Josh from my life. My decision is final," Jasmine recited. She tried to recall the terror of being cornered in the alley, but it was wiped out by the intensity of his shining eyes.

"Goody. Then he's mine," Suz said. She flattened her already perfectly flat hair with her hands.

"No, mine," Jenn corrected. Her freckled arms were covered in goose bumps. She glanced at Jasmine. "Oh, dear, are you okay? You look dead-white. We were just kidding."

Madeline hurried over to Josh, blocking everyone's view. Jasmine watched in horror as Madeleine turned and pointed right at her.

Josh thanked her with a knockout smile and headed straight for their table.

"Don't you guys dare leave," Jasmine commanded.

"I'm not missing this for the world," Suz said.

"We're leaving," Jenn said. But she didn't budge.

With each step that brought him closer, Jasmine felt her heart beat faster.

And what a walk. His loose limbs. The way those hips moved those legs. It was so unfair.

"Is this seat taken?" He stood before them, violet eyes blazing.

"Josh." Jasmine tried not to look happy. "This is Suzie. And Jennifer."

"Hello," they said in unison. They scanned every last inch of him.

The restaurant had gone silent. Every woman stared, open-mouthed. The *ticktock* of the clock on the wall echoed in the silence.

"Nice to meet you." He flashed his million-dollar smile at Suz. Then he turned his gaze to Jenn. "We've met before." He held out a hand. Jenn's hands flew to her chest. Suz licked her lips.

"Nice. You. Meeting. Again," Jenn sputtered. She shook his hand, then didn't let go.

"Nice," Suz added. But she was too frozen to shake.

"Jasmine, can we talk?" Josh asked. He gently disengaged his hand from Jenn's.

"Sure. Pull up a chair," Jasmine said. She tried to still her thumping heart.

Jenn shook out of her lust-induced trance and elbowed Suz. "We were just leaving."

"We were? Good God, why?" Suz still hadn't taken her eyes off Josh.

Jenn stood and tugged Suz to her feet. "Call us!" Jenn said to Jasmine as she pulled Suz away from the table.

"Bye," Suz called to Josh from across the restaurant.

Josh smiled and waved. Women at other tables were taking pictures with their cell phones, and he nodded and smiled at them too.

Despite Jasmine's apprehension about the conversation to come, it was hard not to smile as Suz resisted Jenn's retreat. The friends engaged in a brief scuffle at the door. Jenn prevailed, pushing Suz firmly out onto the street.

Jasmine sat alone at the table. "How did you find me? Wait. Don't answer. Mo."

"She didn't warn me about the blinding pink walls, though. I might not have come."

Jasmine sucked in her breath. *Will not lose my cool.* "You didn't come to rehearsal today."

"I had to take care of a few things in L.A." Josh pulled out the chair opposite her as if he had to hurry in through a sliver of space before it closed forever. He spun the daisy-on-white-painted wooden chair around and sat on it. He rested his arms on the back of the chair, then shrugged. "But I took the red-eye back and made it to New York by nine this morning. I got to the theater but was terrified. I couldn't do it. I passed the place four times and couldn't go in."

Jasmine tried not to melt into a puddle of sympathy. *Hold your ground.* "Did you barf?"

"Twice." Josh grinned. "I miss you."

"Why are you smiling like that?"

"'Cause you look gorgeous. And"—he paused to nudge her shoulder playfully—"you're the only one in the world who *really* understands."

Jasmine was rescued from a response by the pigtailed waitress. Josh refused the menu and ordered a pastrami sandwich. The waitress reluctantly left.

"Why are you here?" *I am not letting you back into my life.*

Into my heart.

Into my bed.

Okay, maybe once more into my bed.

No! She had to hold strong.

"To eat pastrami with you." They stared at each other. Finally, it was Josh who looked down. "Okay, I wanted to talk to you before rehearsals tomorrow. I am going to make it in those doors tomorrow. I didn't think you'd want me to interfere with your work, so I wanted to warn you now that I'll be there." He paused. "Don't you miss me a little?"

I miss you like a part of my own body is gone. Jasmine sat back and crossed her arms. "Josh. It can't be. We've had this discussion. Nothing has changed." *You're still the most beautiful man I've ever met, and you're looking at me like you can see into my soul, and I'm twittering like a leaf.* "We have nothing in common." *Except that you might be my One True Love.*

"Except that I might be your One True Love."

"Stop that!" She felt herself melting toward him.

"What?"

"Reading my mind."

"How's the librarian?"

"Aha. I wasn't even thinking about him. I've been working round the clock. I haven't seen him since the last time we were all together."

The waitress put down Josh's sandwich. Then stood dumbly by the table.

"Thanks," Josh said.

She smiled uneasily.

"Thanks a lot. It looks great."

She didn't move.

"We're fine," Jasmine said.

Madeline came and pulled the starstruck waitress away.

Jasmine shook her head in wonder. *Everyone else is acting crazy, and I'm feeling slightly normal.*

Josh shrugged. "You're wrong about us having nothing in common. We both like pastrami."

"You like foie gras and Bud."

Josh made a face. "Who told you that?"

"Sexiest Man Alive. *People* magazine."

"Forget that and look at me."

"You don't make your own face cream?" She could feel the first layer of her carefully built resistance peel away.

"Look at me, Jas, and tell me we shouldn't be together."

"I want to show you something." Jasmine jumped up and went to the front of the restaurant. When she got there, she considered fleeing. She could slip right out the door. Dash down Broadway and never look back, just like she had done every other time she had been with a man in her lifetime.

She turned. Josh was staring at her. He was so kind. So beautiful. So *right*.

I don't want to run.

She fished around the magazine bin until she found the issue with the torn-off cover. She came back to the table and opened it. "Okay. Do you or do you not cook?"

Josh read the headline out loud. "'He's Sexy, Passionate, and He Cooks.'" He met Jasmine's challenging tone, his lips threatening to quirk into a smile. "Am I or am I not sexy and passionate?"

"I asked you a question first." She willed herself not to blush. Instead, the heat that usually flushed her face flushed, well, elsewhere. Well, that was an interesting development. She wondered where her fluttering heart was going to migrate . . . surely not to her . . . oh. Lovely.

"Chinese. Thai. Continental. American," he said.

Jasmine sighed. "See. Nothing in common."

"Hey, if you eat, then we have that in common." He took her hand and leaned in. "Your turn. Am I sexy and passionate?"

"Oh, yes," a woman at the next table murmured under her breath.

They pretended they didn't hear her.

Jasmine cleared her throat. She lowered her voice. "You're fairly sexy and passionate for an international sex symbol."

He nodded and whispered, "Okay. I can live with that."

"Do you really believe in champagne?" *Make me hate you, Josh, because if you don't, I might be ready to love you.*

He snatched the magazine out of her hands and pushed it aside. He leaned in close and whispered, "Jas, my fans don't want to hear that Cleo and I don't get it on because we're too busy to have a real relationship. Or that my parents are ashamed of me because I didn't go to Columbia. Or that what truly sucks about my life is that I'm so famous, I scare away the one woman who matters."

Her heart stopped. *The one woman who matters.* She couldn't breathe. "What would happen if you let the world in on the real Josh Toby?"

Josh shook his head. "What would happen if you let the world in on the real Jasmine Burns?"

They stared at each other for a long moment.

Jasmine ran his shocking statement about being the only woman who mattered over and over through her mind. *The real Jasmine Burns can't live your life.*

"Jasmine. Why don't we go to your apartment right now? Let me make love to you."

The woman at the closest table clutched her chest.

"Oh. That. Well. No," Jasmine's mouth said, while the rest of her body said, "Oh, *yes.*"

He bit his lower lip and jiggled his leg. "I'm staying at the Plaza." His violet eyes flashed, promising more than a fancy suite. He fished in his pocket and pulled out a hotel keycard. He slid it across the table.

She stared at the card. "What about Cleo?"

"I saw her. I talked to her. She knows it can't be. Mo

will start working on the press release as soon as she talks to Cleo."

Jasmine imagined the media storm that was brewing. She could almost hear the thunder. "No. I can't." Saying no to him was physically painful. Every cell of her body strained toward him.

"Take the card. Just in case you change your mind."

She let the card sit.

"I'm doing Romeo for you."

"What?"

"I decided that the only way to convince you to face your demons was to face mine first. That's the only reason I came back to do it."

He was doing Romeo for her? He was going to let the world see his stage fright, take potshots at his serious acting. He was leaving himself open to insults and ridicule. She felt a flutter run through her entire body. *For her.*

She eyed the Plaza card.

No. She had to be strong. Just because he was charming her socks—or something—off didn't mean that anything about his life had changed. He still had the same impossible life, and she was still her same impossible self. Or was she? She felt so calm.

Josh leaned in. His face was tense with resolve. "Here's what I decided: I'm getting on that stage, and when I leave that theater in triumph, you're going to walk out with me. Gorgeous and on my arm for the world to see. Face your demons, Jas."

Jasmine blinked at the man who sat before her. He was risking ridicule and shame for her.

She looked down at the magazine, which was still open

on the table. Sensual pictures of Josh half-naked stared up at her, but by far the sexiest man in the world was the one who sat across from her right now.

And she didn't have the slightest idea what to do about it.

But just in case, she slipped the Plaza card into her purse.

Chapter 30

Josh was wide awake at 2:35 AM when he heard the knock at his hotel door.

He didn't budge from where he lay in bed. After all, he didn't have any security guards on duty. He couldn't count the times that fans had snuck up to his rooms and knocked on his door just like that.

If it was Jasmine, she had his key.

He waited, hoping.

Then he heard the swoosh of a card sliding through the slot in the door. His heart leapt at the whoosh of the deadbolt withdrawing from its hole. The dogs awoke and stood cautiously at the base of his bed. *Ferocious, guys.*

The door pushed open, and a sliver of light from the hallway illuminated her.

Jasmine.

Josh sat up, his heart beating hard. "I thought you weren't going to come."

She slipped into the room and shut the door behind her. The dogs greeted her sleepily, then curled up again in their doggie beds. Jasmine stood still as her eyes adjusted to the dark.

He flicked on the bedside light. She stood in the living room of the four-room suite, a small package in her hand.

"I brought you something," she whispered, as if afraid of disturbing the sleeping dogs.

"C'mere." His body was on fire. She was here. Had he convinced her to try to be with him? God, he hoped so.

"I came to drop this off." She put the package on the marble coffee table and took a step backward toward the door.

He jumped out of bed, belatedly aware by the look of horror on her face that he was stark naked. He scooped the white terry hotel robe off a wingback chair and shrugged into it. "Wait." Panic began to rise in his gut. He couldn't let her leave.

She retreated another step. "I thought that if you were going to do Romeo tomorrow, you might need this."

He crossed the room to the coffee table and peered into the bag. He pulled out its contents. "A Barbie doll?"

She nodded as if her gift made all the sense in the world.

"Thanks. I think."

"Pretend she's Juliet. You practice your lines talking to the doll. Then when you get in there, it's easy. Well, easier. Try it."

"She's naked."

"Yeah, well, right. She has to be naked so that you practice imagining her at her most vulnerable."

"I'd rather imagine you—"

"You're actually supposed to be naked too. At your, you know, most vulnerable."

He began to open his robe.

"No!" she cried. "I'm just here to give you the doll."

"Bullshit. You can't tell me that you came to my hotel room in the middle of the night to give me a doll."

Her lips betrayed a smile. "Well. Maybe . . ."

He closed the robe playfully. "Nope. Forget it. Let's talk doll therapy." He sat on the couch and pulled her down after him. To his great relief, she tumbled effortlessly into his arms and snuggled against him. He inhaled the perfume of her hair. "Let me get this straight. You think talking to a doll will help me do Shakespeare?"

"Yep." She had become totally at ease against him. The Jasmine he remembered. The Jasmine he prayed for.

"Do you have a Barbie too?"

"A Ken."

Josh's eyes twinkled. "Is he naked?"

"Well, yeah. It was from before we met."

"Did he help?"

"Not much." She blushed. "But I needed a reason to back out of staying if I changed my mind."

Josh's heart leapt. "Did you change your mind?" He held his breath.

"No. But I'm still not entirely happy about this," she said. "It's a real screwup for me, you being so famous." She paused. "And so nice. And so thoughtful. And so beautiful."

He took her in his arms. His heart was beating wildly in his chest. "You don't have to look at me."

Jasmine smiled. "You're a little hard to avoid."

"I'll blindfold you."

She blushed to her hairline. "That might be fun."

He felt something twist inside him at her suggestion. *To possess her. Really possess her. Would she dare?*

Would he? He pulled back. "I can't deal with this back-and-forth, Jas. If you're going to sleep with me, it has to be for keeps." He felt the tension of his challenge in every muscle in his body. His voice felt heavy and thick in his throat. "Trust me."

"I trust you."

"Show me." He could see the desire in her eyes.

"How?"

"You decide."

She met his eyes straight on. "No. You decide."

He stilled his furiously beating heart. "Strip," he said.

And to his infinite relief, she smiled.

Jasmine felt her whole body flare to life. *Strip?* Like a stripper? Naked and bold and *because he says so.* She stood and her heart leapt. Her submission was an act of such supreme braveness, an act of total control she never thought possible.

She slipped out of her shoes.

He watched with smoky eyes. "Slower. Take your time. I'm going to make love to you all night. There's no rush."

She unbuttoned her shirt. Button. By button. By button.

"Tell me what you're thinking," he demanded.

"I want to make love to you," she said, her voice already heavy with desire. Now that they had begun, there was no turning back. She knew it, and a thrill raced down her spine. *Give yourself to him.*

He nodded. "Good. Take off the shirt."

She did as he said, letting the fabric slip to the floor.

The heat of her desire was melting her so quickly, she felt as if she might slide down after it.

"The bra," he commanded.

She unhooked the back and let it fall.

"You're beautiful," he said. "And brave. Do you trust me?"

A delicious shiver raced up her spine. "Yes."

"Turn around."

She did, holding her breath.

"Take off the pants. Slowly."

She did, her heart beating wildly. *To be this bold with a man.*

"The panties."

She couldn't see him, but she could feel the power she held over him in the thickness of his voice. He needed her as much as she needed him. She was naked, exposed, and she was loving every minute of what it was doing to him. And to her.

"Now get down on your knees."

Her body shaking with desire and shock, she dropped to her knees, her back still to him. How far was this going to go? She fought the impulse to flee. *Trust him.*

"Tell me that you love me."

"I do. I do love you."

"Tell me you need me."

"I do. I—"

"Tell me with your body."

She hesitated, uncertain what he wanted. *I know what I want.* She spread her legs.

She could almost feel his smile. She heard him stand and walk across the room, away from her. She heard him open and close drawers, then sink into the bed. For a long, uncertain moment, he said nothing.

She quivered with suspense. *What next? I can't wait.*

"Now come to me. Slowly," he said finally.

She stood and turned. She looked into his eyes and felt the heat she generated in him. The room seemed to go on forever as she crossed toward him.

"Close your eyes," he said when she stood before him. "And turn around."

She did both and then gasped as he wrapped a blindfold across her eyes. Then another tie bound her wrists behind her.

"Trust me," he said again.

"Yes." Her body was on fire.

"I love you," he said, moving her onto the bed so that she lay below him, exposed, vulnerable. And yet, she had never felt so safe.

He kissed her, pressing her into the bed with the weight of his body. "You can't ever leave me again. It'll kill me."

She returned his kiss. *I'm yours.* She memorized the taste of him, the smell of him, the heat of him. And as he slid inside her, the power of him.

She was wild with desire.

She never had to doubt him again. To doubt herself. This was beyond trust. They had entered a pact together: them against the world. They would each fight their demons. Together.

They moved against each other, him grasping, her straining. "Tell me you love me again," he said.

Her mouth was dry with want. "I love you."

He pressed into her, harder, more insistent. She couldn't

see his face, could only see blackness, and yet his eyes were etched in her soul. She couldn't touch him with anything but her mouth, the length of her body. She yearned to claw at him, pull him closer, but the bindings on her hands strained against her wrists. *Come to me. Closer. I need you.* She bit his shoulder. His neck. His chest. As if she could pull him to her with her mouth.

He was teasing her now. Pulling out. Then waiting, suspended, just inside her.

Please, please. Release me.

He waited until the last possible second, then thrust inside her. She tried to pull him closer with her hips.

But he escaped to tease her again.

Release me. Bind me. Take me. Let me go. She was going to pass out from desire.

He thrust inside her again and again, opening her to him. Harder. Faster. More insistent until, with a final thrust, the pounding, blinding wave of release ripped through her. She felt him shudder, too, and wished she could see him. Touch him.

He lay beside her. They both struggled for breath.

He released her hands. Untied her blindfold.

"Hungry?" he asked.

"Starving," she said, finally able to look him up and down.

He disappeared from her side, returning from the mini-bar with a plastic-wrapped plate of cheese, crackers, and fruit. He fed her grapes. One by one. "Fortification for the next round," he said.

"Then you better get some too," she said, feeding him a grape.

"Really? Do you have some tricks up your sleeve?"

"Tricks?" She eyed the blindfold. *Oh, what the hell.* She snatched it up and tied it over his eyes. "It's your turn to trust me."

"Oh, Ms. Burns. I am liking the new, less-shy you."

And they lay back in the bed, grapes forgotten, and began again.

Chapter 31

I am the world's biggest idiot. Josh passed the entrance to the theater for the third time. He couldn't make himself go in. He headed down 47th Street and onto Broadway.

This was ridiculous. It was just a play. He had more experience acting than most of the actors in there. He had read every book he could find about his character. He had his lines down cold. Naked Barbie had given him a definite look of approval after their last run-through.

He could do this.

He rounded the corner, then the next; then he was back on 47th Street. The first snowflakes of the year were starting to fall, and they danced around his head, then fluttered to the sidewalk, where they melted into nothing.

He wished he could melt into nothing. No. He wasn't nothing. He was Josh Toby.

Tell that to his nerves.

"Josh?" Jasmine raced out of the theater without her coat. Her breath condensed into a cloud around his name.

"Jas? What are you doing? You're going to freeze." They had woken up together that morning at the hotel, exhausted but happy. Then she had rushed home (Josh insisted on a limo, but she refused, afraid of what it would look like in the tabloids) to change for an 8:00 AM meeting that morning with the crew.

"They're waiting for you," she said.

Josh shrugged. "I'm just a little late."

"I watched you pass by twice."

He lowered his head sheepishly. "Snagged."

"Who but me would understand passing by a theater, unable to go in?" Her face was glowing from the cold. Or was it from the night before?

He stifled the urge to kiss her shivering lips in public. God, what a night they had had. But they had agreed that they'd pose as friends until Cleo agreed to a suitable press release. "I'm supposed to be proving to you that taking risks is worth it, and you caught me acting like an idiot." Around them, pedestrians hurried by, their chins tucked into their coats, their hats pulled down low against the wind.

"Do you have Barbie?" she whispered.

"I practiced with her all morning," he whispered. "But I would have rather practiced with you."

She looked around nervously.

"Will you come with me to meet my parents tonight? If you say yes, I'll march in there."

"That's blackmail!" Jasmine struggled out of his arms, then rubbed her own arms to ward off the cold. Snowflakes balanced on her black hair, hesitated, then melted.

Josh shrugged out of his coat and put it over her. "Blackmail loosens me up. Makes me feel even more confident than dolls. Say yes."

Jasmine seemed to be inhaling his coat. He would have

done the same if he had something of hers. Just talking to her made him feel better about the rehearsal. If she could be out here with him on the street, where Fat Larry could be, then he could get his lame butt in there.

"C'mon." She dragged him toward the theater. "Get to work."

"One kiss?"

"No!"

"For good luck?"

She looked around nervously, then pecked his cheek.

"That was *so* not what I had in mind."

"I told you last night that Fat Larry's still following me. That's all you get. We're friends."

He looked around once more. The coast was clear. If Fat Larry was anywhere in the vicinity, he would have shown by now. "Screw that. I can pay Fat Larry more than the tabloids will. This kiss is worth at least two million." He grabbed her, leaned her back, and gave her the kiss he was sure they'd both been dreaming about.

When he had thoroughly kissed her, he let her go.

"Oh, Romeo." She wobbled to standing.

He smiled, then pushed through the backstage door. "Oh, and I'll pick you up at nine—we're getting out of rehearsals early tonight. My mom will be thrilled!"

Jasmine took another black olive off the 1920s glass dish and popped it in her mouth. She and Josh sat stiffly on the brown tweed couch, side by side. She could feel each individual spring underneath her. The air smelled of baby powder and roasting red meat.

She was still shaken up by their amazing night together, but right now, she didn't know what was more shocking, the amazing sex they had had or the fact that she was now staring at his mother.

"So, where did you get your education, dear?" Josh's mother asked.

From your son. In bed. Last night.

Josh's mother looked so much like him, and yet, the woman wasn't the least bit pretty. She had his eyes, but they were shriveled and sunken. She had his nose, but in her face, it didn't strike that perfect proportion that made his face sculptural.

Josh's face was more his father's. The strong jaw. The perfect teeth. Even the etched cheekbones were still evident under the older man's loose skin. But Josh's father had an incongruous button of a nose. And perfectly lovely but ordinary blue eyes.

How had this elegant, perfect creature sprung from these two normal, flawed specimens? It made Jasmine aware of the role luck played with their lives: the millimeters of a jawbone's protrusion; the perfect balance of blue and red in a skin tone; her leaving her portfolio in her rush away from Arturo; Josh showing up as her new employer.

Or was it destiny?

The warmth of Josh's leg next to hers was almost too much to bear. She tried to direct her attention to his mother. "Oh, I, well, I'm mostly self-taught."

"She got her master's at NYU," Josh put in. He ate from the spread of pickled appetizers his mother had set before them, despite the late hour.

"That's lovely!" his mother said. "I don't think Cleo ever—oh, well, I guess I shouldn't mention Cleo."

"It's okay, Mom. Cleo is fine."

Josh's father put his hand on Jasmine's. He patted it. His hands were small and soft, the skin paper-thin, like Korean silk. It was obvious he thought Jasmine being with his son was the saddest thing he ever had to witness. She wouldn't have been surprised if he slipped her a twenty-dollar bill as a consolation prize.

"Cleo and I just pretend we're a couple to keep the press off. We're good friends. I told you that before." Josh paused, leaned over, and kissed Jasmine's cheek. "Jasmine's for real."

"Oh." His mother scooped a mound of chopped chicken liver onto a cracker. "Well, then." She chewed carefully.

"And Jasmine isn't a drug dealer, by the way. Or any of those other things you might have read about her in the paper," Josh added.

"Of course she isn't!" his father insisted. He banged his fist on the table, and the mismatched water glasses jumped. They were sour cream cups from the '70s, each decorated with a different color of now-faded flower.

Jasmine tried to change the subject. "Josh is in New York to do Romeo at the Liberty," she offered cheerfully.

His parents met each other's eyes. The look that shot between them said, *Yes, we heard and we're worried sick.*

"How's that going?" his mother asked doubtfully. She coughed lightly into her palm.

Jasmine could feel Josh squirm next to her.

"Fine," she said.

But it hadn't been fine. Rehearsal had been a disaster. From the moment Josh walked into the theater and introduced himself, the scorn of the other actors became a thick cloud, hanging over everything he did. Thelda

Monroe, the actress who played Juliet, threatened to quit. "*I will not take part in a Hollywood mockery,*" she had hissed at Mr. McMann, the director. Josh's face had clouded black when he told Jasmine about it in the cab on the way uptown.

The irony that Jasmine's costumes were emerging from the sewing machines to hushed awe wasn't lost on Jasmine. She was becoming the talk of the show. Sally Wright, the show's publicist, had already gotten her an interview with *Backstage* magazine, which she was dreading.

"She's lying," Josh said. "I was awful. I couldn't get a single inflection right. But I'm working on it. I'm going to nail it."

"Well, Shakespeare is *complicated*," his mother said, as if that surely disqualified Josh from being able to handle it.

"Josh understands emotions better than anyone I know," Jasmine found herself saying. "He'll nail Romeo once he realizes that Romeo is just a kid. Once he stops trying to *understand* Romeo on an intellectual level, he's going to be great."

They all stared at Jasmine.

"Really?" Josh asked.

Jasmine couldn't stand the oppressive apartment another moment. She jumped up from the couch and went to the window. "You read those books about deconstructing the play and finding the images in the metaphors and all that blah, blah, blah because that's how you were taught to learn Shakespeare. But *you* don't have to learn Romeo. You *are* Romeo. Because you understand love. That's all

Shakespeare is—a bunch of humans bungling around on-stage, trying to find love."

Josh's mother gasped.

Oh, God, what am I saying? Jasmine snuck a look at Josh's dad. He was open-mouthed but nodding.

Josh nodded thoughtfully too. He came to the window and stood behind her. She could feel his molecules stretching out to connect with hers. "You mean all that?" he asked softly.

Jasmine looked out at the Hudson River shining below. She whispered so only Josh could hear, "You're going to be the best actor on that stage once you let yourself feel it. I promise you."

They lay together in Josh's bed at the hotel, feeding Lassie and Buster dog treats. It was past midnight, but neither of them felt tired. The dinner had gone on in the same vein—awful and hard. His parents just wouldn't give Josh a break. Jasmine had tried to convince him that they didn't matter, but she knew it wasn't true.

When Josh's cell phone rang, they both startled. He looked at it. "It's Mo." He flicked it on and put it to his ear. "Josh here."

He listened, his face draining of color. "Oh, shit. Right. Okay. Bye."

Jasmine stared at him, waiting.

"Your sister, the psychic—"

"Amy?" Jasmine's body froze.

"Amy told Cleo the name of her One True Love." He got a far-off look in his eye. "I thought I recognized that suitcase in L.A. It was Amy's. I saw it in your apartment the day I met her."

Jasmine felt as if she'd been punched in the gut. Why did she always feel that way when Amy was involved in her life? "Why didn't you tell me Cleo went to Amy?"

"I didn't think it was a big deal."

"Not a big deal!" Jasmine cried. The dogs put their ears back in alarm at the sudden change of mood in the room. Lassie threw herself off the bed, landing with a plop.

"You told me she lost her powers," Josh said. "I didn't think anything would come of it. I thought Amy would just say it was useless. Unless . . . oh, shit." Jasmine could see from the look on Josh's face that he understood his mistake. "Amy lied to Cleo."

"Of course she did."

"And now the lie is out there, and everyone will believe it's the truth."

"What did Amy tell her?" Jasmine asked. She held her breath, sure she already knew the answer.

"Amy told Cleo her One True Love is named Josh Toby, and . . ." Josh's eyes grew dark and stormy.

Jasmine gritted her teeth. "And?"

Josh shook his head wearily. "And Cleo's not going to accept Mo's press release. She's going with her own story. Tomorrow. On *Oprah*." He picked up the phone again. "I have to stop her."

Jasmine reached for her own phone. "You stop yours, I'll stop mine."

Chapter 32

". . . And no longer be a Capulet."

Silence filled the theater. Someone coughed.

"Josh?" Mr. McMann's voice was tinged with irritation.

"Sorry. Right." Josh stood on the stage, his arms at his sides.

"*Shall I hear more?*" Thelda, the actress playing Juliet, cued him with obvious annoyance.

"Got it. I know. Sorry. Shall I hear more?" Josh launched woodenly into his speech while Jasmine, from her spot in the darkness of the wings, cringed. With every advancing hour, Josh seemed to be getting tenser, more nervous. And why not? Cleo had refused to take his calls, and Amy had refused to talk to Jasmine, and *Oprah* was going to be on the air in twenty-five minutes. Mo was trying to get an advance tape but to no avail.

"Okay. Take ten. We'll pick up here." Mr. McMann shut his script a little more loudly than was necessary.

"Break!" the Pugster called. "Back at three forty-seven!" The actors shrugged out of their characters and back into their normal selves as if they were shrugging off clothing. Then they dispersed in clusters for coffee and cigarettes, brushing by Jasmine without noticing her.

Josh turned to the wing, toward her, although he didn't know she was there. He muttered to himself angrily. "Stupid, stupid, stupid . . ."

"Psst," Jasmine hissed as he passed.

Josh looked up, alarmed, then relaxed when he saw her. "How long have you been here?"

"Long enough."

"They hate me. I can feel it like daggers—"

"Amy and Cleo are going on *Oprah* in twenty-two minutes. You can't be expected to concentrate," Jasmine reminded him. They weren't going to watch it. They had work all day. But Mo was taping it for them and would text-message them her spin for Josh's approval by 4:22.

Jasmine gazed into Josh's veiled eyes.

I have to help him get through this rehearsal.

I could. No. That would be insane. But fun. He was crashing and burning out there. It was her professional duty. The show must go on. Plus, she wanted him. Badly. She pulled him into the shadows away from the prying eyes of the nearby sound engineers who were testing equipment on the stage. "We have ten minutes."

"Ten minutes for what? Oh, you mean . . . ?" His eyes brightened for the first time that day. "Ms. Burns!"

"I'm going to inspire you. C'mon. Quick." Jasmine turned Josh's face toward hers and kissed him deeply and fully. She poured her faith into the kiss, willed her energy to him. *I'll be your Juliet.*

Josh grinned like, well, like Romeo.

Jasmine pulled the curtain around them.

He backed her against the wall and pressed against the length of her. He took over the kiss and made it his.

"It's sex, Josh," she murmured into his neck. "Romeo and Juliet are kids."

Josh kissed down her neck. She let her head fall back and tried not to lose her train of thought.

"You know this character, Josh. Romeo's motivated by uncontrollable physical love."

"The kind that makes you do stupid things?" Josh asked. "Like this?" He slid his hand under her flowing skirt.

Jasmine tried not to cry out as she inhaled his warmth, his presence, every inch of him. "Really stupid things." Jasmine moved against him. She couldn't see beyond the dark purple velvet curtain that enclosed them. The fabric must have been a hundred years old, but it was still as dense and lush as a forest canopy.

He glanced at his glowing watch in the semidarkness. "We have eight minutes."

"Then stop talking."

They spun around so that his back was against the wall. His hand scooped back under her skirt, and he felt that she was serious. He pulled her onto him, her legs around his waist. They began to move together as quietly as they could. There was an inch between Jasmine's back and the curtain. She tried to make herself as small as possible to avoid touching the curtain. Then she forgot the curtain completely as she was overcome by him.

He stopped. "Jasmine?"

"Shh."

People returned to the stage, the vibration of their footsteps on the hollow wood a warning of just how close they were. Jasmine knew they were hidden behind the curtain, but still, they had to hurry. She moved more insistently. Oh, God, if she cried out, it would be all over. But him inside her—

"Jasmine."

"For God's sake, what?" Why wouldn't he stop talking?

"You think I can do this?"

"Only if you shut up."

"No. Not *this*. I mean the play. Romeo."

With Herculean strength, she forced her body to stop. She took a deep breath. "I think that you're one of the smartest people I've ever met. You understand people. You helped me so much, Josh. No book could do what you did for me. You taught me to give up the stupid books and get out there. Now you have to do the same. So shut up and make love to me."

He kissed her lips gently—not a passionate kiss but a thank-you kiss—then pulled her to him. They moved together, and Jasmine began to lose herself again in him, in their rhythm.

"So what about you?"

"Are you talking again?"

He was. "You know, I *am* smart about people. You want to know what I think about you?"

"Later!" She grasped his hair.

"I don't think you're hung up on that Raj-in-the-bushes guy at all."

"Josh. Please."

"I think your problem is that you want attention, but you're too proper to admit that you want it, so you run from it, but the problem is you *do* want it. You're allowed to get attention too. You deserve it. Admit it. You want to be in the spotlight." He began to move inside her again.

She bit his shoulder to keep from crying out as she gasped into her climax.

He continued to move until he came, too, an instant later.

He kissed her forehead and whispered, "You want me, and you want the spotlight, and you want it all. And here's what's really important: You deserve it."

He held her against him for a silent moment. Then they separated and arranged their clothes. He smoothed her hair. She adjusted his collar.

"I don't know what you're talking about," she said after her pulse had slowed.

"You do. You're holding back. But you want to go for it."

The Pugster called out, "Let's go! From the top. Where's Josh?"

"That's my cue." Josh pushed out of the curtain, but Jasmine caught his hand.

"Can you do it?" she asked.

Josh bent at the waist and kissed her hand. "M'lady, I am officially inspired," he said. Then he ducked out of sight.

Jasmine went back to the costume shop in a daze. Three elderly women were hunched over sewing machines, running seams down the legs of the black three-piece suits for the first scene.

Oprah would be on by now. Cleo would be telling the world that she and Josh were destined to be. And then

Jasmine would become the most hated woman in America. No—in the world.

Jasmine studied herself in the floor-length mirror.

Not the kind of fame I had in mind.

She ran her fingers over one of Juliet's costumes. It would soon be a purple sparkled silk jogging suit, but now it was a muslin mock-up being worn by a size-four mannequin with no legs. They used the cheap, plain muslin to make the costume until the design was perfect. Then they'd use the pricey, vibrant fabric for the real thing. Jasmine repinned the shoulder.

In the costume room of life, I never get past the muslin mock-up stage. What if this time she took the next step and recut herself out of flashy, gorgeous cloth? After Amy and Cleo were done today on *Oprah,* the world was going to be back on Jasmine's doorstep. Did she really want to be Josh's little mouse? Josh's "Pale, Plain Jane" *Dirt* magazine had called her.

She studied the mock-up, widened the flare slightly on the pants leg. That was better. Not quite right but closer.

She ran the rough muslin through her fingers. Then she went to the closet and pulled out the purple sparkling rayon they would use for the finished piece. She draped it over the mannequin.

Jasmine sniffed.

She coughed.

Oh, hell, was she crying?

So what if she wanted to be noticed? Didn't everyone?

Jasmine took the purple silk off the mannequin and draped it over her own shoulders. She looked at herself in the floor-length mirror. The women at the sewing machines continued stitching, pretending not to watch the eccentric designer crying over purple fabric. Their machines whirred away, the sound comforting Jasmine like a familiar song.

Yes, she wanted to be noticed. But not like this. Not hated by the world for breaking up the perfect couple. It was like coming to Baltimore when she was a kid to be with her sisters. She had hoped she might find a safe haven, but instead she was reviled. Maybe Josh was right—she wasn't scarred by Raj. She was scarred by her family. Her sisters had rejected her.

But this time could be different. This time, she wasn't a sixteen-year-old kid. She could stand up to the world.

After all, she had Josh at her side.

Mo clicked the TV screen to black. They were in Josh's Plaza suite, surrounded by uneaten pizza and one half-eaten slice that Lassie and Buster had snagged off Josh's plate and dragged to their lair under the coffee table. The day had been endless, impossible to get out of rehearsals, impossible to deal with Cleo until now.

Josh, Jasmine, and Mo sat silently on the white couch, staring at the black screen. The only sound was the dogs chomping.

"Ouch," Josh said.

"Not what I expected," Mo admitted.

"I don't think I've ever felt lower in my entire life," Jasmine said. "Cleo made Oprah cry."

Cleo had delivered her best performance ever. She recounted how she agreed to fake a relationship with Josh because she had always loved him and hoped one day he would learn to love her too. She told Oprah she had known Josh was her destiny even though he could never admit to loving a woman "like her." She talked of the horror of living with a man who didn't love her in return, a man who was, perhaps, incapable of love because of his disastrous relationship with his mother.

She clearly did love him. And with her love, she expressed the secret longings of most of the women listening. Who wouldn't love Josh Toby, after all? And who didn't now love Cleo, after her soul-baring performance.

Oprah nodded sagely as Cleo described how she believed that Josh had a problem with needing people to take care of. "He couldn't admit to loving an independent, capable, yes, slightly wild woman like me," Cleo sighed.

I am not Josh's charity project, Jasmine thought. *Am I?*

Cleo said that she believed Josh's need to constantly help others came from his difficult relationship with his parents, who never loved him. "He was never good enough for them," Cleo explained. "Which is why he believes love is conditional on doing good deeds. But me, well, I'm a lot of things, but I'm not exactly *good*." Oprah and her audience sat forward on their seats, spellbound, loving Cleo for being the bad girl.

"You know that's not true," Josh said.

"I know," Jasmine reassured him. But the daggers were working their way in, deeper with every breath. Was she his charity project? Just another waitress to leave enormous tips for? Another stray dog without a home?

Then Cleo told Oprah about Amy. With a breathless introduction for "perhaps the most remarkable psychic Oprah had ever had the honor of meeting," Amy, in full porno-gypsy regalia, appeared from backstage to the applause of a wildly enthusiastic crowd.

Jasmine nearly fell off the couch.

Amy, of course, was dazzling, born for her fifteen minutes of Oprah-granted fame. She described how her powers had come and gone, but how the force of Cleo and Josh's love was so strong, she had for the first time in two years heard a person's One True Love—and, yes, Amy announced (after a commercial break) that Cleo Chan's One True Love was, indeed, Josh Toby.

Oprah's audience clapped wildly. The frenzy had begun. Jasmine could almost feel the wave of support for Cleo and Amy blowing in from Chicago. It was a cold, cold wind.

After the crowd calmed down, Oprah turned to Cleo and asked in hushed awe, "What are you going to do?"

"I'm going back to New York to get my man," Cleo proclaimed.

Over my dead body, Jasmine thought.

A standing ovation. Not a dry eye in the house. Amy stood by Cleo's side looking like a proud mother.

"Did you guys read the spin I texted you?" Mo said after it was all over.

"You'll need to respin it to cover me murdering my sister," Jasmine said.

"Don't stab," Mo said in complete seriousness. "Too much blood. Go with something more photogenic. Poison."

Poison. Jasmine felt too serious for comfort. How could Amy do this to her? *She's lying. God, I hope she's lying or I'm really in for the fight of my life.*

"Why didn't Cleo come to me?" Josh asked. He fed

Lassie bits of pizza crust. "We could have worked something out."

Mo nodded her head toward Jasmine. "That's why, hon. She couldn't win against Jasmine on an even playing field, so she brought in the big guns—public opinion. She knows that you care what people think. And Josh, honey, I hate to tell you, but you look like a schmuck."

"I won't be able to walk down the street without being pelted with eggs," Jasmine said. She waited to feel awful but instead she felt . . . purple. Purple sparkling rayon. *I can do this.*

Josh took Jasmine's hand. "I don't care what anyone thinks. You can't either."

Jasmine scanned her body. No shakes. No nausea. She felt fine. In fact, she felt ready for the fight of her life. "I'm not afraid," she said.

And amazingly, she meant it.

Chapter 33

*L*ater that night, Amy called Jasmine's cell phone. She was at LaGuardia, fresh off the plane from Chicago. Jasmine had to do her best not to hang up on her. *I need to know if she's lying about Josh being Cleo's One True Love. The truth is what matters. Punching her in the jaw can wait.*

Mo had already gone to her own suite to draft the press release, a vague vow of friendship and support—but nothing more—from Josh "to his oldest friend, Cleo Chan, whom he forever holds in the highest regard."

Josh, still overwhelmed from the emotion of watching Cleo spill her guts to the world, wasn't up to an encounter with Amy. He donned his baseball cap and baggy sweats and escaped for the hotel gym with the dogs. Of course, the gym was closed and didn't allow dogs, but a phone call from Josh Toby, superstar, fixed that fast.

Half an hour later, Amy breezed in and threw herself on the couch. She was still wearing the excessive makeup Oprah's handlers plastered on her for the show. The colors were, amazingly, more toned down than her usual bold choices. "You don't have to thank me!" Amy said instead of "hello." "But dinner would be super. There was nothing decent on the plane." She bounced up and down on the couch, testing its springs as if this was where she intended to bed down for the night. Which probably was her plan. "So what are you doing at this swank hotel anyway? Hiding out?"

"Thank you?" Jasmine knew never to be shocked by the depths of Amy's emotional ineptitude. But this was a new low. "You lied to Cleo, right?"

"Nope. It was the truth. But what's the deal with the long face? I solved your problems, right? No superstar boyfriend? Isn't that what you told me you wanted when you were cowering behind the curtains?" Amy opened the hotel guide. "I'm going to order a steak. You want anything?"

Jasmine threw up her hands. "Amy! Josh and I . . ." Jasmine turned red. *Had Amy told Cleo the truth? Had the voice come back?*

Amy looked up at Jasmine. It always took Amy a few minutes into a conversation to actually notice the person she was speaking to. Once when they were teenagers, Jasmine had spent an entire day with Amy before she realized Jasmine had cut off seven inches of her hair. "Really? Oh, my little sister!" Amy leapt at Jasmine and engulfed her in arms and fabric and fumes of clove. Then she released her all at once. "I thought you were just hiding out here. I didn't realize that you guys were shacking up. Although, this joint definitely doesn't seem your style." Amy threw open the walk-in closet, acknowledged the fact of a man's clothes hanging within, checked a few labels for quality, sniffed deeply, and closed the doors, satisfied. "Well for shit's sake, Jas, why didn't you tell me?"

"It happened so fast—wait. Why am I the one explaining myself? I've been trying to call you for days. Did the voice really come back?"

Amy dialed room service. "Oh, Jas. Oprah was the chance of a lifetime. I just knew Maddie wouldn't let me down." Maddie was what Amy called the voice when she was in a good mood. "And she didn't! I think she felt too guilty to deny me my one chance at Oprah. So she came back. I hardly had a chance to get my Web page up and running before . . ." She turned her attention to the phone. "Yes. I'd like a steak. Rare. And a beer. Imported. No, wait, this is Toby's bill? Champagne. Imported."

Jasmine rubbed her eyes. Even the spirits couldn't resist a shot at Oprah.

Amy seemed reenergized by the prospect of the free food. "Oh, honey! Last time I saw a certain someone with Mr. I'm-Too-Sexy-for-My-Pants, she was hiding behind the drapes."

Jasmine was so tired from the endless work on *Romeo*, the extracurricular bonus of the Amy and Cleo Show, plus the time sex was taking away from her sleep, she didn't have an ounce of patience left. "I love Josh and we're going to be together whether the voice really came back or not."

"Well, of course it did, and of course you love him. I'm the one who told you you would, remember? Why does no one ever thank me?" Amy fixed her hair in the mirror. "But what about his Mr. Fix-It hang-up? And what about your sexy-man hang-up? I mean, I'm into boffing a superstar as much as the next girl, but is this guy really worth it? Why not just give him up to Cleo and find a quiet guy? You know, one more your style."

It was so hard to predict what would come out of Amy's mouth next, it was like talking to a crazy person. "He doesn't have a hang-up. And I . . ." What was there to say about herself? *I found love.* Was it really that simple? From hiding behind the drapes to staying in the presidential suite at the Plaza with the sexiest man alive. It *had* been quite an autumn. But then, what exactly had happened to change her? Baby steps and patience and luck and being so fed up with herself at the right moment in time. *And Josh. Just Josh.*

Love was the cure for shyness. But Jasmine wasn't about to talk to Amy about it. Knowing Amy, she'd want to coauthor a book on the subject to hawk on *Oprah.*

"So, no fix-it complex? Cleo made that up? What about his parents not loving him?"

"He's over it." Jasmine felt the doubt creep in, and with it, her fear. She shooed them both away. *Josh and I are in love.*

"Whatever. Hey, do you still want your two thousand dollars back now that you're rich and famous?"

"Yes. And I'm not rich or famous. Well, maybe infamous, as are you, Ms. Oprah Winfrey."

"I did it for you, Jas. I had no idea you two were getting it on." Amy blushed.

"What?" Amy never blushed.

"Oprah invited me back. Next week. To read her audience."

Jasmine tried not to make a face. There was no way to get through Amy's thick skull that she had done something wrong. Jasmine sank onto the couch. "Amy, do you have any idea how angry I am?"

Amy sat down beside her. "No. Go on, tell me," she

challenged. "How angry are you that I helped you find your One True Love and now you're with him in the Plaza Hotel resting from your job as a costume designer and having all that awesome sex?" Amy paused. "The sex is awesome, right?"

Thankfully, the buzzer rang, sparing Jasmine a reply. Amy sprang to the door. She chatted with the room service waiter, clapped when he popped the cork, invited him to stay for dinner.

Jasmine, however, was the one to tip him on his way out.

Amy finally left after she licked the plate clean. Literally.

When Josh came back, he and Jasmine fell into bed in exhaustion.

"I have ten hours of rehearsal tomorrow. I can't deal with all this," Josh said. "This is why I avoid relationships."

Jasmine tried not to cringe. *He has fake relationships because there's no time for real ones.* Ugh. She had to stop letting all this fear creep back into her head. "Maybe that's the answer," she said, trying to sound cheerful. "We'll both work like mad and by opening night, this whole mess will blow over." Jasmine had thought she'd pass out the minute her head hit the pillow, but with Josh beside her, her body clicked back on to full alert. Why couldn't that man wear pajamas?

"If only it were that easy." Josh rolled toward her and took her in his arms. "What Cleo said isn't true, you know. I love you. Cleo's just trying to get under your skin."

"She's succeeding," Jasmine admitted. "And I'm worried that all this is taking away from your work," she added, unsure if it was better to get her fears into the open or keep them inside.

He brushed her top lip with his. "Screw work. It's not important," he said.

Jasmine melted at those precious words.

"I'm going to set up a meeting with Cleo," Josh said. "She's my friend. She owes me at least that." He brushed Jasmine's bottom lip. He pulled her to him. Apparently he wasn't sleepy anymore either.

"What will you say?"

He murmured into her ear. "That I found the most beautiful creature on this earth, and I need to be with her."

Jasmine accepted the irony of that statement with relish. She relaxed and let the sparks of his bites ignite each cell in her body, one by one, until she was sure she was glowing. "You can tell her the feeling is mutual, beautiful creature." She scratched her hands down his back and he moaned.

"What will you say when she asks why a relationship would work now when it never did before?"

"Because this is True Love, dummy," he said. "Boy, you are a slow study. Love is what cured you of your anxiety. Love is what cured me of avoiding relationships. Don't you read your Shakespeare?"

The mention of True Love set Jasmine's teeth on edge. "Josh, Amy said she didn't lie. She said Cleo's One True Love is you. She heard the voice."

"So?"

"You don't believe in Amy, do you?"

"You told me she was a liar."

"She is."

"So why do you believe her?"

"I don't know." But Jasmine did believe her. It was just a hunch, but she thought she could tell when Amy was lying.

"Forget Amy. Forget Cleo."

"I'm trying."

"Here, I'll help." He kissed her forehead lightly as he pressed himself against her. "Forgotten?" he asked.

"Not yet."

And so he went back to work on her earlobe, her lips, the thin skin over her closed eyes. "Now?"

She rolled onto her back and luxuriously put her hands above her head. "Nope. Not yet."

Josh grinned and took her hips firmly in his hands. He dove underneath the covers and licked down her stomach, beyond her stomach, to the place that made her body quake.

And after a few blissful, heart-gripping minutes, all was forgotten.

For a little while anyway.

Chapter 34

They both tried not to read the tabloids or listen to the gossip whispered behind their backs the next day. And the day after that. Amy had disappeared (Jasmine tried not to think too much about that uncomfortable circumstance), and Cleo was flying out to New York on Friday—two days away. Josh had arranged to meet her at her hotel, an arrangement Jasmine didn't like one bit.

But to meet in public was too risky. There was nothing that could be done short of meeting at a lawyer's office, a possibility that Josh and Mo both considered but rejected as too cold. The tabloids would have a ball with it.

Josh assured Jasmine that the meeting would be fine. But fully believing that Amy had told the truth about Cleo's One True Love, it was hard for Jasmine not to worry.

Josh kissed Jasmine deeply, made love to her once, then twice, before she finally relented that maybe she trusted him enough to be alone with Cleo. After all, he had lived with her for two years and had never touched her.

But still. That was before Amy.

The play was in full production now. The sets in place.

The costumes ready for fittings and the endless adjustments that followed.

More industrious, though, was the preopening publicity machine. The excitement about Josh playing Romeo had set the theater world abuzz with speculation. Odds had it that he was going to stink up the place. Pundits, who had never seen Jasmine's work, decided that the costumes, designed by Josh's floozy, would obviously be atrocious.

Not a soul in the New York theater world could wait to see the disaster unfold.

But before it could, the most remarkable thing of all happened.

Josh's parents went on *Oprah*.

After rehearsals ended after eleven on Thursday night, Josh and Jasmine and Mo found themselves back on the couch in Josh's suite—Josh and Jasmine's suite now. The Plaza handled security expertly (not to mention dogwalking), and with everything happening at once, neither Jasmine nor Josh had the energy to worry about Mrs. Little and her water buckets.

Mo had recorded the surprise appearance of the Tobys on *Oprah*. She already had a press release ready for Josh's approval in a purple folder on the desk, a pen standing by for his revisions.

Josh's parents looked tiny and shriveled in Oprah's oversized chairs. His dad wore his best gray suit with a pressed bow tie. His mother wore a red skirt and her "Power to the People" T-shirt.

No matter how many times Oprah tried to direct their attention to her, they kept turning to the camera, which made it feel like they were talking directly to Josh and Jasmine.

"We came here today," Josh's mother said too loudly, as if talking into an old-fashioned telephone, "to tell Josh that we love him no matter what he does for a living."

Oprah, who had asked about their trip out from New York, seemed delightedly shocked at Mrs. Toby's jump-to-the-meat-of-it approach. Either this wasn't scripted, or Oprah was a good actress. Probably both. "But why not tell him in person?" Oprah asked.

Josh's father nodded sternly at Ruth.

His mother took an enormous breath and recited, "It seems that when I'm with Josh, I can be overly critical." She widened her eyes at Josh's dad, then veered off-script, unable to help herself. "I don't think I'm critical. I'm just trying to help—"

"Ruth!" Josh's father put up his hand to stop her. He turned to Oprah. "After we were told about Ms. Chan's conversation on this show, Ms. Winfrey, we felt we had to defend ourselves. And our boy. We're here so that we can say what needs to be said." He pulled a prepared speech out of his coat jacket pocket, put on his dime-store bi-focals, and began to read. There was nothing Oprah could do but sit back and listen, open-mouthed, along with the rest of America.

"We have always been confused by our only son," his father read. "But we had no idea how confused he has been by us. The worst thing a parent can do is make a child believe that they are not loved. And the only thing that matters in life is being good to your family. Josh, you are always loved."

"True, you turned your back on our way of life," Josh's mother put in.

Josh's father scowled.

Oprah watched with raised eyebrows.

"Sorry. Go on. I'm not even here," his mother mumbled. She crossed her arms.

Josh's father readjusted his glasses. His eyes began to tear up, so he said in a rush, "I'll just skip to the end: We are hugely proud of you, son." He took out a bleached, monogrammed handkerchief and blew his nose.

Then Josh's mother reached down and pulled an enormous scrapbook out of a plastic shopping bag by her feet and dumped it on Oprah's lap. "See! Proof!"

Oprah rearranged herself under the book's prodigious weight and paged through it. "Can we get some up-close shots of these for the audience?" she asked, and held up the book for the cameras.

Josh at sixteen, holding up a box of Cheerios and smiling; Josh at seventeen, on a stage in what looked like a high school auditorium; pay stubs from commercial shoots; callback letters for community theater productions; and on and on.

"I have everything," Josh's mother bragged. "Every review, every show, everything! I have six more of these scrapbooks at home. My most prized possessions."

Jasmine snuck a look at Josh beside her. His mouth hung open in amazement. "Why didn't she ever tell me?"

"These'll be worth a fortune someday," Oprah enthused.

Josh's mother looked at the woman as if she were insane. "They're already worth a fortune, dear," she scoffed. Then she patted Oprah's hand with sympathy.

After the segment ended (rather abruptly, Jasmine thought), Oprah moved on to cooking chicken breasts with Charlize Theron. Mo switched off the TV.

No one said a word.

Jasmine thought she saw Josh wipe a tear from his eye during the screening, but now he just stared at the black screen, as if in shock.

Mo handed Josh an envelope. "This came for you today."

Josh handed it to Jasmine. The scratchy writing on the front read, "Josh Toby, son."

Jasmine opened it. Inside was a carefully folded white sheet. *Please come to dinner Saturday night. Bring Jasmine if you'd like. Or Cleo. We don't mind which. We just want you. Love, Mom and Dad.*

Jasmine tried not to react to the part about choosing between her or Cleo. This was about Josh. "They're asking for forgiveness," she said.

Josh let himself fall back on the couch. "Can we watch it again?" he asked.

And they did. Three more times.

After another grueling day, Friday night finally arrived. Jasmine had wished it never would.

She waited in the hotel room, pretending to read *European Costume and Fashion, 1490–1790*. Josh had left to meet Cleo sixteen minutes ago. Jasmine hadn't even paged past Late Tudor waistcoats, and it already seemed like he had been gone forever.

Jasmine stared at a print of a shopkeeper in London. She had to prepare herself for the possibility that Cleo would prevail, that Amy had told the truth. After all, the woman was so sexy, so exciting. And now that Josh's parents had claimed to love their only son, maybe Josh *wouldn't* need Jasmine anymore.

But Cleo wasn't right about the reasons Josh was with Jasmine. She couldn't be his charity case.

Still, she couldn't help wonder if Cleo had known his parents would forgive Josh on national TV. Had Cleo set up the meeting with Josh after his parents spilled their guts on *Oprah* on purpose? After all, Amy had made it to New York in a matter of hours. If Cleo was acting on emotion, wouldn't she have been on that same plane to be at Josh's side?

I'm starting to think like a tabloid reporter: Cleo Chan Maneuvers Back into Josh Toby's Bed.

She had to remember that Josh said he loved her. That Josh made love to her as if he loved her. That Josh was here in New York City doing the play *because of her. I'm in Josh's bed! No more room in here.* She let her fingers trail over the crisp, white Egyptian cotton sheets to reassure herself.

Plus, maybe Amy lied. Maybe fate wasn't on Cleo's side.

The phone startled Jasmine out of her reverie.

"Cleo Chan here to see you, ma'am," the man at the front desk reported.

Jasmine almost choked. "But . . . what . . . ?"

"Shall I send her up, ma'am?"

Jasmine imagined the poor guy downstairs in the lobby, quaking under Cleo's icy stare. "Sure. Yes. Okay."

*Tell her to bust my door down like she does in the movies.
I'll be cowering under the bed.*

Why was Cleo here if she was supposed to be meeting
Josh?

Jasmine threw on a pair of jeans and washed her face
in the bathroom sink. Why did a hotel that had everything not supply its guests with loaded handguns for self-
defense against fake ex-girlfriends?

She looked at the two dogs who were following her
with tongues lolling. "You know, you guys don't exactly
make a girl feel safe."

Lassie put her head down and sighed.

Great.

Jasmine considered calling Josh's cell phone but decided she'd sound too ridiculous. *Um, Josh? I think Cleo
Chan only set up your meeting so that she could come up
and kill me while you were gone.* Jasmine didn't really
think Cleo was coming to kill her. Although, the woman
was a martial arts expert. Jasmine had read all about
Cleo's tae kwon do, kung fu, and karate training.

Jasmine put on lipstick and pulled her hair back in a
ponytail.

*Repeat after me: Cleo Chan is an actress. She is not
really a murderous alien hunter.*

*Repeat after me: Amy is a liar. My Josh is not her One
True Love.*

The knock at the suite door nearly shattered Jasmine's
resolve.

Just a little visit from another superstar. Ho-hum.

She opened the gilded door, and there stood Cleo Chan,
all six foot one of her in three-inch pumps. She wore blue

jeans, a down jacket, and a knit cap. Enormous sunglasses perched on her perfect nose.

Why did Hollywood stars think enormous sunglasses hid their identities?

"Are you going to invite me in?" Cleo asked.

Right. *Try not to stare at her otherworldly beauty.* "Sure. Sorry." Jasmine stood back, and Cleo swept into the suite.

"I wanted to talk to you," Cleo said. "About Josh."

"He's waiting for you," Jasmine reminded her. "At your hotel." She hoped this was just a planning slipup. Did superstars have planning slipups? Were that woman's breasts for real?

"Josh and I are destined to be together," Cleo asserted. "It's not personal. It's not about me against you. It's that I love him. And this might be my only shot at my One True Love." Cleo settled herself in the middle of the couch and draped her long arms over the back cushions. She was so beautiful, it took Jasmine's breath away. Jasmine sank into the wingback chair. The dogs settled at her feet.

Cleo said, "I'm not a bad person. I want you to know that. I didn't go on *Oprah* for the publicity or because I was afraid to speak to you in person. I went on *Oprah* because I needed to let the world know that I really love Josh so that I wouldn't chicken out. I have waited five years for Josh to see that I was more than a friend. I want to have a chance too. That's all. Just a chance."

"I love him too," Jasmine said. She wasn't sure what else she could say.

"Well, in that case, I suppose it's up to Josh to decide."

"So shouldn't you be talking to him?" Jasmine asked.

Cleo checked her diamond-studded watch. "He's on his way."

Jasmine's eyebrows shot up.

"I knew he wouldn't agree to a three-way meeting. That's why I sent him away. I knew you'd let me in. I left a note at my hotel that I'd be here. He should join us any minute."

Jasmine blinked at the flawless creature sitting across from her. The woman was certainly used to getting her way. Jasmine considered taking the dogs out for a walk. Going home to check her mail. Calling Mo for backup. Leaping out the window and hoping for the best. Josh having to choose between this flawless creature and her face-to-face was not an appealing scenario.

A knock at the suite door spared her a decision.

"Jasmine? Let me in. It's Josh."

Cleo flew to the door and threw it open. Jasmine, cemented to her chair, couldn't see Josh, but she imagined the look on his face.

Wait, why would Josh knock on his own door?

"Who the hell are you?" Cleo asked.

Jasmine leaned forward to witness an astonishing sight. Josh Toby, librarian, walked into the room.

"Hi, Jasmine." He came right to Jasmine and shook her hand. He patted Lassie and Buster. "Hello." Then he turned to Cleo. "Hello. I'm Josh Toby. I don't know how to tell you this, but I think I'm your One True Love." He smiled sheepishly at Cleo.

Aha, library boy, who's the crazy one now? Jasmine hid her smile in her hand.

A change had come over Librarian Josh. He seemed

taller, maybe because he no longer bowed his head. His clothes seemed newer, more fashionable. They definitely fit better. Or was it all an illusion of confidence? Jasmine looked closely. Nope, the clothes weren't new. But the man . . .

Cleo dismissed him with a wave of her hand. "Excuse me, we're busy here."

"Amy came to see me," Josh said. "She read the name of my One True Love. It's Cleopatra Chan."

"Amy? But . . . no," Cleo stammered, beginning to see the trap she had stepped into. "My One True Love is Josh Toby. I mean, a different Josh Toby. The other one." A strand of Cleo's hair had ventured out of alignment and fell over her cheek. In the sea of perfection, it hung like a ghastly affront. Cleo squinted. "Do I know you?"

"We went to school together," Josh said.

Jasmine sat up straighter. Fate often threw lovers together in their youths. Maybe . . . no. It was nuts.

Cleo said, "Carrot boy? Is that you?"

Josh's cheeks turned as red as his hair. "I can prove I'm the right Josh Toby for you."

"Really?" Cleo looked skeptical. "How?" She tried to fight the strand of hair back, but it popped loose.

"Fight me."

Jasmine's jaw dropped to the floor.

Cleo's left eyebrow flinched. "Excuse me?"

"Oh, I don't think that's such a good idea," Jasmine said. The dogs sensed the tension in the room and bolted onto Jasmine's lap.

"We were at Master Kun's dojo together. For four years. I trained you when you were twelve," Josh reminded Cleo. "You said one day you'd beat me. But you never did."

"I never got the chance. You moved—"

"To New York."

"Coward," Cleo purred. Something had changed about her. She looked Josh up and down.

Jasmine's mouth, which she had finally managed to close, fell slack again.

All at once, with a tremendous yell, Cleo sprang at Josh. The dogs buried their heads in Jasmine's lap. Jasmine wondered how she could get to the phone and call security. She hoped Josh had brought his inhaler. They struck at each other, a blur of limbs. Josh and Cleo had both lost their marbles. Amy had that effect on people. Cleo was attacking a *librarian*. Surely there were federal laws about that sort of thing.

But Josh didn't hesitate. He sprung his hands into defense mode and leapt aside.

"Bastard!" Cleo muttered.

I've seen it all, Jasmine thought. *I can die now.*

"You're mine, Chan." Josh scowled. He circled, hands at the ready.

To Jasmine's amazement, Cleo smiled. "No way, Toby."

Legs flew. Arms chopped. A beautiful glass lamp shattered to the floor. Jasmine scooped the dogs into the bathroom, where they scampered behind the shower curtain. Then she circled the room to the phone. But just as she got there, the door opened and Movie Star Josh slipped in, his finger to his lips in librarian "shush" mode.

Jasmine gaped at him. The world was not right.

He motioned for her to put the phone down, then waved her over.

Keeping to the outer edges of the room, she skirted the escalating fight and slipped into the hall with Josh.

Amy was there.

"What the hell?" Jasmine began. But they both shushed her. "They're going to kill each other," Jasmine urged. "We have to call security."

An enormous crash rang out from inside the room.

"He won't hurt her. He loves her," Amy whispered.

Josh grinned.

Jasmine turned to Amy. "You told poor Josh that he was Cleo Chan's One True Love and she was his?"

"He'd already heard it on *Oprah*. It didn't take much convincing."

"But, Amy, it's a lie! Well, half of it, at least. You didn't read that poor man."

"I couldn't get a voice on the guy, true. But the minute I told him Cleo was his One True Love, it was like he became a whole different person. It was as if he'd known his whole life."

It had grown quiet inside the suite.

"They're dead," Jasmine moaned.

Josh opened the door an inch and carefully peered in. "They're talking. Josh is showing her something about a kick sequence." He shut the door silently.

Jasmine sank to the floor, her back against the wall. Josh sat down beside her and took her hand. Amy sat next to him and pulled out a half-empty bottle of Coke. She unscrewed the cap and took a swig.

An elderly couple dressed to the nines came out of a

suite three doors down. They nodded at the odd trio on the hallway floor, then scurried past, obviously frightened.

"You were in on this?" Jasmine asked Josh.

"Nope. All my idea," Amy said. She passed Jasmine the Coke, but she refused.

Josh took it and downed the rest. "I ran into Amy and Librarian Josh in the lobby. They were trying to get in, so I helped them through hotel security." He handed Amy the empty bottle.

"I really felt bad about the Oprah-Cleo thing," Amy said. "I didn't know you guys were snogging. I wanted to fix it."

"What are they doing in there?" Jasmine asked. *Snogging?*

"Wait," Josh counseled. "Quiet is good."

"How did you ever convince Librarian Josh to come here? He was so shy. And Cleo—"

"I didn't have to do any convincing. He knew instantly I was right. You know, just because I didn't get a voice doesn't mean they're not meant to be together. They might be perfect for each other. After all, Cleo's One True Love *is* named Josh Toby."

"And it's not me," Josh said, obviously very pleased.

Jasmine shook her head. So that's where Amy had disappeared to for the last few days. She'd been stalking the librarian.

"Cleo loves her martial arts," Josh said. "She wanted me to train seriously, beyond what I needed for the camera. But I hated it. Always. Couldn't stand the fighting."

"See? He's too big a wimp for a woman like Cleo," Amy said.

"Please check if Cleo killed that poor man. I can't stand it another minute."

Josh got up quietly and slid his card through the lock. He peeked in. Then he reached around the door and took out the "do not disturb" sign. He shut the door and hung the sign on the knob. "I better call the front desk and see if we can get another suite for tonight," he said. "I think this one's taken."

Josh's father served them the best pastrami in New York. It was tender and spicy and amazingly moist. Jasmine watched Josh's mother bustle around the small table, worrying over the iced tea and potato salad. She put a fourth pickle on Jasmine's overflowing plate.

"You're lucky I could get this at late notice," Josh's dad explained. He was in his bathrobe and slippers. "It's special reserve. My pastrami man doesn't give his best to just anyone. He got out of bed to cut me this. By hand."

"Come to L.A. I'll get your pastrami shipped every week," Josh said, stopping the conversation cold.

"L.A.? Never." His dad shivered.

"You'll have to come to L.A. soon," Josh said. He took another bite of the enormous sandwich.

"Over my dead body," his mother said. Then she caught her husband's eye and corrected herself. "Of course. We'd love to."

"Good. Because I'm going to ask Jasmine to marry me, and I want to get married on the beach in Santa Monica. Barefoot."

"Oh, my God!" Josh's mother sat down for the first time since the meal began.

All heads turned to Jasmine. Her mouth was stuffed with pastrami.

"Jas? Will you?" Josh pushed away from the table and got down on one knee.

She swallowed. "Marry you?" She took an enormous swig of iced tea. She looked around her. It was so normal; there was nothing flashy or Hollywood about it. No photographers at the ready. No press release. Just Josh and his parents and some really, really good meat.

His mother had tears in her eyes. "There's a beach at Coney Island," she said softly, and Josh's dad elbowed her in the ribs.

"Jasmine?" Josh bit his lip.

Jasmine tried not to leap up in joy. "Well, of course I will."

The table erupted into a cheer. His parents toasted the couple with iced tea and got out a 35-mm camera to snap some pictures. Then Josh's mom cried a little and told stories of how awful he was when he was a kid (a "holy terror; she'd catch him reading the *Hollywood Reporter* after lights out").

I'm going to marry Josh Toby, Jasmine thought.

They all agreed to keep it a secret until Mo got everything worked out between Cleo, her new boyfriend the librarian, and the press.

Josh's dad got out the blackberry wine and poured for everyone.

After the fourth toast, Josh said, "Hey, Dad? Let's go over some scenes from *Romeo and Juliet* after dinner. I think I could use some coaching."

His dad smiled so wide, you could see every silver filling in his mouth.

Chapter 35

Opening night was a mob scene. Not since Laurence Olivier had so many people been this excited about a Shakespeare play.

Scratch that. *Never* had so many people been excited about a Shakespeare play.

Jasmine looked out from the wings. Josh's parents sat in the third row, center. Jasmine scanned the crowd for Librarian Josh and Cleo. They were in the third row, right. Arm in arm. Librarian Josh looked like a million bucks next to Cleo. Cleo couldn't stop smiling. *It's gotta be True Love*, Jasmine thought. Nothing else looked that pure.

Elvis and Jesus sat behind them, freshly scrubbed and grinning. Luckily, Eleanor was nowhere in sight.

Cecelia and her husband, Finn, and their daughter, Maya, sat in the fifth row. Cecelia and Finn's new baby, Emmet, was at the Plaza with a babysitter—Mrs. Little. Finn was in a tux, and Cecelia and Maya wore simple, matching gray shifts.

Amy sat next to them, her gypsy outfit as outrageous and flamboyant as ever. Jasmine guessed that she was hoping to get her picture in the paper. With the hundreds of photographers waiting outside the theater, it would have been impossible not to.

The house lights began to blink.

Jasmine's stomach clenched.

Someone took her hand.

It was Josh. "Showtime," he said.

"How are you feeling?" she asked.

"Never been better," he said.

She looked at him carefully.

"Okay, I just barfed in the men's room. But now I'm fine."

And then the house lights went down, and the show began.

The papers called Josh everything from "visionary" to "electric." All the hours he had spent working through the text with his father, line by line, scene by scene, had paid off in a standing ovation.

But the real excitement was stirred up by Jasmine's costumes. Mo, now Jasmine's publicist, had leaked that Arturo Mastriani had not designed the costumes after all. Jasmine had done seven interviews already (after a little practice with Ken). She had three calls from Arturo's biggest rivals, inviting her for interviews. She was terrified that Arturo would be furious with her, but instead he sent her a dozen pink roses and an invitation to his wedding in Rome.

After the opening-night frenzy had died down, Josh and Jasmine didn't have to worry much about the media. Cleo, Librarian Josh, and Amy were sucking in all the publicity at the moment.

So Josh and Jasmine were able to sneak under the radar.

They stayed in and watched DVDs. Played backgammon. Walked the dogs. Ate with Josh's parents. It wasn't nearly as interesting as Cleo and her new gypsy-psychic-certified lover.

The world would care about Josh and Jasmine later.

Or not.

Jasmine couldn't have cared less.

About the Author

I love to write. That's pretty much all I do. Ask my family about the undone laundry, the unbought groceries, and the fact that I rarely find time to get dressed in the morning. Actually, if you train your family right, they won't notice any of these things. "Popcorn for dinner again, Mom! Cool," say my filthy children. God bless them, they don't know what panty hose are.

Oh, my poor husband.

What else do you want to know about me? I love cats. I love chocolate (not necessarily in that order). And, I love to hear from readers. So log onto my Web site at www.dianaholquist.com and let me know what's on your mind!

More laugh-out-loud humor
and sizzling romance from

Diana Holquist!

❧⁂❧

Please turn this page
for a preview
of her next novel

Hungry for More

available in mass market
Fall 2008.

Prologue

The studio lights were hot and blinding. A bead of sweat slid down Amy's spine and dropped onto the mike pack duct-taped to the small of her back. *Focus on Oprah. Oprah is kindness. Oprah is all-knowing.*

Oprah is really packing on the pounds.

"Three, two, one, go!" The stage manager pointed his finger like a gun, and the "on air" signs lit up green and glowing around the studio. A breath of silence before the live audience exploded into applause.

"Welcome back." Oprah smiled warmly as the applause died down. "We're here today with Amy Burns, the gypsy who has the power to tell a person the name of their One True Love." A pause as the cameras switched to close-up. "Ms. Burns, tell us it's true!" Oprah leaned forward.

Amy nodded sagely as she soaked in Oprah's warmth. Talking to this woman was like chatting with your One True Love. Not that Amy would know; she had never heard the name of her *own* One True Love. Amy's sisters called that sad fact the central tragedy of Amy's life. Amy called it irrelevant. Having her own True Love wouldn't have landed her on *Oprah*, that's for sure. You had to get your priorities straight. "I hear the voice of an all-knowing spirit," Amy told Oprah. "When willing, she can speak the name of a person's One True Love."

The audience murmured in appreciation. Some clapped. Some slunk back in their seats, not meeting the eyes of their companions.

"As we all know, Ms. Burns predicted the whirlwind love affair between Josh Toby, *People* magazine's sexiest man alive, and his new wife, Jasmine Toby."

Now that was something the Oprahites could rally around. But were they applauding for superstar Josh Toby or for the power of True Love? Despite the lights roasting her, Amy felt the focus shift away from herself as acutely as if the whole stage had gone dark.

"Ms. Burns also predicted the storybook love affair between Cleo Chan of the *Agent X* HBO series and her new librarian fiancé *right here on this stage*."

The crowd went mad for the affair between the superstar and the librarian that had been smeared over the tabloids for weeks. Amy sometimes rated a sidebar box on the third page. Sometimes, with a grainy photo attached. She sucked in her stomach further. *I've got more power in my big toe than Cleo Chan has in her entire bloodline.*

Oprah turned back to Amy, if possible more radiant and focused than before. If there was one person in the world who had a slice of True Love for every creature on earth, it was Oprah. Maybe that was *her* tragedy. "So," Oprah begged, "give us details. Does your spirit-voice have a name?"

Amy melted under Oprah's gaze. Or was it the hot-as-hell studio lights? "I call her Maddie, but I made the name up. She never says her name. She only speaks the names of others."

"And she's been with you your entire life?"

"On and off." A tremor of fear raced up Amy's spine, but she shook it off. These last few years, Maddie was mostly off. *But she'll show today. She just has to.* She always showed when Amy needed her most.

Oprah threw back her head, held out her hand, and flashed her magnificent incisors. "So touch me, baby! Tell me the name of my One True Love!" The audience sat forward as one. "Just don't tell Steddy, okay?" She winked.

This woman was amazing. She had no fear. Her One True Love could be anyone. Man, woman, black, white, drug addict, CEO . . .

Amy took Oprah's cool, smooth hand in her hot, wet ones. *Please, Mads. For Oprah. For America. For me.*

Silence. Amy closed her eyes. *One last time. I'll do anything.*

She felt a rustling, a disturbance in the energy patterns. *Yes. Thank you. I knew you'd come.* The warmth that signaled Maddie's presence rose in her. This was going to be the biggest moment on TV ever. *Oprah's One True Love!*

"She's smiling, ladies and gentlemen. Does that mean you're hearing the voice?" Oprah asked. The studio was silent with breathless anticipation. Dust particles hit the hot lights and exploded, microscopic precursors of the fireworks that would explode when America knew Oprah's One True Love.

Amy held still, trying to empty herself so Maddie could enter her soul. *Talk to me, baby. Talk to Oprah.*

Amy felt heat rise inside her. First a pinprick. Then the

warmth of the spirit spread through her like an opening flower. *Oh, Mads. Thank you for coming! I love you. I really do. Sorry. I'll shut up. Go ahead. Give me the big lady's One True Love.*

The voice in Amy's head spoke in a whisper, but its words were distinct. "Good-bye."

And then there was nothing.

Chapter 1

(Three Months Later)

James stirred the melting butter counterclockwise, adding flour with a flick of his fingers, a snow flurry. He watched the flour dissolve in the golden liquid, then handed the wooden spoon to Troy. He checked his watch. Three o'clock. Two hours to opening, three hours to rush, four hours to chaos. "Stir. No. The other direction."

"Why's it matter what direction I stir?" Troy asked. His question was laced with doubt and defiance.

James glanced at the boy. He was just a kid. Barely seventeen. James knew he shouldn't be hard on him, but this was a roux, the classic combination of butter and flour that formed the base of French cooking—the base of *life*. You couldn't go soft on essentials like this. "You wanna be a great chef, you honor the roux. Do *not* question the roux. I'm gonna check out front for the wine delivery."

Troy changed the direction of the spoon with a scowl, which made James proud. A great student asked, but a great teacher never answered because anyone worth his balls in the kitchen didn't give a shit what anyone else said. If Troy was going to be a great chef one day, he'd stir clockwise just to see what happened.

Anyway, if James told the kid he stirred counterclockwise for luck, he'd lose face. And you never lost face in your own kitchen. Worse than death.

James passed through his restaurant's gleaming chrome kitchen, grunting in admiration for Raul's perfectly seasoned stock, for John-John's exquisite mise en place, for Craig's perfectly minced garlic. Each of his sous-chefs told him to fuck off in turn. He loved these guys.

He grabbed a wooden spoon and stuck it into Pablo's soup of the day. "More salt," he muttered. Pablo gave him the finger but added the salt. James passed the boys husking corn on overturned milk crates. The corn was shit. He could tell at a glance—too starchy. "Throw that garbage to the rats. Go across the street to La Terasse and *beg*. *Ahora!*"

Damn. Lousy corn, *plus* his best waitress had just gone AWOL. The night was shaping up to be a nuclear meltdown. A thrill of excitement raced through him. All good chefs were adrenaline freaks; it was in the job description. A meltdown was a test of manhood, of ability. It was all in a night's work.

James pushed through the double swinging doors into the deserted, darkened dining room, thinking about the menu for the night. He was short a first-course special. A delivery of lust-inducing shitakes had arrived that morning, but they'd keep. Better to get rid of the broccoli rabe that was dying in the walk-in fridge downstairs.

His restaurant, Les Petite Fleurs, was the only two-star French restaurant in Philly as rated by *Michelin*. That is to say, as rated by God. The place was going to be the death of him. And what a way to go. *Bury me in foie gras, white truffles, and red wine.* He loved the place like a woman.

No, more than a woman. He hadn't slept more than four hours a night since he'd opened his doors to rave reviews thirteen months ago. No woman had ever been able to keep up with him that long.

The windowless dining room was completely dark. He flicked on the bar lights, grabbed the seltzer spritzer, and shot a stream of the lukewarm liquid into his mouth.

"Can't a person get a bite to eat in this joint?"

James startled.

"Bang, bang, I'm . . . wet?"

James realized he was holding the squirter out like a gun, pointed in the general direction of the voice. Sheepishly, he let it fall. He squinted into the dimness. A woman sat alone at the center table. He could just discern her outline in the shadows.

James put the squirter away and reached behind the bar to flick on the overhead work lights.

He caught his breath. The woman must have just come in from outside, as sparkling snowflakes dotted her tangled hair, blinking in and out like tiny SOS warning beacons. Her face was a valentine heart, her eyes black and slanted as a doe's, her lips a perfect bow. He felt a surge of lust rise within him. "Who the hell are you?"

"I'm here for Roni," she said, not moving. Her voice was deep and layered with sandpaper and cigarettes. She sat like a mobster, her face to the door.

It dawned on him through his lust-induced haze that she must be the temp waitress. He'd sent Joey, his maitre d', out earlier this afternoon to steal help from La

Fondue across town to replace Roni tonight. It was standard restaurant practice to pilfer help. No hard feelings. The scum at La Fondue picked one of James's prep cooks right out from under him in the middle of a Saturday night rush three weeks ago. All was fair in love, war, and high-priced food.

But why was she sitting in the dark? "We do a four-table split, pooled tips, under the table for tonight—on the books if this turns into a regular gig. Whatever bonus Joey promised. And get your paws off the furniture. Didn't your mother teach you manners?"

She leveled her black eyes at him, keeping her feet firmly on the chair. In the sedate perfection of the tasteful beige-on-beige dining room, she looked garish and wrong—like a rosebush in the desert. A mirage.

In one swift movement, she swung her feet to the floor, swept her knee-length shearling coat like a train behind her, and stood. She threaded through the white-clothed tables, yanking off a pair of ragged, black wool gloves with no fingertips as she advanced toward him, smoky and dark, full-bodied and confident. An enormous gold pendant swung against her breasts with pleasing effect. This woman was chili peppers in cream sauce. Hot and smooth.

She dumped her gloves and coat into his arms as she glided past him to the deserted bar. The heat of her body rose off her discarded coat.

"Do I look like the coat-check girl?" he asked.

She ducked under the bar, looked him up and down, then tossed him a wicked smile. "You look like the coat-check girl's fantasy lay, cheffie."

Her sexy, fuck-me smile almost knocked him off

his feet. The aroma of cinnamon and clove, two spices strictly forbidden in his kitchen, rose off the coat in his arms. He slid onto a stool at his own bar like a paying customer, watching her inspect his stock. This woman made him think of sex, and sex made him think of Maria, his last girlfriend. He had created a cilantro tomato bisque after her. Spicy, with an acid undertone. Then Maria had dumped him for his grill man, and he cut it from the menu. Another great dish shot to hell. But Maria was nothing next to this woman. A soup.

He studied the woman before him. She was dressed for a summer's day, in short sleeves and several layers of long cotton skirts, some hanging low, some bunched at the hems. She looked like she had just stridden off the stage after the first scene of *Carmen*—shabby, gorgeous, and dangerous.

Wait, she was *really* shabby. Undone hems on her skirts, the sole of her black boot flapping loose with a thud as she moved behind the bar. Dangerously sexy, but no way was she from La Fondue. That was a classy operation, despite its asinine name. Where had Joey found this one?

She pulled out two glasses, then plucked the most expensive single malt off the shelf. "Drink?"

He shook off her offer with what he hoped was casualness. Four hundred and twelve days without a drink. He was doing fine. He studied the pendant around her neck. It was a gold cross inside a red circle, surrounded by some sort of obscure engraved writing.

She poured two shots despite his refusal. "So where's Roni?" She threw back her shot. Considered a moment.

Threw back his, too. Then repoured. "She's not here. I can read it in your eyes. Shit."

"I thought you were the temp waitress to replace her."

A pause. She pursed her lips. Then, "Oh. Yeah. Right. I am." She didn't even try to hide her obvious lie.

He liked that kind of go-to-hell honesty in a woman . . . er, in an employee. A surge of energy spread through him. Okay, more than energy. Lust. *Down, boy.* "Ever wait tables?"

She downed her drink. "For a few weeks. Mexican joint. Got fired for stealing from the register." She cocked her head and blinked her doe eyes, daring him.

"Did you?"

"Of course. Shit job." She licked her lips, the tip of her tongue a promise.

He checked his cell. No calls. If Joey hadn't looted a waitress by now, he wasn't going to. Stu and Dan could handle at most an extra table each. But an extra set of hands—not to mention an extra set of what was so magnificently stretching out her threadbare, see-through T-shirt—would help, especially with Dr. Trudeau, who came every Tuesday night for his one-night stand of consommé, salade cassis, and roasted duck served wordlessly by Roni, the beautiful gypsy with the big black eyes.

Wordless seemed unlikely with this one, but at least Dr. Trudeau would have those cauldron-deep eyes to stare into as he slurped his broth.

I'll just have to keep an eye on her. The thought made his crotch jump. *An eye; only an eye.* "Do you have a name?" he asked.

She seemed to consider. "Amy," she said finally.

"Hi, Amy. I'm James." He wondèred what her real name was.

She looked him up and down as she leaned forward, planting her elbows on the bar. "It's nice to meet you, James."

He had never heard a woman pack that phrase with so much sex. *Nice to meet you—and nice has nothing to do with it.*

He checked his watch. His roux was probably fused to the bottom of the pot by now. "You'll need to change into something more sedate." He looked over her jumbled, layered gypsy clothes. He could see right through her clingy jersey black shirt to her red lace bra.

"Give me fifty bucks up front for new clothes. I'll pay you back from tips."

Another lie flat and shining on the black bar for them both to admire. James fished two twenties out of his pocket and pushed them across the bar. "Trade you for the necklace. You show for work, you get it back."

Without a second thought, she reached behind her neck to unclasp the necklace. Then she ducked under the bar, glided behind him, and draped the jewel around his neck. The clasp closed with a snap.

The gold was heavy and still warm from her body. "White top. Black bottom. Welcome to Les Fleurs," he said.

"Lays Floooorz," she said, Americanizing the French with exaggerated disregard. "Lays floors, lays coat-check girls, lays Roni?"

"I don't sleep with the hired help." *Two can lie.* Not that he had ever slept with Roni. But as a general policy, not sleeping with the help wouldn't float. They were just about the only people he knew.

"So if you're not boffing her, why would she come back to this dump?" She took the bills and tucked them into her bra. She scooped her coat off the stool.

"I'll take that as a compliment." He wondered if the necklace was a piece of crap. Had he just been conned?

She shrugged. "Take it as whatever you please. You're the boss man now, Jimmy." She shrugged into her coat.

"I doubt that. Now that you have my cash, I've got what? A fifty-fifty chance you'll show tonight?"

She pulled on her gloves. "Twenty-eighty. What are Roni's odds?"

"One hundred percent she'll be back. I've got something of hers she can't live without."

"Hope it's not a dime-store, piece-of-shit necklace," she said scornfully.

He felt as if she had punched him in the gut, but he held his face neutral, then smiled. He'd have to watch this one, if he ever saw her again. He just had to hope she wanted to wait around for Roni badly enough. Or make some cash tonight badly enough. "Four-thirty sharp for the waiter tasting."

She didn't answer or turn to look at him as she strode for the door, but instead raised a gloved hand in a gesture that might have said "ta-ta" or maybe "screw you." A blast of wind and snow pushed into the restaurant as she pushed out.

She slammed the door firmly behind her.

The restaurant had never felt so empty. The seventy-four vacant chairs faced James like a mute audience.

Well, what the hell did he expect? Applause? He had hired an incompetent thief con-woman, and worse, he had enjoyed it.

A lot.

He resisted the urge to touch the lipstick outline she'd left behind on the shot glass. He fingered the pendant instead, and it seemed to emit heat at his touch.

A sudden taste-vision struck him: she was cream sauce with truffles, a splash of whiskey, and chili peppers over orecchiette.

He froze in terror. *She had inspired a first course on first sight.* That had never happened before.

He sat in stunned silence. The dish was original, surprising, and sexy. *Just like her.*

Something was burning.

He sensed it before he smelled it. The roux. He jumped off his stool and pushed past his crew into the kitchen.

The kid was at the stove, stirring clockwise.

James strode past him to the oven and threw open the heavy door, waving away the black smoke that billowed out. He tossed the tray of ruined chives on the counter with his bare hands. Ten years of oven-burn scars made the best pot holders.

He looked over the ruined chives, catching the averted eyes of his crew. They didn't say a word now. But later, when the rush was on full force, they'd rib him mercilessly. He waved the black smoke away. It felt like a bad omen. What did that gypsy want with Roni anyway?

Troy was the only one who dared to look at him—with horror, his spoon suspended over the steaming pot.

"Counterclockwise!" James commanded, proud of the

boy but trying not to let it show. The last thing he needed was a cocky brat in his kitchen.

But the boy didn't move; his eyes were fixed on the pendant.

James left the ruined chives and grabbed the spoon out of Troy's hand. "Have you ever _seen_ a clock? This way."

The boy shook his head. "I wouldn't wear that if I were you."

"Why not?" A chill rose up James's spine.

A long silence floated between them.

"What is this thing anyway?" James asked. "Gypsy voodoo?"

"Voodoo isn't gypsy. It's Cajun. It's just bad luck, man. The worst kind of shit-awful luck."

Yeah. Tell me something I don't know, James thought.

Because despite the steaming pots around him, all he could smell was cinnamon and clove.

THE DISH

Where authors give you the inside scoop!

♥ ♥ ♥ ♥ ♥ ♥ ♥ ♥ ♥ ♥ ♥ ♥ ♥ ♥ ♥ ♥

Book Group with
Lani Diane Rich, Diana Holquist,
Eve Silver, and Mrs. McGrunt

Mrs. McGrunt: Welcome to the Liverpool Public Library. We're here to discuss *War and Peace* by Leo Tolstoy . . .

Diana Holquist: Oh, about that. See, I kind of got to reading Lani Diane Rich's new release, *Crazy In Love* (available now), and I couldn't put it down.

Eve Silver: No way! Me too! The one about Flynn Daly who inherits a historic inn *and* her dead aunt's ghost. Awesome.

Diana Holquist: And that cute bartender, Jake. That scene where he picks her up at the train station and pretends he's not there for her—the sparks really fly!

Lani Diane Rich: You know, that actually happened to me.

Eve: The cute guy, the sparks, or the train station?

Lani: Okay, none of it. But I wish it did.

Diana: Especially the cute guy . . .

Mrs. McGrunt: *War and Peace*, ladies! Now, on page 797 . . .

Lani: Did anyone read Eve Silver's *Demon's Kiss* (available now)?

Diana: Is that the one with long, confusing Russian names?

Eve: God no. My sexy new release is about Ciarran D'Arbois, a lethal, seductive sorcerer determined to save the world from demons while saving himself from the darkness invading his soul.

Diana: Oh, I loved *Demon's Kiss*! The demons try to use Clea Masters to break down the wall between the human and demon realms.

Lani: And Clea unwittingly threatens everything Ciarran is. She steals his magic—and his heart.

(Deep sigh from all three authors.)

Mrs. McGrunt: Ladies? *War and Peace*?

Lani: Ya know, in Diana's new book, *Sexiest Man Alive* (available now), Jasmine has a major war with herself when she finds out that the one man on earth destined to be her "one true love" is the world's hottest movie star. She thinks there's no way she can live that sort of life.

Eve: She sure does find peace in his bed for a while.

Lani: And satisfaction. And bliss.

Diana: And a Ken doll. Er, guess you gotta read the book to understand that part.

Eve: But when the paparazzi catch them and everything falls apart—it was so touching.

Mrs. McGrunt: Touching *and* sexy! Those gypsies sure know how to ride the wild fantastic! That young man on the cover in his teeny towel sizzles. Hoo-ah! You don't even have to open *Sexiest Man Alive* to enjoy it. *Hey, big boy, I'll hold that towel for you . . .*

Lani, Diana, Eve: Mrs. McGrunt!

Mrs. McGrunt: Okay, okay, so I didn't read *War and Peace* either. I was going to, but then I saw Lani's *Crazy in Love.* How hot was that love scene in the cabin, huh? And Eve's *Demon's Kiss* just had me from the start. I'm such a sucker for a dark, tortured hero. And then, I had to re-read that scene in Diana's *Sexiest Man Alive* where they're backstage and . . . well, wowza!

Lani: Let's blow this stuffy library, get a latte, and discuss some hot, sexy, fun romance novels.

Eve: I'm there! And all you readers should join the group by reading these three awesome new releases.

Diana: They're all on the shelves this month. So don't miss a single one.

Mrs. McGrunt: Okay, ladies, let's make a break for it! We can hide behind this enormous *War and Peace* tome. Cover my back. Go! Go! Go!

Happy reading (and discussing)!

Love,

Lani, Eve, and Diana

Lani Diane Rich

Eve Silver

Diana Holquist

www.lanidianerich.com
www.evesilver.net
www.dianaholquist.com